PENGUIN BOOKS

GILBERT

Judith Martin was born in Washington, D.C., and received her B.A. degree from Wellesley College. She worked for the *Washington Post* for over twenty years, covering the diplomatic and political social circuit and serving as a drama and film critic. In addition to writing the nationally syndicated "Miss Manners" column, the basis for her recent best-seller, *Miss Manners' Guide to Excruciatingly Correct Behavior*, she is now critic-at-large for *Vanity Fair* magazine. Ms. Martin is also the author of *The Name on the White House Floor, and Other Anxieties of Our Times*, a collection of essays on White House and diplomatic social life. *Gilbert* is her first novel.

GILBERT

A Comedy of Manners

JUDITH MARTIN

PENGUIN BOOKS

Penguin Books Ltd, Harmondsworth,
Middlesex, England
Penguin Books, 40 West 23rd Street,
New York, New York 10010, U.S.A.
Penguin Books Australia Ltd, Ringwood,
Victoria, Australia
Penguin Books Canada Limited, 2801 John Street,
Markham, Ontario, Canada L3R 1B4
Penguin Books (N.Z.) Ltd, 182–190 Wairau Road,
Auckland 10, New Zealand

First published in the United States of America by
Atheneum 1982
First published in Canada by
McClelland and Stewart Limited 1982
Published in Penguin Books 1983

LIBRARY OF CONGRESS CATALOGING IN PUBLICATION DATA
Martin, Judith, 1938–
Gilbert: a comedy of manners.
Reprint. Originally published: New York: Atheneum,
1982.
I. Title.
[PS3563.A72445G5 1983] 813'.54 83-10537
ISBN 0 14 00.6962 3

Printed in the United States of America by
R. R. Donnelley & Sons Company, Harrisonburg, Virginia
Set in Janson

For Wolf

GILBERT was blessed with good and loyal friends, to whom I am extremely grateful: first, Robert Martin; then, Winzola McLendon, Marion Clark, Leslie H. Whitten, Carol Eisen Rinzler, and David Hendin.

I feel lucky to have an editor, Thomas A. Stewart, who is not only delightful at the primary business of editors, which is having lunch, but can and will edit a book sensitively and brilliantly.

PART ONE

Chapter I

I T   T O O K   Gilbert Fairchild two years at Harvard College (two academic years, from September, 1955, to June, 1957) to learn everything he needed to know.

His enlightened public high school had prepared him. "Feel free to talk back and argue with me in class," each of his teachers had said at the beginning of each course. "That way, I'll know you're thinking." When Gilbert had taught himself to overcome his respect for learning enough to follow these instructions, he made the important scholastic discovery that a student who is belligerently thinking aloud is presumed to have done the reading. This left him time to pursue independent studies.

As his first college project, he chose to study the trust-funded patrician from Pride's Crossing, Massachusetts, who lived down the hall. Freshman year was the appropriate time to do this, because while the Harvard houses mixed the three upper undergraduate classes, they effectively separated the social classes; Harvard Yard housing kept the freshman class separate but mixed the social classes. Gilbert, whose grandfather had been a pharmacist and an immigrant from Estonia, and whose father worked for a New York firm calculating low taxes on high incomes, thus had, for nine months exclusive of holidays, the daily opportunity of brushing his teeth in a basin adjacent to that in which the object of his study, whose grandfather had been an all-American swindler in railroads and whose father was a renowned collector of antique toys, brushed his teeth and occasionally threw up a night's worth of screwdrivers.

After careful observation, Gilbert concluded that it is more effective socially to be tall and barely civil than short and eagerly sociable. This did not affect his height, but it taught him when to shut up.

Sophomore year, he studied Radcliffe and even Wellesley. Through painstaking and painful research, he discovered that nice girls were not looking for nice boys. If these best-of-their-generation women had wanted faithful and loving swains, or, as they called them, creeps, they need only have answered the letters and invitations from their old steadies now at state universities. They dreamed of prestigious passion. They planned to marry above themselves, even the ones who seemed to Gilbert to be high enough already. At first, he wondered how they could so easily distinguish superiority among the best-of-their-generation men who were their classmates. Careful observation gave him the simple formula: Only a person who considers himself too good for you is good enough. Gilbert's conclusion was that in order to be looked up to, and not down upon, one must develop a courtship technique establishing that the object of one's admiration is beneath one's contempt.

After these two rigorous academic years, Gilbert spent a summer preparing to put his education to work. The skinny and anxious young man with plastered hair and button-down shirts who left Dunster House in June, 1957, returned in September a sullen, poetic-looking loner with a headful of unruly black curls and a wardrobe of coarsely knit black sweaters. He did not return to Dunster House. If his birth did not entitle him to an Eliot House river view suite, then surely it entitled him to sink romantically to the slums. He demanded this right of the school, in the name of his mother and also in her handwriting, and was granted permission to live independently in Cambridge. Gilbert had left his crew-cut, crewnecked, crew-rowing classmates to race one another on the mainstream, while he fitted himself out to sail ahead alone.

Had a social historian or psychologist observed the new Gilbert, he might have written a paper predicting the coming decade's fashions in students. There were several such professionals living on the shabby block in which Gilbert had rented a room. Only a non-academic could have noticed that the dingy street, with small brick apartment buildings anchoring the corners and rows of dilapidated clapboard houses, each with more doorbells and mailboxes than its builder long ago would have deemed acceptable to rough laborers, resembled an ordinary working-class neighborhood. To the married graduate students and assistant professors whose only luxuries were their exquisite thesis topics and a bottle of Chianti on Saturday night, it was a temporary and untenured version of the neat New England blocks on which famous professors dwelled in splendid Early American austerity. The aspirants sat over their second-hand typewriters, typing their endless entries to the scholastic sweepstakes, too engrossed to look out the window at one black-clad, counter-establishment, self-improved, sexually liberated undergraduate boy, nonchalantly slouching toward his sagging yellow house with one or another girl apprentice in a black leotard close behind. Much of the clicking that seemed to be coming out of the trees was in the service of explaining the apolitical apathy and social conformity of American youth, as opposed to the exciting European species, and to giving immutable reasons why our own selfish and spoiled youth would never budge.

S PRING ARRIVES treacherously at schools. One day, each student is huddling unto himself, with his failings and melancholia decently covered up, and the next, he sits at his open window, exposing his yearnings to the warm air. In the spring twilight, one can look up from Harvard Yard and see one such unfulfilled human being in each window, like rows of tenement flower pots.

In private quarters, spring is received, as life is lived, with more dignity. What happened to Gilbert was merely that one May afternoon in 1958, he detected a whiff of something delicious moving his burlap curtains. His response was to peel off his gray sweater, into the thick wool of which some forgotten girl had knitted her tears, and to caress his bare chest. For months, he had loved that sweater, stiffened from having been offered to other forgotten girls as a sexual mop, but now it irritated him.

Discarding the sweater was the only thing Gilbert had done since one-thirty, when he had typed on a sheet of paper, "AGAMEMNON AND KING LEAR: A COMPARISON IN PERSONAL MONARCHY." It was now four-thirty.

A rosy girl, slower to detect the spring but then savoring it, arose from the floor, where she had been reading all afternoon, and leaned against the back of Gilbert's chair, placing her cheek along his neck.

"Margery," he said, "cut that out."

Margery smiled, sank back onto the floor, and cradled one of his bare feet in her breasts, or at least on that part of her angora sweater. "You have very aristocratic toes," she said.

Gilbert shook his aristocratic foot free, ripped the paper from the typewriter, and inserted another page, on which he typed, "HELEN OF TROY AND THE DUCHESS OF MALFI: ARISTOCRATIC REBELS." Then he typed the keys lightly, producing a rhythmic sound but not advancing the carriage. He tapped outside-to-inside patterns, and then he tapped inside-to-outside patterns, which were harder. The paper, with its neatly centered title, remained otherwise blank.

"Come on, Margery," he said. "Now cut it out, will you?"

She had parked a rubber band on his knee while she gathered up her hair for a ponytail. "I am trying to write a paper," he said. "Does that mean anything to you, that I am trying to write a paper? An important paper? Do you care?"

She grabbed the rubber band and applied it, then tugged at her hair to loosen some of it over the tops of her ears, which, as Gilbert had pointed out to her, were not quite flat against her head. He seemed to be waiting for an answer. "Yes, I care," she said.

"All right, then. Let me alone, okay?"

"I'm not bothering you." She took up her book and waited to hear that he had gone back to work. "Yes, Margery," he said while she pretended to read. "You're not bothering me. So what are you doing, Margery? Why are you here?"

"Oh, Gil, honestly. Have I said one word, even? I just like being here while you work. Because I love you."

"Wonderful. Look, why don't you go back to your room and discuss it with everyone? Okay? Isn't that part of being in love? Wouldn't it be more fun?"

"Is that it! Honestly, Gilbert, you are so funny. Why do we care if people know? I haven't done anything I'm ashamed of. But honestly, I haven't told anyone. I told you that."

Strictly speaking, only about twenty of Margery's friends knew that she had spent the mid-year break in Gilbert's apartment, and she had explained to them all that he respected her too much to sleep with her. Not many more of her friends had been told, six weeks later, that she was going to spend Easter vacation with him and that, naturally, she slept with him: People did who were really in love and practically engaged to be married. As it happened, Gilbert went home to his parents for Easter and suggested that Margery, unless she had lost all family feeling in her wanton abandon, had better go to hers. No announcement had been made at Radcliffe of this change in plans, however.

Gilbert had told no one. That was one of the things he had learned to shut up about. Boys who bragged about their conquests soon received word that their conquests had been reconquered. (At first, he had wondered how, under this system, word of one's accomplishments in this most important field of student competition would get out. He soon found that that took care of itself.)

"Margery," he said, again freeing a foot from affectionate capture, "what do I have to do? Burn the place down?"

"You're just cross because you have to write a paper," she said cheerfully. "Next time, don't leave it for the last day. I don't see how you're going to make it by tonight, and even if you did, when he said Friday, I'm sure he meant class this morning. Everybody else turned theirs in this morning. Except me, of course. You should have gone to class and asked for an extension. I handed mine in on Monday, because I have another paper due next week." She looked up and saw Gilbert peering at her solemnly, with his face against the typewriter carriage and his nose not quite touching the ribbon. "Shall I go and get us some sandwiches?" She caught his madman eyes. "How about I wash your sweater?" Margery didn't wait for an answer, but grabbed it and ran.

AT MIDNIGHT, it was cold again. Streetlamps provided small areas of light flecked with tree shadows, but Gilbert felt as if he were walking in a moving spotlight toward Harvard Square, where he would enter a fully illuminated stage. The act was loneliness, and Gilbert, a method actor, felt lonely. He walked with his fingertips in the back pockets of his white duck trousers, listening, for eight long blocks, to the sorrowful squeak of his tennis shoes.

Margery, he reflected bitterly, had left him to work

alone. She, like the other members of the collegiate community, would be having boisterous fun in the jolly houses. They could never imagine the life of a poet—the solitariness one had to endure in order to be at liberty when one's first poem would come to one.

But being unobserved was unendurable. He brought his loneliness to the Hayes Bickford cafeteria so that he would not have to bear it alone.

He was not the only one, of course. One could take the Bick for an ordinary working-class eatery, and like Gilbert's block, it did have representative members of that element going about their blunt lives without apparent regard to the academic-Bohemian drama in their midst. Its whitish tile institutional surfaces were theoretically cleanable, although never clean, and it offered none of the ethnic heartiness that was available in the standard variety of cheap food places close to Gilbert's room. Perhaps the only lie that Gilbert told himself was that he went to the Bick to eat quickly.

Actually, it was his club. His freshman neighbor belonged to the Fly. Both of them felt that they lowered themselves to grace an overrated organization, and that they could not assume full equality on the part of the other members, but they both needed some place to go where their special qualities were appreciated and they were assured of respect.

Other members of the Society of Bickford Fellows included a friendly, helpful, perfect student who was one of the two Negroes in the class and who didn't feel comfortable until ten years later, when he was a black and was nominated to the Board of Overseers, and was told how unusual an honor it was for his age, and when he, in turn, told Harvard, in a mimeographed letter, to

go fuck itself, a satisfaction that he came to regret when
he ran for Congress; a Hollywood producer's son who
had some standing in local dramatic activities, especially
when his stepmother came to visit; and a junior who had
had a novel published the year before and had since broken
his leg twice in falls from the best motorcycle in Massachusetts. There was no denying that the Fly had it all
over the Bick in its refusal to admit stray laborers, fresh-
men engaging in tourism, and a variety of nighttime
coffee drinkers.

Gilbert stopped on the sidewalk and studied the illuminated activity contained within the bright square of
the window. The wall hooks were three- and four-deep
in pea jackets and polo coats, and customers were vying
for attention at the counter in the back. An aproned man
who had swept a pile of cigarette butts along the tiled
floor was intoning his complaints against the clientele,
and a bearded student at a center table was yelling at
him to shut up so he could write. For his entrance, Gilbert walked directly to an empty table, the repository of
pie plates, ashtrays, and tin forks no longer needed at
neighboring tables. The table he had chosen was located
next to one occupied by three young women. The girl
he had picked out through the window did not have the
awkward touch of vulnerability that usually told him
which girl in the Widener Library was not really studying, which one at the Fogg Museum had not come to see
pictures, or which salesgirl at the Coop kept a book hidden in the pile of sweatshirts. He could scarcely have
said what signs tipped him off so reliably: unplucked eyebrows, tights instead of kneesocks, a green bookbag carried in a certain defiant way, an absence of lipstick. In
Margery's case the clue had been a leather bookmark—a

child's bookmark, triangular to fit over the corner of a page and stamped "Where I Fell Asleep." Gilbert had spotted it in Dionysus in Poetry, Cult, and Politics (having erroneously assumed that any girl in that class would be eligible), and was not surprised to look up and see the ripe, broadly drawn body of an Edwardian courtesan under high school sorority clothes.

There were no such signs about the perfectly groomed girl sitting across from him now, with her blond pageboy, blue sweater set, and pale plaid skirt—everything screaming Connecticut! Peck & Peck!—things alien to the heart of Gilbert Fairchild. But for all that Erna Janet Boothe looked like the animated part of a wood-paneled station wagon, Gilbert felt that she had a line out casting for just some dark poetic bed as he had standing empty.

He fixed an elbow on his table and lowered his chin into his hand and began staring. The old panic flickered a warning that things might actually be as they seemed, and this could be a self-sufficient young woman who came to the cafeteria to eat with her companions and who would be angry to be approached by a strange skinny kid in a poet's costume. Discipline and experience prevented this thought from translation into the slightest tremor. Not an eyelash interfered with Gilbert's stare.

Four minutes later, Erna's gaze swept around the room. Her eyes rested a fraction of a second too long on Gilbert's, and when she turned quickly away to look out of the distant window, she knocked a book from the table. She stooped to retrieve it and bumped her head coming up, then gave the conversation a U-turn that jerked the heads of her listeners—not missing a beat, she miraculously transformed her saga of romantic woe into nothing that any eavesdropper, or they, either, could understand.

Gilbert left his eyes fixed on her, but shifted his body into a slouch. The movement of his chair attracted the attention of Erna's companions, and the entire situation presented itself with clarity to each of the four. According to the creed, any social contact a girl might accidentally have with a boy took precedence over any bosom-friends-to-the-death bond with other girls. Erna obviously had an Opportunity, and it behooved her friends to scram.

It was their obligation to abandon Erna instantly; it was Erna's to protest and look miffed; it was Gilbert's to smooth the way conversationally from his table to Erna's. It was all as conventionally staged as a ballet, with the corps melting so gracefully into the forest of paper trees that the exact moment of their disappearance from the stage was not observed, and the two principals, having been absently left behind, found themselves drawn shyly into a pas de deux.

(Like any star, Gilbert made even a traditional role his own. Years later, a classmate of Gilbert's, by then a federal circuit judge, tried to describe the technique: "I was sitting there, having a cup of coffee with my girl friend. We'd been at the Brattle to see *To Have and Have Not*, and she'd let me put my arm around her *under* her arm, as long as I didn't move it and we both kept our eyes on Humphrey Bogart. That was a big step in those days. And in comes this shrimp with the curls, and he sits down because he's in my History of Philosophy class, and he starts talking about what is reality and does the fox go around the tree or does the tree go around the fox. And you know what? The next thing I know, he's got my girl.")

In the present instance, Gilbert was doing mime. His

stare lasted until the others had delivered their exit lines about papers to write and hair to wash, and Erna had explained that she needed another cup and promised to join them within minutes. This, of course, obligated her to buy coffee, unless something happened to distract her. Just when she was giving up and getting up, Gilbert reached out his long-fingered ivory hand and lifted one of her books. Erna sat back down, waiting, and finally opened coldly with: "Excuse me, I believe that's mine."

Gilbert held the book high and open with his left hand. His reading voice was sonorous and solemn and derived from a T. S. Eliot record. "A major obstacle has been the presence of those who insist that the demonstration of altered Soviet tendencies must also include the disavowal of the provisions in Marxist ideology for universal revolution and the subsequent triumph of communism." He let the book fall and looked at Erna as if to demand an explanation for such language.

"You were in Emerson, Thoreau, and Hawthorne with me last year," she said. Gilbert said nothing. "Where are you from?" she offered.

"The Seventeenth Century," said Gilbert. "Let's not start that. I understand you need coffee. Get it, and then you can come back and tell me who you are. But not where you're from."

"Are you getting any?"

"No," said Gilbert. "I haven't eaten all day, and coffee might make me sick."

"Why? What's the matter with you?"

"A common, chronic disease," said Gilbert. "It's called poverty. They probably don't have it where you come from."

"I don't really care if I have anything, either," she confided. It was the wrong answer. Gilbert started playing mournfully with the pie crumbs on the tabletop, and she got up. He turned the pages of her book while she was away, and only looked up when she said, "The Red Cross sent you this," and set down a plate of poached eggs and hash.

"You forgot the fork," he said. Erna laughed gaily. She came back from the next trip with two forks, and daintily poked with one at his plate until he pushed the plate toward her and said roughly, "You want it?"

He turned his face away. No matter how long it had been since he had learned that girls found eagerness repulsive, he could never quite get over the feeling that to insult a strange girl was suicidal. He did it, but he couldn't stand to watch.

"No, it's for you," Erna replied. She had trouble with the other instructions, too, and within half an hour, Gilbert knew that the Connecticut looks were a lie, that there seemed to be some question whether the daughter of a Minneapolis tool company vice president was as good as the East Coast upper crust but that it had been settled by one Walter Oliphant, the only son of a moderately rich, very old family from Providence, Rhode Island, who offered a carat and a quarter of engagement ring that entitled her to an eight-bridesmaid wedding, but who was then defiantly thrown over on the grounds of having pale eyes that had come to disgust her. Gilbert listened intently, but offered no comment. He did not consider that a blond girl could have a history.

As it was a first date, so to speak, Gilbert walked Erna home, contrary to his usual practice. He wrote his telephone number in her library book, declined to take hers, and watched her thread her way across the porch through piles of bodies in various stages of embracing, while the watchman clapped his hands and called out, "All right, girls, break it up."

ON SATURDAY MORNING, Gilbert put on the white duck trousers and walked barefoot out to the hallway. From the wall box with his name on it, he pulled three envelopes. He looked over the magazines on the mail table and chose two addressed to the couple across the hall and one bearing the name of the girl upstairs.

Back in his room, he poured himself a glass of milk and put the carton back into the small yellowish refrigerator. The kitten gave a yelp, and Gilbert poured part of his glassful into her Hayes Bickford saucer. He considered the amounts: The saucer hadn't been emptied the night before, so it was almost full now, while his glass was low. Holding the kitten at bay with one bare foot, he reached down and poured some back into his glass.

He drank his milk while leaning on the table-high refrigerator and examining the mail: A letter from his parents, the telephone bill, and a crinkly pale blue envelope. Once, he had received a similarly crinkly letter with a mouth imprinted on the back in lipstick and had fastidiously dropped it into the garbage, but this one had only a Lesley College return address, so he tossed it aside, but not out, with the bill.

He did not intend to read the letter from his mother and father, but only to pocket the aquamarine check for which it had served as wrapping paper. Gilbert knew that he caused his parents no trouble. He neither smoked nor drank, nor swore, for that matter, although they sometimes did when talking about the government. Taking drugs had never entered his mind, even when his high school had shown tantalizing movies, on rainy days when they couldn't have track, suggesting how thoroughly and casually one could arrange to be lost to society forever as a dope fiend. Nor had any concept of political unity with other students for common aims, much less for ideal- istic goals, ever occurred to him (it was certainly not what was meant then when people acknowledged that Harvard trained statesmen). They had never thought of wondering whether he was a virgin, a question that was burning up females' parents. Yet he knew that the affec- tionate letter would be aquiver with worry, and he knew that he couldn't help reading it.

It was written on the back of a syllabus page from a course in The Dynamics of Space. Ginerva Fairchild, who had given Gilbert his curls, was the longest continuously enrolled student at the New School for Social Research. Twice a week, she asked him whether he had given any thought to what he was to do when his own four-year education should come to its neat ending.

He didn't understand his parents' worry about his future. Harvard had been their idea, and they had made great efforts to instill in him a preference for that brand name. It wasn't as though they had chosen it for any professor or special field to which they thought him suited, or in which he had expressed an interest. In fact, he had had to sublimate his academic interests in high school to get into Harvard. It would have been pleasanter to ponder the causes of the American Revolution, as stated in the textbook, than to have to make up selfish psycho- logical motives for its heroes; to shed tears over *Silas Marner* instead of tearing it apart; to memorize the French phrases in the book, instead of bits of Verlaine with which to sidetrack the class. While other students plodded on, some doing the suggested as well as the required reading, writing papers containing information and conclusions they had read in textbooks and noted in lectures, Gilbert argued, criticized, ridiculed, and talked back. He worked so hard that it began to cut into his recreation, which was reading good books at home in his room. He found he needed not only grades but popularity. His high school's college counselor had explained to him the concept of the Well-Rounded Student, object of all good college recruitment programs.

Gilbert was appalled. He had, at best, been socially inconspicuous at school, but it was a natural result of his new self-expression that nobody liked him. He hardly blamed them. He didn't much like what he heard when he talked in class, either. The counselor had suggested his trying out for the school newspaper, but every bright pupil wrote. What Gilbert did instead was to found a literary magazine and to publish in it his own obscure writing and the work of a few other loners. This was in tenth grade. The newspaper's teacher-adviser noticed, and recruited him to add creativity to the newspaper. In twelfth grade, Gilbert became editor of the newspaper, in recognition of his superior sarcasm, while the literary magazine, bequeathed to a sophomore poet, had disappeared. That year, Gilbert also became the first president of the Literary Society and the first vice president of the Philosophical Society, having founded both and held early elections.

The day the letter came from Harvard, his father kept running around the dining room table whooping, and his mother couldn't stop laughing. What other teen-ager put so much effort into getting his parents what they wanted? And what did he do when he got to Harvard College? Flunk out? No, he made the Dean's List. He was even popular, if you counted Margery and her ilk. What did parents with such a son mean by greedily demanding to know what he was going to be when he got out of Harvard? He was going to be a Harvard graduate, of course.

"Have you thought about lining up a summer job?" his mother had written.

Gilbert's ingenuity and energy worked in spurts. It never failed him in important matters, but there wasn't enough left over to line up his shoes.

GILBERT WAS SCRUPULOUS about following his professors' instructions on the length of papers. He had never written one that exceeded the specified minimum, and he felt this entitled him to some leeway in the matter of time. It meant, though, that his papers had to be delivered, with oral explanations. He finished his toilette and headed up the old wooden staircase in the hall, to a door with a large embossed card in flowery script, announcing "Mrs. Betty Pergino." He had not forgotten taking her magazine, but after seeing what his kitten had done to it, had courteously refrained from troubling her with the remains.

"Who is it?"

"Me," said Gilbert. "Can I borrow your bicycle?"

The door opened, closed, the chain was taken down, the door opened again, and a young woman in a pink quilted housecoat smiled out at him. Gilbert, who found all the young women in his life to be alike, possibly because he steered clear of any who might not appreciate him, thought Mrs. Pergino exotic. "It's only the kid, Frank," she called. "I'll get the key. I keep the bike locked now. You never know, do you?"

Frank appeared from the kitchen in trousers and undershirt, holding a plate on which ham slices alternated with slices of paper. "Why don't you quit bothering her, nerd?" he asked sociably.

"Why don't you quit sponging off her?" asked Gilbert, who came to his shoulder. "Why don't you go back to your six children, ape?" He smiled.

Betty returned with the key, and Gilbert moved close to her for safety. "Like some breakfast, honey? I bet you never eat right."

"Thanks, anyway, I have to go."

"Let him. Little fag spoils my digestion," said Frank, lowering a slice of ham into his mouth.

Betty took it as being witty, Frank not being her husband, and put her arm around his big waist while beaming at Gilbert. "That's a beautiful kid," she said. "Smart. You still the best in school, honey?"

"I guess so," said Gilbert, in a hurt tone to show that she should have said something more passionate, although the attitude was what he had just been wishing his parents to take. He was whistling happily as he tossed his paper into the bicycle basket, and took off, only stopping to tuck the paper into his shirt because the pages had been fluttering. After the long winter of huddling against buildings, looking to them for protection against the weather, people were out walking freely on the sidewalks. His Cambridge neighborhood was ugly, but without its black-edged patches of used snow, it looked jaunty and smelled fresh. Gilbert turned off at an old brick building, leaned the bicycle against a tree, and skipped down the steps to his English section-man's basement office. The professor who gave the course did not deal with students. Gilbert was sliding the paper carefully under the door when it opened.

"Hey! Rupert Brooke, isn't it? Hi there, Rupert."

Gilbert had nothing to say, but at least he knew not
to smile. One of his earliest lessons, learned on the elementary school playground, was not to pretend to enjoy
being ridiculed.

"Okay," said Gilbert. "I won't take your time. Here."
He flicked the paper onto the scratched wooden desk.
"You obviously don't want to talk to me."

Gilbert had never yet had anyone resist that word-
ing. "What about?" asked the section-man, sinking down
into his standard-issue Harvard armchair until his head
rested casually against its back.

"Nothing. Advice."

"You asking or giving?"

"Asking," said Gilbert, exiting, but allowing the instructor to stop him before the third step.

"You don't want my advice, old man. Not worth anything. You know, I got overruled on your Thomas Dek-
ker paper. I had in mind G for Garbage, so I don't want
you to think the A-minus came from me."

"Okay," said Gilbert. "Never mind. Hey, not even
O, for Out of the Ordinary?"

"How come you don't come to section once in a while?
I wouldn't ask you to come *all* the time. I'm hoping that
instead of a raise this year, they're going to let me flunk
you." The voice was kinder than it had been.

"Maybe I'm leaving, anyway. That's part of what I
wanted to talk to you about"

It wasn't that the section-man didn't know he was had.
But the pause was too much for him, and he asked, "What
do you mean?"

"I don't know what to do," said Gilbert. "The *Atlantic*
people tell me one thing and Mr. Thomas said another,

and while I'd like to strike now if they want me, I don't know if I'm ready. I've got to talk to someone."

"What are we talking about, Rupert? What *Atlantic* people? The *Atlantic Monthly?*"

"That's right. I have a piece there they said they'll take if I re-do it, but they don't say how, exactly."

"Who's Mr. Thomas, one of the editors? I knew a Mr. Braithwaite there."

"No, no," said Gilbert. "Dylan Thomas. You know. He was at my prep school once, and I showed him some things. He wrote me letters for a long time, about writing and stuff, kind of strange, and then he just stopped. Now I don't have anyone to show things to. Look, I'm sorry. You're busy. I'm sorry the paper's late."

"That's all right. You know, if you're really serious, I'd be glad to look at your work."

"Okay," said Gilbert, leaving. "Let me think about it."

"Wait a minute. Do you, um, still have the letters?"

"From Mr. Thomas? Sure." Gilbert gave his teacher a sad little salute, and went outside to pick up Betty's bicycle. The section-man brushed his thick eyebrows with one finger as he watched Gilbert from the bottom of the steps, and then went in and picked up "ANTIGONE AND OTHELLO: THE PASSION TO SET THINGS RIGHT."

MARGERY WAS SITTING on the hall floor when he came home, after stopping at the Coop and a grocery store. She had his gray sweater on her lap with the sleeves neatly folded behind the body, as if it were a present. He unlocked the apartment door and was about to close it again from the inside when she scrambled up, ran in, and held the sweater out to him.

Gilbert sniffed it under the arms. "What did you do, boil it?"

"It could have stood it," she said happily.

"What's the matter, don't you like the smell of my body?"

"How can you say such a thing?" She trotted around behind him as he put two cartons of milk into the refrigerator and a Chianti bottle on top. A paper cup of Chianti was always served after initial lovemaking sessions. Margery got them only occasionally now. The last bottle was still in the trash. It was one of Gilbert's principles not to use Chianti bottles as candlesticks.

"Who knitted the sweater?" He didn't answer, so Margery added generously, "Not that it matters. I know it was before you met me."

"Louisa May Alcott."

"Is that the same Louisa May Alcott who did the drawing?" Above Gilbert's bed was a drawing of him, also lying on a bed.

"The girl who did that drawing is now dead. I'll thank you not to joke about her."

"Gilbert?"

"What is it?"

"Gilbert? Don't you love me any more?"

Oh, there it was. All year, girls had been accusing him of not loving them any more, when he had never said he loved them in the first place. He was careful about that. Not saying it was his virginity that he was saving, while collecting theirs. It was also supposed to be protection against being promiscuously quoted, when they went around confiding their stories to whole dormitories. His legalistically noncommittal answer was a passionately intoned "What do you think?"

Margery was blinking at him, and he recognized the

approach of the emotional cracking point. She would let out a flood that would swamp his whole evening and leave the place mildewed. "What do you think?" he asked again, more gently, and he walked close enough for her to collapse against him.

Holding on to him enabled her to fit the cracked parts back together. Gilbert, who had been about to assist the rescue, let his hands hang down at his sides, and Margery held him and sobbed, "You make me so happy."

"Do I?" he asked. He took a step backward, so that Margery had to stand alone, unfastened the white duck pants, and let them drop. He wore no underwear, and after he had kicked off his sneakers and pulled the pants legs over his feet, he lay down on the bed in his shirt, clasped his hands under his head, and looked up at her with his body alert.

Margery started pulling and tugging and struggling with her clothes in several directions at once, while she used one foot to scuff off one flat shoe from the other. As a show, it was more comic than erotic, but Gilbert watched her, and when she uncovered the poster-sized body that looked so stocky under clothes, he pulled her toward him by a curl of her pubic hair. She opened her mouth into a smile, and rushed to him, but Gilbert pushed her away with a thumb in one of her wide nipples. Suddenly, he got up on his knees and forced her to hers. They faced each other, a foot apart and not touching, and then he reached a hand underneath her and drew the pads of his fingers along in a slow stroke, like a pops conductor drawing out the last echo from the second violin section. Margery's eyes were shut, and Gilbert stroked her, noting when she switched her breathing from nose to mouth. It occurred to him that no one ever did clever things like that to him. The telephone rang.

"Shall I answer it?"

"No."

But he stopped touching her, folded his hands primly over himself, and did nothing while they both listened to the ringing. "Oh, go ahead."

Gilbert leapt up and said, almost whispered, "Hello."

"Well, hello. Is this the Seventeenth Century?"

"No," said Gilbert, "it's Kleberly 5-2387."

"Gilbert Fairchild?"

"Yes?"

"It's Erna. Erna Boothe. From last night?"

"I remember. Good of you to call." He shrugged helplessly across the room at Margery, who stopped pretending she wasn't listening and maintained a question mark on her forehead.

"You asked me to."

"Yes," said Gilbert.

"Yes. Well, I was wondering, did you notice if I left my glasses at the Bick last night?"

"No."

"Oh. Well, I don't remember if I had them there. I don't need them, except to read. I just thought maybe you'd noticed. They're tortoiseshell."

"Do you want me to go down and look?"

"Oh, no. It doesn't matter. I'll find them. I probably just lost them somewhere. Well, how are you, anyway?"

"About the same," said Gilbert.

"Oh. Well, you know, this is sort of embarrassing, but I know we talked about getting together, and I don't remember if we said anything definite. Except that I should call. So I did."

Gilbert was observing Margery, who had picked up the fact that he was talking in an English accent. "I can't tonight," he said, back in his more or less normal voice.

"I have a lot of work to do. Suppose I call you tomorrow, or you call me."

Margery jumped out of bed, snatched her wired brassiere from the pile of clothing she had left on the floor, and tried to fasten it behind her back. The telephone had a long cord, and Gilbert was able to walk across the room, cradling the receiver on his shoulder, crooning, "I really feel I should work tonight, but maybe I could put it off, after all," while with his free hand, he scooped up Margery's jumper, blouse, half-slip, and underpants. "You're very understanding," he said into the telephone as he pushed the bundle out the window.

Margery shrieked, and Gilbert smiled at her proudly. "I'm terribly sorry," he said into the telephone, "but there seems to be some sort of disturbance going on here."

"What is it?" the voice asked, but Gilbert hung up. Margery and he faced each other across the room, she tense with fury and he dancing with excitement. "You get me my clothes, you bastard," she hissed.

"What'll you give me?"

"You better, if you know what's good for you."

"Oh, yeah? What's good for you?" He leered.

Margery lifted her arm in the beginning of the standard feminine movie slap—a good, long, wide crack—but Gilbert grabbed her wrist in mid-air and forced it behind her back until she suddenly went limp. When she cried, he let her go. "Lie down," he said. She did, but with her back toward him and her face to the wall.

Gilbert sat down on the bed and gently extracted the rubber band from her hair. "Margy," he said, combing the puppyish brown hair with his fingers. "Margy, do you want me?" There was no reply, so he took her shoulders in his hands and turned her over. He arranged her hair prettily on the caseless pillow, and peered worriedly into her face.

She looked at him, not crying now, but with an accumulated reservoir in her eye rims. Gilbert took off his shirt, which he had been unbuttoning while he was on the telephone. She lifted her arms toward him, as if it were a dying embrace, and he leaned into it, but then stopped. "Margy, I'm not going to take you unless you say you want me to. Margy? Answer me. Do you want me to?"

"I want you," she said. "Want" came out in two syllables. It was two or three minutes before her enthusiasm returned. It had not taken much for Gilbert to teach Margery to love a good romp.

She lay with her head on his stomach to recuperate, until he slapped her playfully and said, "Time to get to work."

"Not yet, Gil."

"You lie there, then," he said, tucking in the dirty covers around her. She was smiling and still, like a good child, while he dressed, but when he turned and went out the door, shutting it behind him, she sat up nervously.

But then he was back, and Margery snuggled into the covers again, feigning luxurious sleep. A slight weight fell on her legs. Gilbert had dumped her clothes there. While she tiredly replaced them on her body, Gilbert read, sitting in the desk chair with his feet in an open drawer.

"Will I see you tomorrow?"

"What are you, a sex maniac? I have to study."

"You never study," she said.

"Whose fault is that? If you cared about me, you'd see that I did."

"You made a date over the phone. I heard you."

Gilbert swirled around. "Here," he said, grabbing the blue letter from the morning mail and waving it in her face. "You want to read my mail, too?"

Margery looked precarious again, although her lips were pressed tightly together. "Margery, I think you better go home and get some sleep. You had a rough day. You got to take care of yourself, love." The word *love* was a present.

After she had gone, Gilbert picked up the cat and gave it a pleased squeeze, which it didn't care for. "Turned out to be a pretty good evening, didn't it?" he asked.

Chapter II

SUNDAY MORNING, two weeks later, opened with
the distant sound of church chimes, those ancient heralds of
the day of boredom. Gilbert tried fooling it by faking
energy. He jumped out of bed, wrapped himself in a
blanket, and ran out the door, but the people across the
hall had already taken in their Sunday paper, and he returned empty-handed. He looked in a bureau drawer
with the thought of changing the bedsheets, which had
been on since March, but there was only one clean sheet,
and it hardly seemed worthwhile pulling the bed apart
just for that. He opened his door when he heard footsteps, but Frank said, "Close the door and mind your

own business, you little fag," without pausing on his course upstairs. The kitten shot out the door during that moment.

There was no staying in the house after the faint tin voice of a television preacher began to seep under the door, but there was nowhere to go. What could he say to the pairs of girls in bowl-shaped veils and navy dresses and black suede best pumps, who would be coming out of churches?

He had to make do with known and available resources. He reached for that instrument of desperation, the telephone.

"Margery isn't here," said a stern voice. "Is this Gilbert Fairchild?"

Oh-oh. Margery had a romance counselor. Gilbert, who knew a thing or two of dormitory life, recognized the officious tone of the peer-adviser issuing instructions for plots to bring errant lovers to their knees. Last fall, when he had been newer at all this and friskier, Gilbert had seduced such a counselor and then left her and her client to talk over abandonment together. If, indeed, they were still talking. His intention had been to get the word out, among all womanhood. If he had neglected Margery for a short while, it should have taught her to appreciate him more, not to contemplate insurrection.

"Gilbert Fairchild?" he asked. "That cad? The rotten one?"

"Because if it is, she doesn't want to talk to him."

"Supposing it isn't, does she want to talk to him?"

"What's that?"

"Nothing. Where is she?"

"Out. For a long, long time."

At this point, he heard some verbal scuffling, muffled

by a hand over the speaker, until Margery said coldly into it, "What do *you* want?" She would never have talked like that to his face, he knew—she was playing for the home audience.

"Will you give me a bath?"

"I wouldn't give you the time of day," she replied, in a triumph of wit.

"No, really. Like Japanese women do. Scrub my back."

"I'm not Japanese."

"For heaven's sake, even American women have instincts about spring cleaning. I haven't been washed for months, did you ever think of that?"

"No," said Margery.

"You're not the domestic type, are you, Margery?"

It was a significant challenge, artfully designed for Margery's weak spot. One of the things girls appreciated about Gilbert was that they could talk to him. He listened attentively, at least in the early stages of courtship, to all their hopes and dreams and fears. In two sessions, at most, they had handed over to him every weapon capable of felling them.

Margery's was that she wanted to be a doctor. As a little girl, she had confided this to her father, who had gradually given up owning a car, smoking, going to the theater at night, and going to theater matinées, as he budgeted four years of Radcliffe, four years of Harvard Medical School, a year of internship, and three years of residency. From the first expensive year, Margery brought home the question of how this could be reconciled with her being a woman, by which she meant a married woman.

Mr. Vagelos expressed the fervent hope that if Margery should happen to look up with love in her eyes upon, say, the anatomy class partner handling the other side of her assigned cadaver, it would at least be at someone whose parents had budgeted as carefully as he.

But the more sophisticated people Margery met at Radcliffe explained to her that even this wouldn't do. Medicine took years of drudgery, first in school and then in horrible hospitals, before you got rich. Margery would have to spend those years launching her husband's medical career, and statistically, they reasoned, she would also be bearing and rearing children. And that was if she happened to get a husband at medical school. They knew that male medical students never thought of their few female classmates as real girls. And no wonder. What kind of girl would deliberately go after a career that would interfere with being a woman?

It was Margery's timid hope to do both. The girls had a point, she knew, but there was also something to the plans that she had made with her dear, naïve father.

After all, her classmates did not actually admit that they had the nasty motive of using the college as access to the most valuable male community in America. They valued themselves. Like Miss America winners, they could recite their statistics without embarrassment: their IQs, their college board scores, their grade averages. Some bragged that they had never been invited to a high school social event. Now they were wildly interested in the history of art or child psychology, and it was not their fault if these would be suitable hobbies for fashionable wives and mothers.

The college always said it was sending its students off on the pure road toward the ivory tower, and seemed mildly puzzled that each one of them was ambushed and carried off to a suburban castle. Although entire classes

were waylaid every spring, the administration never
seemed to realize that it had a highwayman problem.

The victims of these kidnappings were amazed, too,
although some upperclasswomen got impatient if they
were kept waiting for their amazement too long. With
access to Harvard College and its graduate schools, Radcliffe girls were surrounded by lawyers, corporation presidents, and doctors, all aged eighteen to twenty-five, but
with two-car futures absolutely guaranteed. Elsewhere,
a Harvard Law School student might be considered the
next step down from royalty, but these women were so
privileged as to be capable of turning one down for the
honor of going to work to support, say, a doctoral candidate in Chinese Studies or Romance Philology. One of
Margery's classmates actually did turn down royalty.
How was she to know, she wept later, that that nasty
little Indian who had bragged to her about his fancy
English schools was literally a prince?

So Margery pretended to be pretending to be interested
in medicine. She was always afraid of being revealed as
masculine, not only to others but to herself. In the game
tests people did of masculinity and femininity, such as
whether you looked at your own fingernails with the tips
curled toward you or whether you spread out your hand
with the fingers pointing out, Margery anxiously waited
to hear if what she did was right. And now here was
Gilbert, whose mistress she was, suggesting that she wasn't
domestic.

"I guess I'll come over," she said. "I have something
important to tell you, anyway."

"You're a good kid," said Gilbert, hanging up. It was
not, perhaps, what every girl longed to hear, but it could
be categorized as a compliment.

There were tributes to Gilbert in the way Margery showed up. The fact that she came later than he might have expected showed that she was learning from him the value of suspense and anxiety, or would have, if he had not been too busy with his preparations to notice. The way she was dressed showed his influence, along with some conflicting, older influences. Gilbert had taught her to dress in black if she wanted to be taken seriously, and she had used manicure scissors to remove the bright cutout of a poodle, in felt with a jeweled collar, from her black circle skirt. She had a stiff white crinoline under it, though, and a knife-pleated scarf brightening her new black shirt at the neckline. Margery was still subject to lapses in faith, in which she wondered how Gilbert, clever as he was, could know more than the fat college issues of *Glamour* and *Mademoiselle.*

Gilbert was returning to his apartment from the dark hallway, where he had carefully placed a sign on the bathroom door, and he ushered her into his room with a bow. He was wearing a wine woolen bathrobe, edged in navy, and it was hanging strategically open. The gift box in which it had arrived two Christmases ago was open on the floor, and he kicked it to one side to make a path for her. "Good morning, Mikimoto," he said courteously.

"Hi," said Margery. "Gilbert, I have to talk to you."

"Aren't you forgetting something?"

"I said hello."

"That's not it," he replied. "Margery, I noticed this morning that the tub is dirty. Now, I realize that is not your fault. Other people used it. But the fact remains that the bathtub is extremely dirty."

"It's flooded," said Margery. "You can't use it. You're supposed to use upstairs."

"Don't believe everything you read," said Gilbert.

"Look, I really do have to talk to you. I'm not kidding."

"Okay, okay, but I really need a bath, and I'm not kidding, either. Can't you talk to me at the same time?"

"I guess so," she said. "Am I supposed to get undressed?"

"Please, this is a respectable bath, not an orgy. I will get undressed, if you please. When the time comes." He took a plastic soap container from a drawer and said, "Follow me. Leave your coat here."

Margery wriggled out of her raincoat, the reversible one she had to wear out before she could follow Gilbert's instructions about buying a trenchcoat, and followed. He locked the bathroom door from the inside, and she squeezed against the wall to keep out of his way as he bustled about. He hung up a towel marked "Hotel Commander" and produced a can of scouring powder and a brown sponge from beneath the sink. Flicking powder into the bathtub, he knelt and turned on the water, sponge in hand. "Here, let me do that," said Margery. When the tub was full, Gilbert turned his back to her, and she absently helped him remove his robe.

Her wandering attention prevented her from seeing what a wonderful time Gilbert was having. He stepped in regally, and sat down with a majestic splash. Gingerly lying back with the porcelain edge under his neck, he closed his eyes and pointed somewhere in the direction of the sink. Margery pried the soap out of its gummy dish and rubbed his body hypnotically.

"Darling?"

"Hmmmmmmmmmm?" he sang out, smiling, his eyes closed.

"Gilbert? Can I ask you something? Do you know a girl named Erna Boothe in my dorm?"

"Shhhh," said the watery figure. "This is so peaceful. Thank you. Let's just be quiet and enjoy it, shall we?"

The quietness had turned tense, however, and Margery, blocked at one point, tried another. "I should have gotten my period yesterday or today," she remarked.

"What do you want me to do about it?" There was annoyance in his voice, but it dated from the mention of Erna's name and did not seem to intensify with the introduction of the new topic, which he was taking firmly as just another possessive trick.

"I don't know. I just thought I'd tell you."

Gilbert sat up in the tub. "Just remember, toots, you weren't exactly a virgin when I got you."

"I was, too! I was, too!"

"Well, maybe technically, but that's all. Don't force me to be nasty, but I haven't forgotten all those sordid confessions, you know. What about Dexter, huh?"

In flushes of post-coital warmth, Margery had confessed not only her small collection of deeds but the thoughts, too. Dexter had been the 'cello player from her high school orchestra whom she had loved from afar but never spoken to. Possibly Gilbert was confusing him with Donald, with whom she had gone steady last year, and who had had his hand inside her clothing from eleven-thirty to midnight on Fridays and until one on Saturdays, from October until June. Donald was an engineering student and had given her a flannel sleeping shirt marked "Massachusetts Institute of Technology."

"Gilbert! You know perfectly well—"

"I'm just trying to show you how silly you're being. I'm getting tired of hearing about your plumbing. You're always late. I think you're using a Gregorian calendar."

"But suppose—"

"Come on, Margery, stop it. You're embarrassing me.

I'll tell you what. Let's go out to a restaurant. That'll take your mind off it." He settled back in the murky water, his brow smooth again, and closed his eyes.

GILBERT HAD an actual friend, a psychology major who frequently reminded Gilbert that he didn't like Gilbert, but was interested in him from an academic point of view. They were put in the same room freshman year and stayed together until Gilbert had worked the apartment deal for himself.

The friend's name was Buddy Loomis, which he often volunteered embarrassed him, as Buddy, his real full name, was such an obvious attempt of his father's to be reborn in his generation. Gilbert had volunteered that it wouldn't take him far socially, and had suggested "Bentley." This seemed ingenious to the former Buddy Loomis, who began to feel reborn himself, but the change was ineffectual because Buddy's former classmates from the Taft School kept divulging his old name at the most inopportune moments.

He was waiting in Gilbert's apartment, looking through the mail and papers on the desk, when he saw Gilbert enter in his open bathrobe, with Margery behind him, blouse soaked, carrying a towel.

"Jesus Christ," he said.

"Hello, Bentley," said Gilbert. "What's the matter?"

"I don't know how you do it," said Bentley, unable to keep his mouth shut in front of the girl.

"Whoever said you did?" asked Gilbert. "Bentley's in love with me, too," he explained, having unfortunately been entrusted with a day-by-day recital of Bentley's analysis.

Buddy, now recognizing Margery as someone who could hear what men said, started to protest, but since he had originated the theory, he could only, in all honesty, come up with "No, I've worked it out and I don't think that's what it was."

Margery perked up and was darting about, smiling hospitably and shutting doors and drawers.

"Am I interrupting something?" Buddy asked. It sounded crude to all of them.

"No, you can go out with us. We were just going to get something to eat."

"Is it really okay if I come along?"

"Try to show a little confidence in yourself, Bentley. Don't you think your company is worth having? Can't you believe that anyone would ask you to eat with them?"

"Thank you," said Bentley humbly.

"Fine. You want to go out with us?"

"Sure. But look, there's something sort of personal I want to discuss with you."

"You, too? Margery, dear, would you excuse us, please?" Gilbert guided her shoulders toward the door. "You can come back in about five minutes," he whispered conspiratorially.

After she had left, with the choice of waiting in the hallway, in the wet bathroom, or on the porch, Buddy's mesmerized glance followed. "I know her now. Jesus, Gilbert, I don't know how you do it. I had a blind date with that girl once, and I never noticed anything. What the hell were you doing in the bathroom?"

"Having a bath. Is that what you wanted to discuss?"

"No. The two of you?"

"No, just me. Now what's your problem?"

"I don't have any problems I can't cope with. I just

wanted to tell you I'm doing a paper on you. It's confidential," he added, jerking his head meaningfully in the direction of the absent Margery.

"Abnormal Psych?"

"No, I'm sorry. Just regular. Cognitive Process in Personality, if you want to know."

"Are you using my name?"

"Of course not. You'll be part of a type. Don't worry."

"Oh. Well, I don't know, Bentley. I'll think it over."

"Okay, but hurry up, will you? Because I have to have a conference next week, and I don't know what other type I can get at so easily."

"What about Margery?"

"For the paper?"

"Why don't you ask her? You want me to?"

"I figured I already know all about you, so it would be easy."

"Is that all you wanted to ask me?"

"Jesus, isn't that enough?"

Gilbert had been dressing while he listened to Buddy, and he stuck his head into the hall and shouted for Margery, "Let's go!"

"All right, I heard you," she said from the floor just outside his door, where she had been squatting. Gilbert looked down in amazement. Margery was decidedly getting tricky. She could have been eavesdropping.

They walked down Mount Auburn Street, the three of them, with their arms linked, Margery's penny loafers skipping along between Gilbert's sneakers and Buddy's white bucks. In Cronin's, they found a pewlike booth just vacated by four Harvardy-looking men in their tweedy twenties who probably taught at Simmons College and commuted to Cronin's in their Volkswagens. It was a friendly mid-afternoon meal, with beer for Margery and Buddy and an ostentatious glass of milk for Gilbert.

"It's your turn to pay," Gilbert said, when Margery left them to go to the ladies' room.

"Oh, no, you don't. I don't have to buy people's respect any more." Buddy's eyes were big and wavy from the old-man lenses of his glasses, and he always looked on the verge of tears.

"I thought you might have gotten to the point where you had enough confidence to be generous."

"Listen, you invited me. I'll pay for mine, but that's all."

"You want me to leave you alone with Margery?"

"Nothing doing. My adviser told me to stop taking sloppy seconds from you."

"Your adviser? Can't you afford an analyst any more?"

"My adviser in the Psych Department. He says I'm not ready for analysis again."

"Gee, I hope you make it. All right, we'll split it." To show his own generosity, Gilbert not only paid a third from his pocket but added a dollar tip after Margery returned, as she got her share from her red wallet, bursting with girls' autographed high school graduation pictures.

"It's all right," she said to Gilbert. "It's here."

When Gilbert realized what she meant, he moved fastidiously away from her.

"You know, Margery here would make a great subject for one of those papers of yours," he said. "Bentley does studies of interesting people," he added to Margery, in the polite tone of a hostess informing a bird watcher that she is introducing him to a beetle collector.

By the time their change arrived, it was all settled, the

last point of negotiation having been where the interviews would take place. Gilbert offered his room, Buddy said no, and Margery settled the matter by saying she wouldn't do it otherwise.

GILBERT WOULD come home to find Margery and Buddy deep in conversation that would cease while they both looked up to greet him and followed him with solemn eyes as he looked for a book or put away a purchase. His trash was overflowing from their carry-out meals.

Looking for places to rest, he sat in his art lecture hall, listening to the soothing whir of the slide projector and watching the colorless beauty of its long beam, which picked up the smoke from students' cigarettes and spun it into soft, revolving spirals. "Notice how the triangle formed by the two angels leads you to its apex, the face of Jesus," he heard as he dozed off. He took Erna out for walks and cups of coffee and museum visits.

Other times he planted himself in their midst. "Of course, it wasn't my fault that my brother was killed in Korea," Margery was saying as Gilbert, in his new robe, got into the bed she was primly sitting on the edge of. "But I think I've always felt guilty about still being alive. Maybe that's why I feel I have to be the boy in the family now, you see what I mean, to replace the son my father lost. My mother, too, I guess. Because you see, if I hadn't been a girl, I might have been drafted, if I'd been older, of course, and then I would have been killed instead of him. He could have been home in my place, except he'd be a son, of course, and my father would still have a son left."

Gilbert put his hand in Margery's lap, but she seemed to take no notice. "It's not that I wanted to be killed, you understand, but just that I felt that if someone had to be, it probably should have been me. See, I'm also the second child. The first child is a big thing, but when you have a second child, you already have a child. Sometimes I think my father is overcompensating because he feels bad because I'm only me. He really does make a lot of me, and he doesn't have to."

"Gilbert, cut that out or go away," said Buddy. Gilbert took his hand out of Margery's lap and put it back on the pillow behind his head.

"*You* know what I mean, Gilbert," Margery said, but then she went back to addressing Buddy. "By being so good, he creates these expectations in me that I don't know if I can live up to. Sometimes I resent it because I think he's only doing it out of guilt, and then I feel guilty about thinking that way, because he's really a good man. I think."

"I'll tell you something interesting," said Gilbert. They both looked at him as if he had decided to stand up and profess personal faith in an Episcopalian congregation.

"No, this is interesting. I gave up feeling guilty. I can't say I never did, because I used to have this sort of embarrassment, but it was more when I felt I had blundered than done something wrong. But anyway, I stopped. I know what I'll let myself get away with and what I won't, so I do only what makes me feel comfortable, and I never have a moral backlog."

"You would like my father," Margery said to Buddy.

"My father's a real pain in the ass," said Buddy.

"Mine's a really nice man," said Margery. "A good man."

"No," said Gilbert, "shut up and listen a minute. This is important. You deal in a realistic way with expectations—your parents', society's, whatever. Look at what they really want, not what they say they want or even imply. Then you figure out how to do the best you can, and what it is you can't possibly get away with. Let's say we're all going to make it through school, which is something, when you think about it, and we're never going to commit murder. Of course, we may not get to be President of the United States, either. Well, who knows? I'm not even going to concede that. But my point is, we're doing all right. Our accounts are basically in order. Anybody can look at them, there's nothing to hide. If there is, you erase it right away. So if you do that, you never feel guilty."

"Gilbert's father's an accountant," said Margery.

"I don't think my father means to be the way he is," said Buddy, "but he can't help it. He feels guilty because he's neglected my mother, so he thinks if I become a surgeon, too, that will justify him, so he makes me feel I have to, for his sake. But then I keep thinking, All right, but do I want to justify him? Isn't that betraying her? So I end up feeling guilty no matter what I do."

"Unless you refuse to," said Gilbert.

"You can't," said Margery. "Everybody feels guilty. When my brother died, and I know he felt guilty because he hadn't wanted to go to Korea and yet he felt it was his duty to his country—"

"I don't!" said Gilbert.

"You don't what?"

"I don't feel guilty!"

"So you say," said Buddy. "I guess we all know what that means."

"Are you two getting out of here so I can take a nap?"

"You see?" said Buddy. "You see?"

WHEN THEY HAD GONE, he summoned Erna. The Margery-Buddy sessions, plus Margery-without-Buddy sessions to keep his hand in, so to speak, had taken up his apartment, if not all his time, and so the courtship pattern he had formed had no longer been possible. Accidental abstinence having excited him, he experimented with deliberate abstinence.

He put Erna into his desk chair and undressed her and, turning the gooseneck lamp on her, looked at every part of her small-breasted, angular body. It was a slow, methodical, gentle exploration, and it weakened her. When he put her back together, including the gold brooch at her collar, he knew she was soaked in desire for what she would have considered granting a favor if it had taken place at the proper time.

"You're a bitch," he told her one night, as they sat stirring whipped cream into bitter coffee at the Mozart Café. She smiled proudly. "I have a girl home waiting for me right now who is worth ten of you. Love is just a big stupid status thing to you. If I wanted you, you'd sit up nights thinking of ways to get out of it. I just happened to get in there first at not giving a damn."

"Let's go to your place. I want to meet her."

"I don't have any money to pay for this."

"I do," said Erna. "I'm a rich bitch." For a while they stared at each other, while all around them couples leaned toward each other across the flimsy tables and spoke of being totally honest and wanting to do what was right for both of them, and one member of each couple plotted a cruel way of breaking up, and the other fell in love.

When they got home, Margery and Buddy had left and there were slimy paper cartons from a Chinese carry-out on the bed. There was nothing else to do but to push the trash on the floor and make love, just the two of them.

GILBERT BEGAN to wonder if he was slipping. One of his better midnight inspirations, a paper for his History of Religion class, came back marked "C — I do not accept mystical experience in lieu of scholarship." It was the lowest mark he had ever received.

What if the skills he had learned were not enough? What if his parents were right about his having to exert himself all over again for a new career?

The blank summer was approaching. His friends were running about making plans of their own instead of waiting to see where he would lead them. Margery had sublet his apartment for the summer, and although she invited him to stay there as her guest, it seemed to Gilbert that she was not pressing him desperately enough. Buddy had a job as an orderly in a psychiatric ward. Erna had invited Gilbert to visit her in Washington, where she would be interning in a senator's office, but it seemed to Gilbert as if she were appraising his appearance while she issued the invitation. He told both girls that he couldn't let them know, because his mother might have cancer.

He tried to remind himself that, for someone who was once an adolescent, it was no small achievement to carry around inside himself a voice that was always commenting on how devilishly clever he was, and looking forward to the wonders he would think of next. It was true that the voice was not as adulatory as it once had been—its honeymoon with Gilbert had passed, and they had settled down together—but at least the other voice, the one that had once told him he was an ass, was silenced. If the new team had any complaint now, it was a need for more outside stimulation; domestic peace was no longer enough. Having his own home, inspiring love, eluding others' demands—what did they add up to? A dusty room, a clingy girl, an empty calendar.

THEN, one perfect day when there was warm sand and chilly water and fresh lobster and cold drinks awaiting anyone with the freedom to take off merrily for Hyannis Port, the examination period began.

Gilbert stretched stiffly out on the auditorium chair, extracted half a chocolate bar from his pocket, and settled back, leaning on the writing arm. Trapped, he stared at the unintelligible mimeographed questions.

Outside, he could see the tops of freely swaying trees through the two-story windows. The class's regular lecture hall was comfortably creaky, with movable chairs, its side walls hung with enormous canvases depicting Flemish gaiety. There, he had found slide identification quizzes to be exciting sport. But the examination was antiseptically administered in a physics classroom with cement tiers for flooring and rigid chairs. An instructor walked over to the greenboard and wrote in large chalk numbers: "10:15."

Gilbert looked at the small, smeared purple sentence on his copy of the papers that had been distributed in each row. "Discuss the transition from Romanesque to

Gothic architecture, illustrating your points with examples from the course."

He drew a picture of a Romanesque church and labeled it "A." Then he drew an arrow and began to sketch another church, "B." The next arrow went half an inch to the right and then doubled back to the left-hand side of the page for church "C," on which he did fancy shading by smudging the pencil marks with chocolate spit. He was putting pilgrims on the paths when he suddenly crumpled the booklet. He walked down the cement steps to pick up a fresh booklet while everyone else looked up, realizing with alarm that they hadn't yet filled one booklet apiece. When he returned to his seat, he put the last square of chocolate on his tongue and wrote, "In order to fully understand," and tore out the first page and the corresponding last page and wrote in the thinner booklet, "In order to understand fully the development of the Romanesque style of church architecture to its natural philosophic fulfillment in the Gothic, it is necessary to comprehend the religious and emotional currents that inspired such massive tributes, built, as it were, in their images. Just as our modern churches, with their straight lines and empty surfaces, seek to capture a democratic God—that is to say, one bland enough to prove inoffensive to the greatest variety of people—so the Romanesque church, reflecting . . ."

Gilbert began to smile. His handwriting was getting less elegantly precise with every line, but a bubble of recognition was on his lips. Somewhere he had read that the professor's Gaudiesque design for a chapel had been passed over for the work of one of the School of Design's most famous and austere graduates.

He had, after all, taken in enough knowledge to save

himself. He put the cap of his pen into his mouth. But the professor didn't grade his own papers and would probably never see this one. Yes, but the graders were graduate students of his and no doubt sensitive to his interests.

". . . and so the Romanesque church, reflecting the religion of a people whose spiritual fervor was administered not by a popular authority interested in preserving its popularity, but by a holy officialdom wholly bound in the . . ." He laughed. A girl in front of him turned around and glared.

Gilbert wrote quickly. Spoiling the freshness of the first page was the only really hard part; once started, he had been able to answer the three-out-of-five questions without hesitation. When "11:30" was written on the board, he was finished. No one had left, though, and while being among the first dozen to finish was a triumph, being the very first looked bad. At 11:45, a boy who he knew hung around art museums, apparently not even to hunt for dates, got up from a first-row seat, and Gilbert decided to go ahead and be the second. The other boy returned to his place with a fresh booklet just as Gilbert was walking out the door.

"I didn't know you took art appreciation," said Buddy, who walked into him just outside the entrance.

Nevertheless, Gilbert felt he had successfully completed the school year. Gilbert Fairchild, honors student and beloved of two intelligent, attractive nineteen-year-old girls, had survived another semester. Perhaps, after all, his skill would get him through college, graduate school, assistant-, associate-, and full-professorships, and retirement, when he could rest. As his train clacked toward New York, he felt the blessed relief of speedily leaving it all farther and farther away.

Chapter III

"'C O M E O N , I'm trying to read."

The hand withdrew from his hair.

"Oh, come on, Mother. It's just that I can't read while you're messing with me."

He looked up to find that Mrs. Fairchild had gotten on her hands and knees, and was crawling slowly toward the dining area. She was picking fuzz off the new rug and collecting it into a ball. "Okay?"

"I can't see what you're reading," she said.

He held up the paperback, but she was busily harvesting. "*Moby-Dick*," he said. "If you bought a good rug, you wouldn't have all that mess. This place looks like a motel room. No, a VIP suite at an in-town motel. You really like it?"

"I thought you already took Melville. This is a good rug. I hate to tell you what I paid for it. Besides, good rugs shed just as much."

"I did. Remember, I sent you the paper on why the whale was white? It got an A? It was really one of my better papers. So I thought I'd read the book. It's like after you see the movie, you want to read the book. Oriental rugs don't."

"You know," she said, sitting back on her haunches, "you really are a scholar. I mean that. Most kids don't do any schoolwork in the summer, much less for a course they already took. Here you did so well, and you still want to go deeper into it. I must say, it's a pleasure to educate you. Don't what?"

"Don't shed. Or at least if they do, they shed on the Orientals before they even get here. Why don't you get an Oriental rug?"

"Gilbert, dear, are you going to sit around all summer in your underwear doing nothing?" At home, he wore underwear, even when he had clothes on.

There it was. Gilbert couldn't figure how they had gotten there from scholarship and Oriental rugs. "I'm reading," he pleaded. "I'm reading *Moby-Dick*."

"Pooh. You're nearly twenty years old. It's time you got out of the house. It's not healthy."

"I told you I wanted to go to Europe. That's out of the house."

"So go. Darling child, you want to go to Europe? You get yourself a job and buy yourself a ticket. That's what we were told when we were kids."

"Yes, and you never got there, did you?"

"I beg your pardon. Your father was born there."

"That's hardly earning his own way, is it?"

"All right. Grandfather Fairchild crossed the ocean, didn't he, on his own money, with a wife and a little baby, too? It was the other direction, I grant you, but he crossed it instead of sitting around in his underwear all day, complaining about nothing."

Now Gilbert was miffed. He had known Max Fairchild as a querulous old man with stains on his ties and tobacco crumbs falling out of his sweater pockets. The family story was that he had had imagination, courage, and foresight to coin an optimistic surname for his branch of the family and bring them to a life of quickly earned luxury. In contrast, it was pointed out as the moral of the story, Uncle Alex, who had had everything except daring—looks, a singing voice, fluency in Russian, German, and French, and a wife with a dowry—had remained home and been killed (forty years later) by the Nazis.

The mere mention of Max Fairchild fermented Gilbert's previously sedentary emotions. The six-section sofa on which he had been sitting began to send up wiry blue hairs to prick his legs. He got up, waded through the marine blue rug, opened the center of the three-part window, and leaned into the woolly summer air. Then he went back to the regulation apartment house chill, so unnaturally uniform like a block of frozen vegetables, and tried out a blue and green tweed armchair, experimentally leaning his back against one of the narrow, slanted arms of orange-colored wood. "Mother?"

"Want an apple, dear?" She was writing at the dining room table, a walnut rectangle surrounded by six walnut chairs, all leaning away from the table at a slight angle, like overfed guests, and for a moment he thought she meant the walnut bowl of matching walnut fruit in the center of the table. "In the kitchen, dear," she said patiently.

"This place looks awful. This is the second time you've done it over just since I went to Harvard. What is all this Danish junk? Didn't we used to have real furniture?"

"No, dear, this is the same junk. I just changed the color scheme. Remember it was orange and yellow? See—now it's blue and green. Don't you like it? That was two years ago that we got the furniture."

"I hate it." He opened the color-toned refrigerator, saw nothing but a whole city of cartons—tall ones, squat ones, round ones, square ones—and shut it again. "Why don't you ever fix up my room?"

"You don't like change, dear. I do."

"Why didn't you just change your address without telling me? Wouldn't that have been simpler? No wonder you can't afford to send me to Europe." He listened to the clicks of the refrigerator, readjusting itself after having been violated. "The problem is, How are you going to get my room back, so you can redecorate it the way you like it; isn't that right? How're you going to get old Gilbert out of the house, huh? Once and for all."

"Why don't you call up a girl? You used to know some nice girls."

"Leave me alone!"

"Don't be cross, little one. I know you had a hard year. Truthfully, I don't care if you get a summer job, so long as you have something useful to do. I'd like you to have a good time. Darling boy, you know what the secret of happiness is? Keep busy, because when you're busy, you're happy, because you don't have time to notice whether you're happy or not."

"No kidding."

"Bert, I don't like that. That sounds rude. It's not my fault you're bored."

"I know it isn't." Gilbert ruffled her gray and black

curls, but she had gone back to her reading and shook her head free. He looked past her, leaned over, and combed a ball of green fuzz out of the rug.

EVERY PLACE he had ever been had been redecorated so that he wouldn't recognize it. Grandpa Fairchild's pharmacy, long since sold to a chain, turned out to be simply a busy, popular drugstore, full of bright, slick, cheap merchandise that was sold and replaced daily. In his memory, it had become like a New England spa, quiet and full of dusty metal boxes and toothpaste cartons and magazines that had tables of contents for covers.

There was a vast newsstand now, and Gilbert picked up a magazine that said on its cover, "What Elvis Made Me Do!" but put it back after he had studied it for several minutes without being able to discover what Elvis had made the author do. He picked up another one and was skimming a short story about a widower and his son and the two women in his life, one a chic career woman and the other a homebody who loved animals and children, when someone said, "You want to buy that?"

Gilbert was startled. He didn't buy dumb magazines.

"Then put it back. This isn't a library."

Gilbert wanted to burst into tears and report the clerk to his grandfather. He had been used to having the run of the aisles, with everyone acting delighted when the princeling reached for a bauble.

Paula's apartment house had a new buzzer system. You had to push a button so that someone upstairs could push another button to open the door you were standing in front of. After he had mastered that, he went up and buzzed the apartment door and found himself face-to-face with Paula's father, who, Gilbert was sure, didn't use to have a face. It wasn't a nice one, even now. "Did you come to see Paula?" the man inquired by way of greeting. Paula's mother appeared and said, "Oh. It's you."

Wait a minute, thought Gilbert. This is new. Over the years, they had treated him to their emotional repertory, and it had consisted of impartiality ("Oh, yes, you were here before, weren't you?"), hospitality ("Would you care for a Coke while you're waiting?"), suspicion ("Maybe you'd like to tell us what the movie was about?"), inclusiveness ("Come and meet Paula's aunt and uncle from Great Neck!"), and bitterness ("I suppose you'll be meeting lots of new people at Harvard University?"). This greeting, he interpreted as fear.

What could they be afraid of? Was it possible that Gilbert Fairchild, who had been fading out of existence, whose childhood had been painted out, was a threat? He drew himself up to military bearing before letting himself down into a graceful slouch.

Paula had heard the commotion at the door and cut through it by saying, "Why, Gilbert Fairchild, I hardly recognized you."

"Hi," said Gilbert. "If I can't come in, can you come out?" At this, the two-person crowd dispersed, and Paula led him through the door, gesturing toward the living room sofa he had stained with his first grown-up, misaimed conquest. He checked to see if it had been reupholstered. No fair—it had a summer slipcover, and as the conquest had taken place in winter, he couldn't tell.

Paula Davies had loomed so large in his life at some times, and shrunken so much at others, that he was surprised to see her a regular-sized girl. What was it in her face that had made him think she looked like an Indian princess? The small eyes? If she looked like anyone, it was the Miss Subways he'd looked at in the poster rattling over his head on the way over to Paula's house.

Their romance had been characterized by social inequality, and the excitement of crossing class lines. First it was Gilbert who, as an oddball, was favored by the secretary of the student council and president of the girls' choir; then it was Paula who, as a prospective Florida State student, had been honored by the attentions of an embryo Harvard man.

"Gilbert! Aren't you going to say you're happy for me?"

"What?" He had been reminiscing; now he re-ran in his mind all the things she had been saying to him, but this time examining them for meaning. She had said she was getting married to a potato chip heir. "What?"

"Give the bride a kiss!"

Gilbert stared at her until the smirk left her face, and then pulled her onto that sofa. He did kiss her, and meanwhile, he bunched her nylon panties in his fist. "Paula," he said, "what are you doing to me?" The last time he had checked his feelings for her, they had consisted of discomfort at having neglected her letters. Now she had joined the conspiracy to deny his existence. His mother had renovated an apartment he had dreamed in, his grandfather had died neglecting to leave instructions that he was to continue to have the run of the drugstore, and now his girl friend was passing herself off as a bride.

It didn't help that Paula was kissing him back with wriggles and noise. He felt it was just a ruse and she would return to her sham engagement. He pushed harder, and was succeeding in getting on top of her when they heard dish-rattling so energetic that its meaning even penetrated to their situation. Gilbert got up and turned his back on her.

"I guess you'd better go," said Paula.

He slammed the door behind him, trying to convince himself that he had stained her bridal act.

''He sleeps too much. I worry about him," said his mother, waking him from a nap. "Maybe it's his heart."

Gilbert had discovered sleeping, and the last two weeks had passed groggily, but they had passed. He heard his immediate and general occupations slipping away as she spoke.

"Ginerva, you know there's nothing wrong with his heart. He's just—well, he's sensitive. Not like other kids, you give them a couple of dollars to go to the movies and they're happy. It's a funny age to be."

"You know he's got paroxysmal atrial tachycardia," she said primly.

"No, he doesn't, Ginerva. We don't even know what that is. I can't believe you really believe that." Albert Fairchild was running his fingers rapidly through his hair as he always did when they had that particular conversation.

"Doctors don't just make things up."

"Ginerva, darling, please. Remember you told him you would kill him if he didn't make up something to get Bert declared four-F?"

"Of course I did."

"All right, then."

"I just find it hard to believe a doctor would."

She went to the kitchen and back for the sole purpose of indicating that the conversation was over, and ignored Albert's attempt to cap it off, which was: "He would if he's your cousin and you told him to.

"Shall we give him a little money?" Albert asked. "Maybe let him travel?"

Gilbert lay perfectly still on the sofa.

"Send him to Europe? He's not ready. I've thought of it."

"Oh, not Europe. Florida? Bermuda? Washington—doesn't he have a girl friend in Washington? I bet she'd be happy to see him."

"Why not Europe?" asked Gilbert from the sofa.

"Oh-oh," said his mother.

"Washington," said Gilbert. "I'll take it."

PART OF Gilbert's travel arrangements was to show his parents how much more lively a son about to go off on a journey was than one engaged in the occupation of hanging around the house.

"Let me teach you what I learned at school," he announced one night at dinner.

The senior Fairchilds exchanged looks of pleased anticipation and put their chins on their hands like children promised a story. Gilbert thought how much more satisfactory this was than Margery's and Buddy's behavior when he condescended to impart wisdom to them.

"I have developed an answer," he said. "An all-purpose answer. It goes to everything, understand? So you don't have to know the question to give this answer. Are you ready?"

"Ready!" they both called out gaily.

"Ask me a question. Anything. It doesn't matter."

"Right," said his mother. "Let's see. Did you have a pleasant day today?"

"No, no, no. A philosophical question. Or literary.

Something like that. I'm trying to explain education to you."

"All right," said his father. "What does it all mean?"

" 'What does it all mean?' Is that the question?"

"Yes. Is that all right?"

"Perfect. I'll tell you." He leaned across the table to them, his mother having moved closer to her husband and taken his hand. Gilbert looked first into her eyes, and then into his. "It's a kind of yea-saying," he said.

The two were silent. "Well, yes," said his father finally.

"That's rather charming," said his mother. "I like that."

"You understand?"

"Sure," they replied together.

"Are you sure? You do understand, don't you, that if you had asked me to explain the Bible or the French Revolution or anything at all, I'd have said the same thing? That is was a kind of yea-saying?"

His parents moved apart from each other, and Ginerva Fairchild took some plates into the kitchen. "That doesn't make it any less true," she said from the safe distance.

"No, wait. Don't go away. Figure out what it costs you that I say things like that. You want to know the truth? You want to know what I do at school? I learn this technique. This is a simplified version, but the point is that I have said something that doesn't mean anything, but it doesn't not mean anything, either. You get it?"

"No," said his father. "You're not saying anything."

"I do," said his mother. "But I don't think he's right. I think the professors know more about you than you do, my darling, even about your own self. You may not grow up to be President, but you'll do fine. Sometimes I think you'd be better off teaching. As you say, you know the system."

"If you're saying we're not getting our money's worth,

I can appreciate that," said his father. "But if we're satisfied, and the school is satisfied, and you are doing well, why should it bother you?"

"But I will grow up to be President," said Gilbert. "That's the point. The school knows what it's doing. It's a very good technique, and I'm catching on to it very well. Doesn't that scare you? What I'm learning is a very sophisticated way of putting things over on people. What do you say to that?"

"Yea," said his mother, who then giggled until she had to rest her head in his father's lap.

Chapter IV

ERNA WAS THERE for him to fall on when he stepped out of the airplane chill into the thick Washington heat. He could hardly see her, because the slowing propellers whipped his tie across his face; he couldn't hear her, because engines were shrilling; and he didn't much care, because a hot-wind glue had pasted his clothes to his body. Putting a heavy arm across her shoulders, he staggered into the terminal like a wounded soldier leaning on a crisp nurse.

"You know what they told me?" she asked by way of greeting, although as far as the deafened Gilbert knew, it could have been the pop quiz at the end of a complicated lecture. He said nothing. When his parents had taken him to Washington as an elementary school graduation present, he had been awed at stepping from the plush-and-grime train into the stately splendors of Union Station. He had moved his eyes upward, past the tantalizing displays of candy bars at his own level, and discovered a world where calm statues representing what he took for the ideals of government were presiding from high niches over a vast kingdom of space. The airport was blank.

"They told me I had to be back in an hour. I haven't had a lunch hour in two weeks. Besides, I have to work late."

Gilbert looked at her. She had not translated the New England schoolgirl look into summer; she looked like a clerk. He hadn't remembered her nose as being that angular, but it was noticeable now, the nose being if not burned, then singed. Vertical cracks of worn-out lipstick gave her the lips of an old lady. She wore a checked cotton suit with a cotton carnation at the lapel, realistically drooping.

"I see," said Gilbert. "Welcome to Washington." He made a negative gesture at the baggage claim area, to which she had led him, and pulled off his tie. Everything he had was in his father's attaché case, which he carried. The young congressman look, which had pleased his parents that morning, seemed to be a failure.

So was the sticky cab ride, and the lunch Erna impulsively decided on, in a rathskeller where she had to produce her driver's license to get a beer, and Gilbert had to pick sauerkraut strings off his hot dog before he could eat it. Erna never looked at him. She sketched in the office setup and how it conspired against her, named her roommates and their most offensive habits, offered some minor gossip about people he had never heard of, and supplied no clue to what was wrong. By the time their next cab pulled up at her four-story Georgetown row house, which was next to a dress shop of some apparent antiquity, she was also frightened about going back to the office late. "Just go on in," she said, disengaging the house-key from a flowered keycase and giving it to him. "They know you're coming. I'll call you later." She re-entered the cab, backside last, and motioned Gilbert to the window. "Mine's the blue bedroom on the fourth floor. You're supposed to be in the dressing room off it. Don't tell anyone any different." She left Gilbert standing in front of a narrow structure of brick that had once been painted white, but was re-claiming its natural red.

He couldn't find the front door. Checking up the block, he saw that the other houses had iron steps and recognizable front doors, but his didn't. He thought of asking a woman who was coming down the street walking two dogs, but let her go by because he couldn't frame the question.

The house threw a grand archway over an open garage space next door, and when Gilbert went in and his eyes became accustomed to the dark, he saw that just inside its entrance there was, on one side, a door with a brass lion knocker. Erna's key opened it. He found himself in a tiny hallway, papered with red-inked trees and pastoral lovers. There seemed to be no other room on the floor, but one flight up he discovered a living room in which genuinely decrepit, if not antique, furniture had been supplemented with Louis XV chairs of the sort that are sold unpainted.

This floor also contained a closet-sized kitchen, piled with pots and dishes and food cartons anad soda bottles. The next level up had two crowded bedrooms and a stairwell window giving a long view down to the brick backyard, with its iron-and-glass furniture and flapping newspapers. From this vantage, Gilbert heard the door slam way below, and two figures crossed the yard. There was a neat head of tightly pinned-up hair, with a billowing white dress under it, and a white-haired male head over a gray suit. They embraced passionately by the back fence, as Gilbert watched from his mezzanine position, and the black hair and white dress re-crossed the yard alone.

He sat at the top of the steps, waiting for this fascinating company to come up and open the dialogue of the play with him, but the slam of the back door was soon followed by the slam of the front door, and he rushed to the street-side window only in time to see the white dress disappearing quickly down the block.

ERNA HAD the smallest room, on the hot top floor, and the so-called dressing room was an insult to her guest. There was no clue there to what Erna was doing with herself in Washington, much less what he might expect to do. But the house was quiet, so he considered it adventure time. At first, he picked out a room piled with department store boxes as being that of the lady in the white dress, but then he changed his mind in favor of the largest room, which had formal invitation cards stuck around the frame of the dressing table mirror, a half-written letter in French on the desk, and a closet full of evening dresses. There was nothing in the drawers except boxes—quilted boxes of handkerchiefs, scarves, and underwear in the bureau; ivory-colored pasteboard boxes full of writing paper in the ladylike desk. There was a jug of Chanel No. 19 perfume (Gilbert had heard only of No. 5) on the bedside table, along with a leather-covered notebook that proved to contain menus, table seating plans, and shopping lists.

All the beds in the house were unmade, so he didn't think much about this one as he sat down to read the notebook, but he flinched because it was damp. There was a towel in it, too. It made Gilbert uneasy. This lady would be the one to introduce him around Washington, and she seemed unnecessarily busy. If she fell in love with him, Gilbert, would the ensuing complications take up too much time to get them outside, where the real Washington was?

Gilbert decided he was too sleepy to deal with it. Back in Erna's room, he re-hung two dresses on the hanger of a third so he could have one free for his jacket and one for his shirt, and he got into her bed naked.

HE AWOKE in late afternoon, when he heard another series of door slams, first downstairs, and then on the floor below him. With some hope, he peeked into the hallway, but it was the shopper's door that was now closed, not the Chanel room. He tried to sleep again, but couldn't, and was angrily searching Erna's room for some way to telephone her when she called.

"There's some crazy girl here making a pass at me," he whispered on the hall phone. "I got to get out of here. Where shall I meet you?"

"I still have to drop by this terrible party," she said.

"You said you had to work late," Gilbert said cannily. Was he supposed to play Margery?

"I do. It's an office thing. That's part of the job, getting around and talking to the other staff people. I won't be late. It's really boring, going to those things."

"What do I tell the cabdriver?" Gilbert insisted, and she told him.

It was not in the Capitol itself, as he had hoped, but the Old Senate Office Building, which was being deserted by flocks of blowzy women and quick-moving young men with briefcases. He listened to the directions the policeman gave him but got lost anyway, among the corridors of oversized doors, as if the architect had assumed lawmakers to be two or three feet taller than their constituents. Erna's door said "Mr. Talbot"; when he entered, he found her sitting at a walnut desk reading *Vogue*. The only thing in the outer room that wasn't heavy—curtains, carpeting, and furniture were all loaded down with dignity—was her silly summer handbag, made out of straw in the shape of a cottage.

"Why doesn't it say 'Senator Talbot'?" he asked. "Instead of 'Mr.' On the door."

"Because everybody knows he's a senator. It's like saying 'Mister,' not 'Doctor' at school, because you know everybody's got a Ph.D."

It was the first piece of information Gilbert had heard all summer that he thought worth memorizing. "Do you call him Mister to his face, or Senator?"

"Senator. Look, do you mind if we just stop by this thing quickly? Don't expect me to show you around, because I'll be there officially. I just want to go in and out, and we'll get something to eat at home."

"Oh, stop being ashamed of me, will you? What's the matter with you? Listen, can I meet your senator?"

"Nothing's the matter with me. He's not here."

"Can I see his office?"

"Oh, I suppose so. Don't touch anything." Gilbert was already walking through the outer offices to the senator's quarters. He could feel the carpet thicken under his feet.

The office was all soothing surfaces of polished wood and soft leather, the luxury underscored by the dull gleam of silver picture frames. There was a state flag and a United States one on eagle-topped floor stands behind the desk, and a beautifully typed and framed card on the desk with the senator's schedule for the day. It showed him to be out of town; the meticulous routine was being carried out in his absence exactly as if he had been present. The walls were covered with framed photographs of the senator—smiling, speaking, shaking hands with presidents and movie stars and kings and beauty queens and crippled children and ambassadors.

"Is this a typical office?" Gilbert was an eager tourist. He was lifted outside himself for the first time in years, curious, alert, happy. What was stirring his heart—patriotism?

"I guess it's typical. Let's go. I don't want anyone to find us here. I'm in trouble enough."

It was something like patriotism, he decided. It was the feeling that the country held limitless opportunities, and that there was no honor to which a smart citizen might not aspire. He was ready to work, beginning with examining all the details around him.

"Let me ask you something, Erna. Aren't the pictures a mistake? I mean, this way you know whom he knows, and you all know he doesn't really know them or he wouldn't be shaking hands with them, would he? Don't you think? Erna?"

"I don't care."

He wanted to look at the artifacts on the desk and the mounted samples of homestate products on the bookcase, but he was feeling generous, so he kissed Erna's angry cheek. He knew it was one of those kindnesses that throw desperate people over the brink, but he did it honestly to relieve the irritable Erna. She burst into tears. "They don't want me back after graduation," she said.

"So what? You don't want to come back, anyway. You're taking the Foreign Service exam."

"Fat chance that'll be. Anyway, what would that lead to? Spending my youth in some backwater dump?" She took a deep breath and walked out, Gilbert following her down an Alice in Wonderland corridor, up a wide circular staircase, into a packed room and, with something of a struggle, to their destination, a tableful of cold cuts, potato chips, and soft drinks. Erna left him the minute he turned his eyes from her to the food.

Gilbert looked around. He found a girl to stare at, but instead of looking away and then shyly back, she marched up and shook his hand heartily and announced that she was with the Vice President. Gilbert looked behind her, but then realized that she meant the office. "Do you like it?" he asked, hardly up to his usual standard of opening.

"Are you kidding? It's the best internship there is. Bar none, and I mean including the Casa Blanca itself. You get to learn more."

"What do you do?"

"Everything. You name it. Plan his trips, organize his schedule, screen his phone calls. Today," she announced triumphantly, "I went to his house!"

"Really? You're getting that thick with him, huh?"

"Sure. I picked up his suitcase. His wife gave it to me herself. He was going to go home before he left, but we were running late, and he didn't have time."

She seemed to be examining Gilbert for signs of intelligence. "The African trip? You've heard of his African trip? Well! I did an awful lot of the planning on that, I can tell you. Air schedules, hotels, everything. I'm keeping a diary of everything I do. It's history in the making. Excuse me."

It had been years since Gilbert had been dismissed like that by any girl. He flushed and closed his eyes. It was the stupid party situation, he thought. The girl hadn't had a chance to listen to him. He mustn't go to parties. Was she really keeping a diary based on someone else's engagement calendar? He'd always known he shouldn't go to parties. He hadn't been to a party since freshman year. His proper area was—that one crummy room in Cambridge? Gilbert promised himself that this ordeal would soon be over and that none of it counted, because no one he knew could see him. He numbed himself enough to try again. Pure tourism. A young man, this time. Safer, although he hadn't usually found boys safe socially. "Who are you?" he asked gruffly of a person standing next to him wearing Harvard summer clothes.

Everybody in the vicinity burst into laughter. Gilbert hadn't realized that his target was the center of a group, because the group had left a circle of space around him. Now Gilbert was in the arena with him. "I'm sorry that's so funny," he said evenly, holding back his inclination to cry. "I'm from out of town." They laughed again, but the young man's smile was not unkind. Gilbert heard his own name come from that terrible laughing chorus. He hadn't realized, either, that Erna was in the group.

"Don't you know what you did?" she murmured with her eyes closed as soon as she could elbow him away. "That's S.B.—Samuel Brewster. Didn't you ever hear of Small Boy when you were a kid?" He shook his head humbly.

"Yes, you did. Small Boy ate his cereal, remember? Small Boy let everybody play with his toys. Small Boy invited all the polio children over to play. Small Boy

saved his gum wrappers for the war effort. And he did
cute things, too, like let frogs loose in the Cabinet Room.
You must have heard this. You were supposed to feel
sorry for him because his parents were dead, but you
wished yours would die, too, so you could live in the
White House. Where were you brought up, for God's
sake?"

"Oh, God," said Gilbert. "He was the President's
nephew. Grandnephew. Oh, yes. What's he doing here?"

"He just graduated from Yale Law School, and he's all
over the place. He's waiting until he's old enough to run
for something."

"Do you know him?" He gathered so, from her having
spirited him away so as not to let the Small Boy crowd
know that Gilbert was hers.

"I've met him."

Small Boy found them out, even in the corner where
Erna had tried to hide. He strode toward them through
parted waters. "Erna, you look terrific," he said. "I'm
going to come by your office one of these days."

"You look terrific, too, little boy," said Gilbert.

"That's Small, friend, Small, like my brother Pox. Seriously, though, hello there. I'm Sam Brewster. I'd like to
know you."

Gilbert said nothing. His inclination was to be flattered
and to submit his name, but he stopped himself and felt his
face go hot.

"Don't tell me," said Small Boy. "You hate me, right?
You're just the age. You grew up when I was the world's
hammiest little kid. Well, okay. All I can say is I'm sorry,
and I wasn't nearly as good as your mother told you."

Gilbert gave in and smiled.

"Now will you tell me your name, friend?"

Everybody laughed at the prompting. Gilbert had to

say his name and to put out a hand to meet S.B.'s firm shake. "Where're you working, Gilbert?"

"I'm not."

"Me, neither," said S.B. "Don't tell anyone. See you around, okay? 'Bye, Erna. I'll be seeing you."

Gilbert was stunned with liking for S.B., but he roused himself and called, "Brewster? What was that about childhood? Did we know each other as children or something?" He wasn't even trying to top S.B.; he was trying to stop him from getting away.

But Brewster only laughed and waved his hand over his head, his back still turned to Gilbert. They distinctly heard him say, "At last—someone who dislikes me for myself!" and the crowd laughed with him.

"Are you ready to go now, Gilbert? Are you sure there isn't anyone else you'd like to meet?"

Gilbert held up a conciliatory hand.

"Don't think he won't remember, either," she said. "He remembers every person he ever met in his life. By name, too."

JŪST BECAUSE the sun had gone down, it wasn't any less hot outside. They walked for a while, Gilbert too humble to decide whether she would be pleased or annoyed if he put his arm around her. The fresh grass of Capitol Hill restored his spirits, and he took her hand. "I got to admire him, you know. What he does is anticipate you. How can you show contempt for him if the first thing he does is to tell you you've got to have contempt for him? Then you've got to switch to avoid letting him be right. And then if you switch—wait a minute, let me figure this out—what have you got to switch to, except the opposite, which is liking him? It's really ingenious. Except, why does he have that little businessman haircut?"

"He looked the same as everyone else."

"No, his is just a little shorter on the sides and longer on top. It says, 'I'm trustworthy, but I'm not a Marine.'"

"What do you want him to wear? Curls and a black sweater?"

"All right, Erna. That's enough." That pose seemed dumb to him, too, now that he pictured himself as S.B. They were silent on the way home, taking a streetcar, Gilbert enjoying seeing the leafy city, empty of people, to the pleasant railroad whine of the car shifting its weight. The woman in white was coming out of the living room as they went up, and Gilbert was presented. "Diane?" he asked, pronouncing it in French. "Diane what?" He was practicing being S.B.

"Liane, with an *L*," said Erna. "She's French."

"Canadian," said the girl, without expression. "How do you do?" She left without waiting for a reply.

He thought her ballerina looks startling. Her face was oval and bony, the black hair pulled back, with a center part, into a bun. She had long eyes and a delicately curved mouth, but none of it had moved. He watched her sweep grandly and tragically past, up the stairs.

"She's a bitch," said Erna. The confidence implied renewed comradeship with Gilbert, proven when she deposited a carton of cottage cheese on the spot they had cleared on the kitchen table.

"How old is she?"

"Old. Twenty-five. Maybe thirty. I knew damn well she was Canadian—she's the one who always says 'French.' Pretentious bitch."

"What'd she do?"

"To me? Nothing. She doesn't talk to any of us. She

works at an African embassy, and she plans all these
dinner parties, so she's out most of the time. And then
she's having this wild affair with some crazy old guy—I
mean, really old. This is his afternoon. I hope you didn't
spoil it." She laughed. "He's got white hair and he's married and he has I don't know how many children—our
age, I mean, they're in college, for God's sake, and she's
crazy about him. They meet here at lunchtime, and nobody's supposed to know because he's some big cheese
at the State Department, and so we're all supposed to
tiptoe around and not let him know we're here because—
get this—because it might scare him. She's really cuckoo.
She's not bad-looking, if she'd fluff up her hair or something and not go around looking like a schoolteacher.
Everybody says she used to have all these boy friends and
she thought she was too good for any of them, and now
here she is, making an ass of herself. If he breaks a date
or he goes on vacation with his wife or anything, Liane
goes into a trance. I've never seen anything like it. She
doesn't eat; she doesn't hear you when you talk; she can't
see anybody. He's supposed to call about now, but he
doesn't always do it. He has to tell his wife he's going out
for cigarettes, so I guess he has to smoke everything at
home first. It'll probably kill him."

As Erna spoke, the telephone rang. She got up and put
her hand on the kitchen wall phone, but didn't pick it up
until the ringing had stopped, and then she handled it
gently, listening and afterwards soundlessly replacing the
receiver. "He says he can't go on like this," she reported
gleefully. "He's going to take a week and think it over
and he'll call her when he's got it all thought through,
and then he hung up on her because his wife was waiting
in the car." Erna was beaming.

Gilbert had been scraping the last of the cottage cheese

from the carton, and was getting curls of wax on his spoon. "How high up in the State Department?"

"Who knows? He's probably near retirement anyway."

He knew that she could give him only the penny-ante gossip, and there must be a more important theme to Liane's story. It didn't sound as if the romance were connected with career advancement, but you never knew. His own accumulated wisdom about love, reducible to the formula that the world consists of masochists and sadists and it's less painful to be the latter than the former, seemed simplistic in this larger world. He didn't even bother to put it into effect to subdue Erna, and just politely overcame his disgust at her ignorance in civic and diplomatic matters enough to occupy her bed, so he wouldn't have to sleep on the dressing room cot. He had a crowded head tonight, and merely emptied his body so he would be free to concentrate on S.B. and on Liane.

But when they unstuck their wet bodies, Erna was still restless. "It's not just the dumb job, is it?" he asked her. The psychological excursions of undergraduates no longer interested him, but after all, there he was. A guest had to earn his keep.

"It's everything."

"Like what? What about if we open the skylight, would that let some more air in?"

"It wouldn't help. Nothing helps. I'm going to end up like her, with a bunch of thirty-dollar nightgowns I wear to bed by myself." Gilbert had glimpsed Liane on their way upstairs, she on her way to the bathroom trailing yards of negligee, and Erna's mentioning it got him all excited. He discharged the mattter quickly and searched for the thread of her spindly conversation.

"I'm sure you could get married if you wanted to.

Who've we got? Also, what about all that Foreign Service stuff? Was that just for show?"

"It's all hopeless. Yes, I could marry some jerk, or I could go run errands for some ambassador's wife someplace."

"Why don't you marry a jerk who's an ambassador?"

"Thanks."

"Oh, you thought of that."

"I'll tell you one thing," she said. "I'm not going to spend the rest of my life in Cambridge. Or worse. Minneapolis, for Christ's sake."

Cambridge? That was he. Who had asked her? "Spare the personal remarks, please. Let's look at this rationally. Why don't you go after Small Boy? He looks like a good bet."

"Ha."

"Tried it, did you? Okay, what about Whatsiz, the cross-eyed one you were engaged to? Isn't he in the Foreign Service? Maybe he's in Washington now."

"Yes, as a matter of fact, he is."

"Pay dirt," said Gilbert. "Got it in one. God, I'm clever. You rejected him, and now it's his turn."

"I wouldn't touch him with a ten-foot pole. He lives right down the block from here, as a matter of fact. He and three other guys who think they're God's gift to the world, and they give candlelight dinners and they all have MGs or Triumphs."

"Triumphs," said Gilbert. "You'll tell me about them tomorrow."

H E S T A Y E D fuzzily half-asleep while she dressed for work, and leapt up when he heard the front door close.

He ran downstairs, and there it was, in the shade-darkened living room, the great statue with the dark hair, staring sightlessly at the space through which Gilbert was walking.

He walked straight up to her and knelt before her. "Liane," he said, "I love you. I have always loved you. I know you can't hear me, but I had to tell you. I can't sleep, I can't eat, I can't do anything. I can't go on like this."

It smiled. The china lips moved ever so slightly, but they were definitely curving. "Who are you? Erna's beau from college? Get up. Don't be so silly."

"I can't. I froze this way."

"Oh, God, everybody's crazy," she said, but the smile went up a notch.

"Like a date for breakfast? I don't want to complain, but that is the most disgusting kitchen I ever saw. You girls are rotten housekeepers. You tell me some nice place we can go, and I'll take you there and I promise I'll devote my whole life to making you happy. Or suffering with you, if that's what you'd prefer. I'm yours. I don't have any money, but my heart is yours."

"Go away."

"Never."

"What do you want?"

"Breakfast. Your love. Either. Both. How about we start with breakfast and work our way up? Stay right there. Don't go away."

He ran up and returned dressed and with the change from Erna's ashtray. In a way, Liane had followed his instructions; not only had she not moved, but she had gone back into her trance. Gilbert had to jog her elbow. "I'm back. Remember me? Gilbert Fairchild. Coffee.

Love." The last word triggered a look of alarm. "Coffee. Just coffee."

"Is this going to cause trouble with Erna? Please, I don't want any more trouble. It's not worth it."

"No trouble. Just coffee. I have a project for you to get your mind off all your troubles"—she looked at him suspiciously—"if you have any. Why would a beautiful woman like you have troubles?"

"I'll tell you what. I'll give you a dollar, and you go on ahead and have a good breakfast."

"You can't buy me off."

"Well, then don't tell Erna."

"Your heart carries too many secrets," he said, beginning to be aware that he was talking like Prince Valiant.

AFTER ALL, one of his minor techniques seemed to work in Washington. At a cafeteria not unlike the Bick, over scrambled eggs and coffee, she responded to his questions about her history. Her parents were teachers in Quebec, she had come to Washington as a secretary to the Canadian Military Mission, had become an American citizen, to her parents' dismay, because she never knew when she might want a government job, although she hadn't yet, and had a good job now as a social secretary. So many new African countries were sending diplomats who considered French the only language of diplomacy and didn't care to learn English that she had pretty much free range.

"Have you ever been in love?"

"No."

"I only ask because I'm jealous. I know it's hopeless." He gave her a version of a hopeless little boy smile until

it made her laugh. Well, yes. There had been someone in
Quebec and it had to do with her leaving, and for a long
time there had been a count from the Swedish Embassy,
and then one person or another. It wasn't true that
Washington had too many women; in her experience, at
least, it had too many anxious men.

"Sounds like a terrific life."

"It is," she said defiantly.

"Who was the man who visited you yesterday?"

"A friend of mine," said Liane. She rose to leave, and
while he left change on the table, she did leave.

He couldn't tell whether she meant to walk out on him
or had assumed he would catch up, but he dashed after,
grabbed her, and kissed her cheek, as people tried to brush
past them on the street. "You forget that I'm in love, and
people in love sometimes make fools of themselves," he
said. Tears came to her eyes. "Can we do this again?" No
answer. "Tomorrow morning?"

"I don't know," said Liane. "I don't want to cause any
trouble."

HIS BEING in love with Liane was a joke, of course.
He had meant to satirize her own posture of exaggerated
tragedy. It was the notebook of seating plans, with its
tantalizing abbreviations—"H.E.," "Sec. St.," even an
"H.R.H." on a plan that had been redone on the next
page without the "H.R.H." (what excuse did royalty
offer for dropping out?)—that attracted him. He could
just as easily have attached himself to Small Boy, had that
been possible.

Indeed, Liane proved to be a source of exactly the sort
of information Gibert sought, and she was observant and

cynically amusing about unspoken interplays of power and symbolic detail. Gilbert, by habit an attentive listener, was wide awake all the time now. He followed her, asking questions, wherever she would let him—in the house, on shopping excursions, partway walks to her office, a tiny re-converted town house—until she said she was late and dipped into a taxi. Once he showed up at her tennis lesson and handed her a cold drink as she came off the court.

It was like beginning college again, among the ivy-covered brick buildings of residential Georgetown. Long dormant with the inertia that followed his Harvard successes, Gilbert was now in a state of nervous and eager anticipation.

He made good use of his education. Knowing that the one essential part of any academic course was learning the jargon and fashions of the discipline, he understood that his proper field of study in Washington was the dress, traditions, manners, customs, patterns of speech and behavior of his new field. As much as he had always yearned toward cloistered scholasticism, he knew that he could no more afford it now than he could in high school. He had to master the tools of a practical trade.

She lectured him about Washington diplomatic life. His picture of a court of aristocrats and jewels and whispered state secrets was nastily dispelled, but he found her version, of a society precariously based on one's current job title, where international civil servants anxiously performed tasks made obsolete by worldwide telephones and newsmagazines in order to clutch at a few remnants of government-sponsored old-style luxury, more convincing and more interesting.

She explained the social hierarchy among countries. France and Great Britain were always best, and then the rest of Western Europe plus Argentina. The Soviet Embassy was considered exciting, but the Eastern European embassies were worse than the Asian, American, and Latin American. A few countries on those continents had enough special fans to make them of general importance—China, Japan, Israel, India. But as she saw it, the opportunity to advance a new embassy such as her employer's was through assuming dramatic command. Her employers were uninteresting, but rich and willing to learn, she said, and her dinner parties—of course, they were hers, although she never ate at them but faded into the pantry in her evening dress when everyone sat down according to her chart—featured strange foods and famous wines, and there were always two or three aloof black beauties about, wearing French couture clothes and admitting to law degrees from the Sorbonne. The dinner invitations were beginning to be accepted by cabinet ministers, and the offers of free trips were not being rebuffed.

The only subject on which Liane failed him was that of the United States Congress. Only members of the Foreign Relations Committees were of even marginal interest to her. The rest were all captives of the standards and styles of their remote constituencies, she said.

She refused to talk about the non-work aspects of her present life. Gilbert could see that she was in costly pain, and that the project of educating a bright student was a merciful distraction to her. Sometimes she would stop talking gaily and close her eyes and clutch his hand, but when he moved to embrace her, she flinched so genuinely that he didn't try it again.

He found he was building his schedule around her. When she wouldn't see him, he would ask her what to do, and go where she sent him: to an art gallery, on sightseeing tours, to walk about neighborhoods whose character—always in terms of its symbolism to the social structure—she had explained to him. Erna was gone all day, anyway, and tried to avoid taking him to the marginal social events she attended. He was reasonably good to her, because his mind was preoccupied, and he shared her bed and suppers with guest-like manners. She had an occasional flare of jealousy, when she asked him about Liane, but he defused each episode. He was too busy to deal with Erna's getting interested in him again.

ONE MORNING Liane greeted him cheerily and said, "Keep out of the house all day tomorrow."

"I will not," said Gilbert.

"Oh, yes, you will. Until five o'clock on the dot." She kissed him on both cheeks and roughed his hair.

"I'm going to come in, in the middle," said Gilbert. "And I'm going to make the most colossal scene you ever saw. I'll be your brother the French fisherman. Or maybe I'll be your illegitimate son; how would you like that? I know! I'll be the man you picked up in the park last month and gave the clap to. I hope none of your guests are timid."

"I'll take you out to dinner next week, just the two of us, and we'll have a wonderful time."

"Friday. And you have to give me a report."

"Friday's our national day party. I'll be too busy."

"Plus you have to invite me to the party."

"You are a pest," said Liane.

"Okay. You want to take your chances tomorrow?"

"You're not really a pest," she said. "You're a dear, loyal boy and the kindest friend I ever had."

"Oh, no, I'm not. I have no conscience, I'm a liar, and

I never gave a moment's consideration in my life to any-body but myself." He said it because he had been touched, and he felt it honorable to tell her the truth. The fact was that he was learning, when holding her hand and watching her close her eyelids against her pain, to enter into another person's feelings, rather than to analyze them as data for determining his reaction.

"I know," she said, "but you're my horrible boy, and I love you."

"How can he get away from the State Department that long? Do they know where he is? Suppose there's a crisis in his territory?" Gilbert was testing her love for him, and when he saw her stiffen, he became frightened of failure. "Five o'clock?" he said, claiming her hand to see if he still could.

"Better make it five-thirty. This is my house, you know. I could throw you out. Let's say, dinner Monday. Oh, and the party on Friday."

That night, Gilbert bragged about the party to Erna, who came alive with anger.

"You think I would stand for being on the edges of glamour as a mere secretary, like some poor relation?" she demanded while throwing her baby doll nightgown on the floor.

"I tell you," he said, "S.B. is your only chance."

Chapter V

LIANE AND GEORGE had met two years before at the State Department, for the purpose of discussing whom Colonel Bwamati might want to meet in Colonial Williamsburg.

George Beaufort was a career man, assigned to the West African regional planning office. His New Orleans French had been tuned during a year in a Parisian lycée, but his parents had run out of money, and he had never led the merry student life at the Sorbonne that his knowledge of Parisian bistros and slang implied when he engaged in old-school talk with West African diplomats who had.

George and Liane had planned the state visit of Colonel

Bwamati more meticulously than any other three-day Washington-area run-through by a king, queen, prime minister, president, or dictator. They spent hours poring over guest lists, maps, menus, and suggestions for state gifts. They discussed the visitor and his country in historical context with psychological and sociological influences, viewing the prospect of his three days in the United States as a crisis of international relations, with potentially favorable or damaging repercussions on the safety and peace of the known world. Occasionally, the mere edges of their fingers touched over a freshly typed sheet of paper. The first time, it was no more than a hair from the base of George's thumb against the side of Liane's hand, but both of them went momentarily faint. George was in Liane's small office the next morning, and their fingers accidentally met in a full touch and stayed that way for long seconds, until Liane slowly drew back. They both had to sit down that time, and when they looked up at each other, it was an acknowledgment that they both knew.

Circumstances, in the shape of Liane's blustering, humorous friend, the assistant military attaché, had separated them before they could acknowledge it in words. Twice that afternoon, George had called from the State Department to ask the spelling of a name, and the third time, when he needed to know Colonel Bwamati's birthplace, it was obvious that a working lunch was imperative.

This was held the next day. George chose the Rive Gauche restaurant, which he had visited once previously, on his twentieth wedding anniversary earlier that year. Liane tried conscientiously to get up a conversation about their mutual interest, the Colonel, offering sketches of people sure to be in the official entourage, but there was a conversation problem in that neither of them had enough saliva in the mouth to talk for long. George quickly announced that he was happily married, had three teen-aged children and a summer cottage in Maine, and was subject to reassignment abroad within three years.

Liane said she thought it all sounded wonderful—mar-riage, children, Maine, foreign assignments, everything. When she began an account of her own life by mention-ing that her parents were schoolteachers, George eagerly broke in to say that he himself had an aunt who taught school!

This coincidence stunned them into silence. They were having trouble with the meal, too. Neither of them could finish an entire venison-burger, and each of them had spilled a bit of wine on the white tablecloth. Once George made a remark in French about the bordello décor, and Liane answered him in French, and then they had to stop at the marvel of their sharing their own secret language, while the waiter, who was from Marseilles, stood waiting for them to say something about dessert, one way or the other.

At three o'clock, they emerged from the restaurant and were shocked to encounter daylight. George took Liane's elbow, and they steered each other to the corner, but he made no move to hail any of the empty taxicabs that swerved by them to hurtle down M Street. This failure of transportation to return them to their proper lives seemed providential. They were left stranded in time and space. George took Liane's elbow again, a grip that made both of them shut their eyes involuntarily until they could collect enough of their senses to cross the street safely, and they set out on foot.

As the State Department would be a long walk in one direction, and Liane's Dupont Circle chancery in another, they compromised and walked through Georgetown along the canal. Only one bicyclist passed them on the dusty path along the old commercial bargeway, and they felt strangely isolated. No one in the whole world knew exactly where they were. George had told his secretary that he had an afternoon dentist appointment, and Liane had told her office-mate that she was going to the florist's after lunch. If the *Queen Mary* had slowly appeared on the puddly canal, they would have boarded without another thought and never been heard of again.

The *Queen Mary* did not, however. Even the mule-pulled canal barge was not in sight. Instead, a street they both knew suddenly loomed into view at the end of the path. George panicked. Pushing Liane up against the wall of somebody's miniature canal-front house, he shoved his tongue into her mouth and his hand up her stockinged leg.

Approximately every five years of his adulthood, George had had a secret affair, lasting about four months each, although one had continued into a sentimental correspondence of two years' duration. Each time there had been lengthy discussions of geographical and emotional logistics preceding physical contact. Where could we go, and where do we say we are, and how do you think this will affect our families, and how can we make sure we don't hurt anyone else? This usually took numerous lunches before even a kiss was performed.

George heard a thud and was stunned into realizing what he had done. The sound was Liane's purse falling, so that she could use both hands to hold on to him.

Anything definitive was hopeless, even for two maniacs. Summer heat aside, office formality required that Liane wear stockings, which required a garter belt, and there was the usual quantity of other underwear, gloves, and a dress. Also, because it was a special day, she had worn her lapis lazuli necklace, and the clasp caught in his hair. George was well armored, too. He had on a seersucker suit, now even more badly wrinkled than it was supposed to be, and was complete with white shirt, diagonally striped tie, discreet gold cuff links, and the requisite underpinnings. He had stopped wearing a hat when he had decided it made him look too old.

They were standing in front of a row of stage-set houses which, however small and cute, were inhabited by real people. This picturesque spot was in the middle of a neighborhood where she lived and in which each had a couple of hundred acquaintances. It was the busiest time of a working day.

"Let's sit down," said Liane when she realized that anything else was hopeless. George stooped to pick up her purse and kissed her wrinkle-stockinged leg. They staggered to a bench.

"My God," he said. "My God."

"I haven't slept in a week," she answered.

"Neither have I. I can't eat."

"I had to taste something this morning, a sample for the dinner, and I didn't know what it was. I said it was a good dessert, and it turned out to be the pâté. The chef was furious."

"That's nothing," said George. "I got lost yesterday, outside my office. I was walking down the hall a mile a minute and got into the wrong elevator and I didn't know which button to push."

"You're in good shape," said Liane. "I got lost *in* my office. I sat down at the wrong desk."

"Darling." He patted her hand exhaustedly. "What do I call you—Liane?"

"Well, yes. That's my name."

"I know. Mine's George."

"I know."

"What do we do now?"

"I don't know. I guess we go back to work. Do I have lipstick all over my face?"

"You're beautiful. Do I?"

"No. George. What shall we do, George?"

The conversation continued in this vein for an hour, until they both realized that they had to check in at their offices before they could go home. Once Liane put a hand on George's leg, but he snatched it and held it so tightly that their respective rings—Liane's mother's cluster of sapphire chips and George's wedding ring—cut into their fingers.

In the taxi, they both took out combs and made individual repairs and then asked to be inspected by the other. George took one of Liane's hairpins out of her mouth while she was fixing her hair and put it in his wallet. She kept the linen handkerchief he had given her for dusting her shoes. In the modest residential street near her chancery, a diplomat waved at them. The man continued down the street normally, but George and Liane felt the enormity of having been discovered. "I'll call you tomorrow," he muttered as she summoned superhuman strength to walk up the doorstep of her office.

WEEKS LATER, she was amazed to count ten whole days between their first meeting and their engulfment in emotion. She told him how she had tried to get a messenger to send her lists to his office, and that if she had not gotten fed up waiting for the messenger service, they would never have met. They shuddered delightedly at the horror of that. She had slammed down the telephone on the messenger service. Imagine!

They were lying, spent, on her bed, their bodies glistening with perspiration and the damp sheets wrinkled beneath them, as she reminisced. Two hours of constantly renewed lovemaking—George kept boyish count and announced that he had broken his teen-age record—had left them too tired to move, but unwilling to let go, so they lay with locked hands. Liane narrated every step she had taken that first fateful day, down the grubby State Department corridor, and said that at the end of it, she had merely noticed a large white-haired man sitting behind a gray desk.

"Liar!" cried George. "I have a wooden desk. Only secretaries still have those gray metal desks. So you don't care, after all."

"Well, you're certainly an old gray government fixture," she said. "You can't deny that." It was his great mane of white hair she loved best, and the way it showed off his taut pink healthy skin. Unruly white hairs from his chest were on her body now, and she dreaded the idea of showering them off to accompany his pre-departure cleansing.

"You're right," said George. "Too old and too gray. I'm going to find a young stud for you and watch. You'll let me watch, won't you? I won't disturb you. You just tell your young lover that you have some pity for an old man who adores you, and you can laugh at me together. I won't mind. Hey, I know. I'll send my son over. He looks like me. How would that be? Because you're right, I'm too old for you." They both watched his penis rise as he talked. Liane bent over it, her black hair curtaining her

face, and stored away in her head the fact that it was the
first time he had mentioned his family since the original
luncheon announcement of its existence.

HER STORE of facts to go over in private grew in time,
and she didn't mind the time she spent alone because there
was so much to taste and ponder in memory, from their
two afternoons a week. There was the martyred expression on his face as he hung over her, and the groans that
escaped him, the smile he flashed from a taxi as he left,
and the whispered words of love later, from a pay phone
near his house. Sometimes she found a precious white
hair on her bed. It was so rich a life that she dreamed of
nothing more.

She loved the unedited way he reported the details of
his life, good or bad. The other men who had courted her
always spoke of the flattering things in their lives, keeping the unflattering ones to themselves or lying about
them. George's openness seemed to bespeak an enormous
self-confidence. She never heard him apologetic. If he
had anything embarrassing to tell about himself, he told
it without the slightest request for pity or forgiveness.
If he had been slighted by a superior at work, or was
suffering from his spring allergies, or a car had splattered
him with mud, Liane's heart leapt to his protection, but
he hardly noticed. Reprimanded, sneezing, or splattered,
he maintained the same rather pokey, absent-minded dignity she had found so sensual and so different from the
tense, self-serving quickness of the men she had known.
He didn't treat Liane's love as an honor, but as a burden
which, on consideration, was probably worth it.

He told her funny stories about his eccentric southern

family, about his comic posts abroad, about slapstick diplomatic incidents and bureaucratic entanglements. His wife and children sometimes figured in the stories, but never as the butts of jokes or complaints.

Doodie Beaufort was an object of respect to both Liane and George. She looked strong and frank in the wallet snapshot, taken aboard the family boat, also named *Doodie*. Liane declared that she liked her enormously and wished she could meet her.

Once Mr. and Mrs. George Beaufort had attended a large party at Liane's embassy, and Liane had had a glimpse of Doodie, gamely talking to stray, low-ranking wives. George had been off in a corner all evening, treating with exaggerated gallantry a young but undistinguished Dutch woman. Liane had felt sick, and was desperate by the time their next Tuesday rolled around. It wasn't for herself, she explained; she had been perfectly satisfied to have George pass her by without notice because he was protecting their secret, but she thought his behavior an insult to Doodie. She liked Doodie, she reminded him.

Besides, she trusted him with Doodie.

Another time, she got herself into a state over what she was willing to concede must only have been the illusion of indifference on George's part. She had brought it on herself by breaking the rule about calling him at the office (there was no need of a rule against calling him at home because she would have died rather than allow her fingers to dial that number) to tell him that her nephew had been found to have leukemia. There was no provision in the system for her calling him; she was not supposed to have emergencies. George had cut her off abruptly, and had said afterwards that he had been frantic, because the Under Secretary had been in his office at the time.

He had not remembered to ask about the nephew.

Liane was surprised at the rages and despairs such incidents could cause in her. She learned to hold it all in,
molding the wild emotions into small packages of pleas
when it would be convenient for George to listen to them,
but she never got satisfaction. He didn't scold; he never
scolded. He merely said that it was all too much for him,
and that they had better give it up.

THE DAY on which Liane had cleared her house of
Gilbert was her and George's second anniversary. That is,
it was the closest weekday to the date they had met. Any
pain Liane had felt during those two years was washed
away by tears and semen, and only the odd beauty was
left: the redemption through pure love of (as she saw it) a
formerly heartless flirt and a man who had been wearing
away without ever having had magic in his life.

In a new silk suit and a small hat, Liane sat at a center
table in the Rive Gauche, sipping water and keeping her
eyes down for fear of meeting those of strangers. It was
understood that George could always be late—Doodie
might call, or the Under Secretary. At one-fifteen, she
ordered a glass of wine, and by putting ice from her
re-filled water glass into it, and then water, she made it
last until nearly two. Her face ached from looking im-
passive, and a hatred for the waiter, who had twice
asked, "Does Madam care to order now?" burned in her
heart. But she was prepared to wrap in love whatever
crisis George would bring with him.

He arrived at two-twenty, taking her hand as he
slipped into the heavy leather banquette, and looking
stricken as he said, "Darling, I'm so sorry."

Liane beamed at him. "George, never mind. I love you. I want you to know that these have been the two happiest years of my life."

"You're marvelous," he said. "There's no one like you. Mine, too."

They had agreed not to exchange presents, but she handed him a flat square package, beautifully wrapped, and in it he found a dozen of his special kind of hem-stitched linen handkerchiefs, to symbolize the one she had kept on that first day.

"But I don't have anything for you. I thought we agreed."

She smiled and extracted the minuscule diamond on a chain that she had worn night and day, with some discom-fort at night when it tangled in her hair, since exactly a year ago. They laughed and congratulated themselves on the kind of trust and lasting love that never happened to anyone else any more, and they tried to remember what they had eaten—or rather not eaten—that first lunch, so they could order it again.

"What kept you?" Liane asked pleasantly, after the menus had been taken away and they had entwined their feet.

"Oh, nothing," he said. "Arlene stopped me just as I was leaving—I was just walking out the door. I was even leaving early. I thought I'd shock you by being here before you."

"Darling," she said gratefully, squeezing his hand on the table and then withdrawing it quickly in case any of the three other diners who were left should be State Department spies. "What'd she have for you?" Arlene was George's fat secretary, whose crush on him Liane didn't particularly like. It wasn't the possibility of rivalry, which was so remote in this case as to be ridiculous; it was the idea that George's tremendous sexuality was visible to another woman. Liane considered it her unique discovery.

"She's got some stupid problem with her mother. I don't know why she has to tell me about it."

He reached for Liane's hand, a rare public gesture, but her hands were clutching the edge of the table. "On my time?"

"Well, on my time, I guess. She's really pathetic."

"*You kept me waiting an hour so Arlene could tell you about her mother?*"

"What's the matter with you, Liane? Please keep your voice down. I told you I was sorry. Listen to me. Arlene might be suspicious about us. You do persist in calling, you know. And she does answer the phone."

"I never call you. You're the one who calls me. I have an office, too, you know. Maybe people wonder about me."

"You called yesterday."

"I wanted to ask about your *God-damned dog being run over. Remember?*"

"Yes, I remember. For God's sake, keep your voice down. I am not quarreling with you, Liane. I am merely saying that Arlene knows your voice, and I don't want to antagonize her."

Liane threw down her napkin and walked rapidly to the door. Outside, she ran and ran, but when she sat down, on that very same sacred park bench, he didn't come. Her sorrowful rage bore her up for a long time, but when it drained, she felt shipwrecked. She began to tell herself that he had had to stay in the restaurant to do something about the food they had ordered. That he was frightened of scenes. That he was always too kind to dismiss bores, and that he couldn't conceivably be accused of preferring

Arlene's mother to a luncheon at the Rive Gauche. That she was a fool and had probably ruined the only love she had ever known. That these sudden rages weren't really like her.

She walked around until four-thirty, going into shops without looking at merchandise or answering the offers of clerks, and then found herself at the Department of State. There she stood, leaning against a wall in the lobby, until George walked by at five-fifteen. It was a desperate gamble. If this was one of Doodie's days to pick him up, Liane's action would be a further, fatal offense.

He was alone, and he greeted her heartily. She walked with him to his car.

Outside, the smile left his face. She had forgotten, in her shot-in-the-arm relief at his initial expression, that he was, by profession, a diplomat. "Liane," he said, "I can't go on. I can't take this. I'm just the right age to have a heart attack."

"George, I'm so sorry. Please. I don't know what got into me. I'm so terribly sorry."

"I know you are, but it never helps. Liane, I have a wife and a family. I work for a very straight-laced, nosy organization. We don't wear brown shoes, and we don't know women who make scenes. This could ruin me, personally and professionally. All I ask is that you don't come after me in the office, and that you don't make public scenes. And here you are again."

"Please, please, please. I'm leaving. Right now. I love you. Please tell me it's all right."

"It's not all right. I know you love me. That's the trouble. Can't you love me without all that drama?"

"I'll try. I promise."

"Couldn't you have waited until tomorrow to talk to me? Did you have to waylay me here? Now I'm going to be home late, and everybody's going to ask questions."

"No, you're not, George. I'm leaving right now, and you haven't gone an inch out of your way. There's your car. Good-bye, George. Okay?"

"Liane, it's not okay, any of it. I'll call you in a couple of days."

"No! George, don't say that! Please. Tell me it's all right."

"See?" he asked, looking at his watch.

"George, just tell me you love me, and I'll go."

"I do love you. That's the trouble."

"And you'll be over on Tuesday?"

"See? Now it's five-thirty."

"George, please."

"Okay, we'll talk on Tuesday. But I mean it."

Liane had run away before he could dilute this concession with qualifications.

As Liane lay looking at the ceiling, there was a knock on her bedroom door. Unreasonably, because George was tucked away in McLean for the night, her heart thumped.

"It's me. The one who loves you."

"Go away."

"Take pity on me."

"Gilbert, not now. Go away. Please!"

Gilbert closed the door behind him and sat down in the flounced chair next to the bed. "There's nobody home but you and me," he said.

"Please don't torture me, Gilbert. I really need to be left alone." He moved to the bed and took her in his arms, and she cried and sobbed until she hiccoughed.

Then she pushed him away and lay back on her pillow and smiled at him. "If you think you're getting in this bed, you're crazy."

"Why not?"

"Because you're a sly little twerp and you think you can take advantage of me, but I'm not yet that desperate."

"Thanks, pal."

"Can I tell you the truth? I really like you, Gilbert. In fact, I love you, I think, in a funny way. We understand each other. But I haven't got the slightest romantic interest in you, and I'd hate myself if I went through the motions just because I don't feel well."

"That's okay," said Gilbert. "It's not what I came in for, anyway. I got Hot Erna, remember? Why should I serve the whole silly household?"

She laughed. "You know, you do make me feel better."

"That's what I came in for," he said, returning to the chair and putting his bare feet on her bed. "I'm here to tell you how to stop that jerk from walking all over you."

"Mind your own God-damned business. And *get out*."

She was sitting up, looking as if she were going to throw something at him, but Gilbert refused to be cowed this time. "Liane, Liane, listen to me. I'm the only friend you've got. You're lucky to have me, because I know how to help you. I can teach you to make that man your slave. I do it all the time, myself, with girls. It's foolproof. Honestly."

"What man? I don't know what you're talking about."

"George. I'm talking about George."

Liane tried to ask, "George who?" but her voice broke. She got out of bed, on the other side, and started brushing her hair swiftly in front of the window, not acknowledging Gilbert's rapid patter. It was his sadist-masochist theory of romance. He told it in a long and repetitious speech, filled with examples, the latest being that of Erna's rejected beau who was now rejecting her. The moral of the story was: "Kick him in the teeth." He said that several times.

Liane's only motion was the flick of her hairbrush.

"Well? You understand the idea?"

She sat down on the bed. "You think you're so smart, don't you? Gilbert, dear, every maître d' in a restaurant knows as much as that. Insult people, and they tip higher and come back for more. Is that what you want me to do?"

Gilbert was so floored he was silent.

"Gilbert, it just so happens I'm a lot older than you are, and I have no interest in spending the rest of my life playing childish games. Sure, I know plenty of men who love to get kicked in the ass. I got sick of them. My foot got tired. I come from a family where people happen to love each other. I like loving someone, and I like being good to him, and if you can't understand that, too bad for you."

Gilbert looked abashed, but he said, "Does it work?"

"It works fine. Good night." She pushed him out the door.

AN HOUR LATER, she knocked on his door and said she was ready to go out for a drink. At a four-table café, two blocks up from the Rive Gauche, they sat with a candle in a glass wind-protector between them, making spitballs out of the paper placemats, Liane consuming three Manhattans while Gilbert drank one Coke, and she told him the whole story.

He argued for giving George one good kick, as an experiment. For the sake of science. Just one.

"I know," said Liane tipsily. "I'll have someone call and cancel his invitation to the party Friday, saying we need it for someone higher up. We did that once to somebody, I forget who. Of course, that was a dinner, not a big free-for-all like tomorrow, and we were in an emergency, and the ambassador invited him for a special lunch the next week."

"Hey, terrific. Let's do it."

"I can't. What about his wife? She's invited, too. I can't do it."

"You've got to. The hell with her. Let's let him worry about her, for a change. Let's let him worry about you for a change."

"I can't. He'd feel humiliated."

"That's the idea, Liane."

"No, I'm sorry. A joke is a joke, Gilbert, but I'm not going to hurt him. He worries about his job, and he'd take this as a bad sign. He probably wouldn't even think I had anything to do with it."

"Then cancel next Tuesday."

"Are you crazy?" He only looked at her with raised eyebrows. "Oh, all right. I'll think about it."

SHE WAS all business Friday morning, when he heard her up early and followed her to the kitchen. "You have to obey the ground rules tonight," she said. "I'm very serious. I had no business inviting you, and I could get into trouble." She handed him a pasteboard invitation with a gold crest.

"First, I want you to be on your own. I'll be too busy

to talk to you, and anyway, it wouldn't be a good idea. You can talk to anyone you meet, so long as you don't say anything that arouses any curiosity about you. If you want, you can be a friend of the ambassador's son. He's gone back home. He was at the University of Iowa last year, studying animal husbandry, and as far as I know he never had any friends, but if he had and they were here, we might have invited them."

"Animal husbandry? You want me to look like I'm an animal husband from the University of Iowa?"

"They have an enormous plantation back home. He had a choice between that and mining engineering. There's a buffet, but don't go back to the table more than once."

"Are you going to tell me not to get drunk and rape the hostess?"

"No, but don't, anyway. Let's not have any, shall we say, unusual socializing?"

"I'm surprised you invited me at all," said Gilbert.

"So am I. Any questions?"

"Who else is going to be there?"

"Nobody much. National days are a bore, and some important people have to stop by, but the rest is just a catch-all. If we really want to see anyone, we ask them to dinner. These are mostly freeloaders."

"Then why have them?"

"What do you think any embassy's for? To make friends, of course. Which reminds me. I don't want you to talk to George."

"How do I tell who the important ones are? Will they be more dressed up?"

"No, less. They won't bother changing their office clothes just for us. Or they might be in evening clothes, but I don't know of anyone who's giving a dinner tonight. The cocktail clothes are the nobodies. If our party is the highlight of anybody's day, that person is in big trouble. The big people will either be going someplace better afterwards, or home, which they'll consider much better. What color's your tie?"

"Navy blue. That too flashy for you? I wouldn't want to embarrass you in front of George."

She snatched at the invitation, but he held it out of her reach. "Watch out for name-dropping in reverse. It's interesting. The in people say 'The President' or 'Senator So-and-So'; people who call them Ike or Bill or Joe or whatever don't know them."

"Right. What else?"

"I've got to go." She gathered her purse and an assortment of leather notebooks and pasteboard boxes. "Can I ask you something? What are you going to do with all this stuff I've been telling you? Why on earth do you care?"

"I'm trying to better myself," said Gilbert. "I don't want to be a secretary all my life."

SIX-THIRTY to eight-thirty, it said in engraved script on the invitation card. As nearly as Gilbert could make out, the gold crest on top was of two crossed birds, grasping rolled flags in their claws and scowling at each other.

All afternoon, he had felt the clock creeping maddeningly, but while he was in the bathtub, it leapt ahead, and when he raced out to the street, it was ten minutes after six. Those ten minutes—he had meant to leave half an hour to get there—were gone out of his social life, like ten years out of his life. To his surprise, he captured an empty taxi on Wisconsin Avenue, after having calculated that the rush-hour traffic, combined with the perverseness of the world, would rob him of the rest of his Washington debut.

It rattled Gilbert that the taxi driver had never heard of the embassy. He took the card, which Gilbert was afraid he might smudge, announced that it was in the park, and asked Gilbert's advice on how to get there. Failing an answer, he set out bravely, anyway.

In the streets, people were coming home from work, the men carrying their jackets over one shoulder, the women carrying bundles and shopping bags. As Gilbert saw people going slowly up to their Georgetown door-stoops, one by one, he found it incredible that the owners of these genuine, historic, narrow dwellings, complete with gas lamps and brick sidewalks, had not been able to achieve entrée into the diplomatic whirl he was about to enter.

Then the diplomatic car plunged into the park, free of the slow city traffic. Gilbert lowered the window to create an artificial breeze. Soon they were winding along what seemed to be blank country roads, although he knew they still had to be in the middle of Washington. He had a panic of disorientation, and then remembered that the chancery, where he had sometimes met Liane, was the office, while the embassy was the ambassador's residence, where the entertaining was done. Just when he was wondering how two people ignorant of the city's geography would ever find their destination, he observed what seemed to be a segregated automobile party. Long lines of brightly colored cars were parked on both sides of an uphill road, and another line of cars, these all black, was going up in the middle. A policeman stood on the road separating the cars—beckoning to black ones, and directing colored ones to park on patches of grass, under a row of No Parking signs that were, like Gilbert's invita-

tion card, partly printed and partly filled in with handwriting.

Gilbert's taxi was allowed to join the line of limousines,
although its orange and black gaudiness made him feel
an intruder, like a commuter car sneaking across a funeral
procession. He leaned an arm out of his shabby window
and tried to slow the pace of his expectations to the very
slow progress of the line. The owners of the self-driven
colored cars were making the trip up the hill on foot
faster than the car-borne guests, but they looked funny
trudging in their party clothes and were peering into
the black cars, where the guests sat in back and chauf-
feurs drove.

When their destination came into view, it turned out
to be a large but ordinary-looking stone house. His
door was opened for him, just as he was opening it for
himself, and he saw that he had to walk through the house,
although he had been able to spot the party taking place
outdoors behind it. It was the ceremony of the receiving
line, which Liane had warned him not to attempt escap-
ing. A butler asked his name, listened to his hoarse
whisper, and repeated it embarrassingly loudly. Gilbert
shook hands with five people: a man in long blue robes,
a young woman in swirls of white and gold material with
a fabric headdress, another man in robes, a woman in pink
lace, and a huge man in a dark business suit. He said,
"How do you do?" to each one, and was surprised to hear
each answer, "Thank you." He shot an ear out behind
him, and found that the other guests were murmuring,
"Congratulations," as they passed from one handshake to
another.

Somehow the other guests all got around him and out.
Gilbert was stranded with those five strange, smiling
people. They stood patiently, now and then glancing

expectantly towards the front door, and Gilbert was frozen into place. Finally, the man in the business suit noticed his difficulty. "I am so happy to be in your beautiful country," this personage announced. "I do hope you will go and have a drink on the occasion of our independence." He gestured to the left, and it uprooted Gilbert, who shuffled ahead, feeling disgraced.

On one side of the hall, he saw an empty drawing room, furnished with gold chairs, white silk sofas, and tigerskin footstools. To the other side was a dining room consisting of a filled table entirely bordered, several thicknesses wide, in outstretched human hands. Through the door, on the flagstone terrace, he saw four different bars, each with its covering cloth gently flapping, and each with its own small clientele. Just to have a destination, he set out for one of them, maneuvering sideways through the crowd around it. No conversational possibilities presented themselves, and he soon found himself face-to-face with a bartender over plates of cherries, limes, and peanuts.

"Champagne," said Gilbert grandly, as a kind of Noel Coward parody. He was feeling reckless since he had managed to become a failure in five minutes. Champagne was sloshed into a thick but shallow stemmed glass, from one of five open bottles in a bucket of melting ice. The trip back across the terrace, which was filling now, was more difficult because he had to protect his brimming glass and also because he didn't know where he was going.

He parked the full glass on the edge of a step, which already had collected a row of glasses, some empty, some half-full, and entered the dining room. Using his hand as a wedge, he got through the three-deep ring of people around the table, and found himself facing a vase carved out of ice with real flowers in it, and a tall structure, papered in silver, which showed the remnants of having once been studded with shrimp-bearing toothpicks. By stretching dangerously, Gilbert could just reach a platter beyond it, and his hand returned to him with a tiny tomato, bursting from an injection of cheese. It expired with a swish as Gilbert's back teeth closed on it. That done, he took a look at the enterprising eater next to him, a woman in turquoise chiffon, efficiently picking shrimps off their silver wall—she had cleverly discovered that the back wall had been overlooked during the original invasion.

"Hello, there," said Gilbert.

"Nice to see you," she said.

"Do I, uh, know you?"

"Probably you know my husband," she said. "We were three years in the Cameroons, and he traveled around a lot. Shall I find him for you?" She left, and Gilbert contemplated making the terrace round trip again, enough time having elapsed, according to his calculations, for the bartender to think it plausible that he had drunk his drink. Probably all the bartenders were in secret communication.

On the way out, he spotted Liane, in poison green. She was talking to a fancy white uniform, and Gilbert's joy at seeing her froze when she gave him the barest nod without altering the fixed smile she was displaying for her companion. He had to stumble backwards to get away.

A table was spread on the edge of the stone terrace, where steps led to the swimming pool below. There were strawberries on it, in potted arrangements like miniature trees, and plates of éclairs apparently iced in church-candle wax. Gilbert plucked a strawberry, but it was too large to eat in one bite. He was nibbling away sideways, prepared to let it drip into his cupped hand, when someone else came up to seize a pastry.

The man faced him. "Pakistan Embassy," he said.

"Gilbert Fairchild." They shook hands.

"I have six months in this country; I like it very much indeed."

"Good," said Gilbert. "Me, too."

"I like perhaps to meet Americans."

"What kind of Americans?" Gilbert asked suspiciously.

"All kinds. I do not share unfortunate American prejudices, unworthy of your people. But I find Americans very interesting indeed. Perhaps more so than they do themselves. You are a student, please?"

"Sort of," said Gilbert. "Thank you."

"I, too."

"I thought you were in the Pakistan Embassy."

"Yes. I work in embassy, and also I am candidate for Ph.D. in the American University. Perhaps you mistake me for Pakistan national. You think we look alike."

"What do you do at the embassy?"

"Drive."

"Okay," said Gilbert. "Excuse me." But then he turned back. "You're not by any chance a friend of the ambassador's son, are you?"

"No, indeed. I should be pleased if you would introduce me."

"I'll be right back," said Gilbert. "Don't go away. Say, how did you happen to be invited here?"

"I am the boarder of the third secretary."

"See you," said Gilbert.

He made his way down to the pool, pleased that he was catching on, but feeling that this person's invitation had cheapened his own. A bald man who looked familiar to

Gilbert was walking away from the bar with three glasses of tomato juice, delicately balanced. Gilbert asked a bartender for tomato juice and the time. Seven twenty-five. One way of calculating it was that he had thirty-five minutes to fill before he could go home. Another was that there were only thirty-five minutes left for him to make it socially in Washington, D.C.

He closed his eyes momentarily and headed for the first group he saw when he opened them, swerving only when he discovered it contained the woman in turquoise. She saw him and shifted, turning her back to him. Gilbert closed his eyes and opened them for another attack. This is worse than high school, he thought.

"Was this your drink?" he said to an old woman in a sleeveless blue coat, handing her his tomato juice.

"No, but I'll take it if I may. I'm Margaret Gates. I don't think I know you."

Gilbert gave her his drink, his name, and his best smile. "I'm new, but you'll be hearing from me," he said.

The woman's grandmotherly looks turned cold. "Oh, good," she said, turning slightly.

"I'm sorry. I'd like to impress you, and I don't know how."

"My dear, don't waste your time. I assure you I'm not worth it, and I really must go."

"Is your husband a diplomat or something?"

"I've never been married."

"Oh," said Gilbert. "Do you work?"

"I work for the government," she said. "Excuse me. Please." She turned around, but found herself blocked by S. B. Brewster, who smiled at her and repeated his name.

"Oh, dear, yes," she said. "How's your uncle? Do remember me to him, won't you?"

"He told me to keep away from you because you're

the most vicious woman in Washington. So of course, here I am."

"Well, silliness must run in your family," she said, taking his arm.

Brewster waved at him as they went off, saying, "Gilbert Fairchild."

And Gilbert Fairchild stood there, so obviously bereft that a strolling accordion player gave him a free smile.

"Tell me who that is," Gilbert pleaded.

"Oh, my, that's Small Boy. I remember him from way, way back. He used to ask me to play 'Hail to the Chief.' It's good to have him around. Like the old days. I miss the old days."

"No, the woman."

"Are you kidding? That's Miss Gates." Gilbert looked puzzled. "The Secretary of the Treasury?" the musician asked, as if he weren't sure that he was getting through.

"Thanks," said Gilbert. The musician nodded and did an extra blast on his accursed instrument in Gilbert's honor as he walked off.

The party was thinning, and Gilbert went back to the dining room table, which had been still further ravaged. He found a lonely deviled egg, pulled off its parsley camouflage, and pushed it whole into his mouth. On the other side of the table, he discovered one triangular piece of toast covered with a triangular piece of salmon. Not one shrimp was left. He went back outdoors for a last try, and walked smack into the first man he had shaken hands with in the receiving line.

"I hope you are enjoying yourself," the man said. "Do you, by any chance, speak French?"

"*Un peu*," said Gilbert. "Actually, *non. Rien.*"

"It's of no importance. English is very difficult for my wife. She takes lessons, one hour every morning."

"You speak it very well," said Gilbert.

"Thank you very much. I was posted in London for eight years. Before that, I taught at Oxford University. Come and have a chat with my wife."

Gilbert watched with horror as the young woman who had stood next to the host in line approached with her hand out again. "*Enchantée*," she said.

"English, English, English," said the ambassador. "You are in America now."

"I am enchanted," she told Gilbert, who understood it as a cry for help from a fairy princess under a spell.

"Do you like America?" Gilbert asked, wishing he were dead.

She looked at her husband before facing Gilbert. "It is enchanting," she brought out.

"Yes, isn't it?" said Gilbert.

"Good, good, good," said the ambassador. Gilbert thought he had passed the test, but realized it was addressed to her. "Excellent. I shall leave you two together. You must speak English with our American friends."

The two of them watched him depart. "How is your son?" said Gilbert.

"Only four month. Baby. So I did not come here before. Arrived in America one month ago. I am very happy here."

"I thought your son went to school here. University of Iowa."

"Oh, no, no, no." She laughed. "Son of my husband. I am second wife. Son's mother is dead. How old you think I look?"

"I'm terribly sorry," said Gilbert.

"Thank you," said the young woman. "It is all right." She took a deep breath and said, "I am so extremely enchanted to have made your acquaintance. America is

a beautiful country, and I find the people friendly."
Gilbert wanted to tell her she had said it right—he was
beginning to identify with her—but she left him for the
woman in pink lace, who had been next to her in the
receiving line. They whispered together and broke into
laughter, renewing their merriment by fresh peeks at
Gilbert.

The hell with them, Gilbert thought. He walked away
and smack into Small Boy. "May I work for you?" Gilbert asked him quickly. "I graduate from Harvard next
June. Would you give me a job? Anything; I just want
to learn."

"Gilbert, I don't have a job myself," said Small Boy,
with an amused smile. "If you hear of anything, let me
know. See you, Gilbert."

"Sure," said Gilbert.

Then Liane came up to him, deliberately, right to him,
on purpose. He was thrilled. "Time to go home," she
said.

"Fine. I'm ready. Are you?"

"No, you. We're not together. 'Bye."

He fled. But not before he found he had to run through
the re-formed receiving line again. His clothes were
sticking to him, and he felt faint. Suppose he dropped on
the floor; wouldn't they have to call an ambulance that
would take him out of there? What if they put him up
in the guest room instead?

"My wife tells me you had an interesting little chat,"
said the ambassador. The wife immediately busied herself
talking to her pink lace friend.

"We did," said Gilbert. "Remember me to your son.
I miss him."

"Ah," said the ambassador, his eyes flickering with
pleasure. "Of course, of course. He will be so sad not to

have seen you, but I will tell him all about this charming encounter. He misses his American friends. Please consider this your home. I hope you had a chance to chat with our Minister of Justice?" He handed Gilbert's hand to the big man in the business suit, who had wandered out of line. "This is a dear friend of my Louis." The minister nodded and stepped back into line. Gilbert scanned the horizon for another departing guest to take his place, but no one appeared. "You will come one day and visit us at home," the ambassador told Gilbert. "Louis speaks often of his American 'pals,' as he calls them. He is anxious to return their hospitality. You will like our country. It is unlike anywhere else on earth, if I may be permitted to say so. I will arrange something. Perhaps very soon; who knows?"

"Who knows?" Gilbert admitted. He walked out, forgetting that he had no car and was in the middle of a park, miles from public transportation.

''I DIDN'T DO SO HOT,'' Gilbert announced to Liane the next morning, having caught her as she was about to leave the house. He was hurt that she had come in late that night and even this morning hadn't sought an opportunity to reassure him.

"It doesn't matter."

"No, it does. Don't give up on me. It's just that the practice is a little harder than the theory. Also, I suspect this wasn't such a hot party, if I may be permitted to say so."

"That rat!" she said.

"No, it's not his fault. He was trying to be nice to me."

"George, you idiot. He didn't even show. She was there—he sent her with that stupid admiral friend of theirs. Did you see them?" She flounced out the door, slamming it behind her.

ON TUESDAY, Gilbert opened the door and said, "Madame isn't in. She had a lunch date. You might try the Rive Gauche; she often goes there. It's just down Wisconsin Avenue at M. Would you care to leave your name?"

George didn't care to. From the second story, Liane watched him walk droopily away. Three times that afternoon, Gilbert raced her to the telephone and kept his hand over it until it stopped ringing.

"If he leaves me, I'll kill you."

"Nobody ever left anyone for one broken date," said Gilbert. He was bitterly disappointed in wrinkled old George, and in old Gilbert, too, for that matter. Liane was not accepting his instruction, and would be on the telephone begging the minute he relaxed his vigilance. Erna was bothering less and less to pretend that he was anything except a poor consolation for a wasted summer.

"Mother," he said on the telephone, "I want to go home."

"You know," she said, "you're the only teen-ager I know who would think of interrupting his summer fun to spend some time with his parents. Your father and I are very pleased and proud."

Chapter VI

THE AIR CONDITIONING in Gilbert's parents' building hadn't exactly broken, but it had faded away, and the inhabitants, having long lost their ancestors' survival habits, didn't know how to use fans, sit outdoors, go to the movies, or even open windows strategically to achieve cross ventilation.

Gilbert's parents had lost the will to live. His father, with a green plastic awning over each lens of his eyeglasses, ready to be snapped down as sunglasses should he go foraging for food, kept saying, "This is unbearable," and his mother kept adding, "Me, too."

Gilbert alone had detected a noseful of cool air, a

quick breath of autumn briefly cutting through the dense heat. It started him thinking of the sharp life ahead, in which he would keep alert, so that every minute thing he did from that moment on would be executed perfectly.

Being perky upset his home schedule. Having lost his early summertime apathy, he couldn't even sleep late. He tried to arouse his parents as they sat looking blankly at their dinners.

"Present for you!" he said one night.

They looked at him distrustfully. He couldn't make it cool, and anything else would be a cruel joke.

"I've picked a career."

"Good," said his father. "I can't eat corn on a night like this."

"Listen! I'm going into government. Politics. I've been thinking about it, and it's the ideal thing for me."

"So don't eat it," said his mother. Gilbert was looking at her. "Why?" she asked dutifully.

"Why? I thought you'd be pleased. Because my country needs me, that's why."

"Your country needs Englishmen, too."

Gilbert's father looked at her thoughtfully. "I don't think so," he said after a while.

"English majors, I meant. English professors. Whatever. Who cares? We had ice cream last night, but I don't care. So what if we get fat? At least we'll survive."

GILBERT LEFT THEM to try, explaining that he had to go to Cambridge a week before school started to get his affairs in order. Actually, he was still trying to go home.

Coming in from Logan Airport, he felt a flow of kindliness at how happy Margery would be when he walked, unannounced, through the door. "Margery," he would say, "I've come home to you." (Perhaps he would just say, "Margery, I've come home." No point in getting her overexcited.)

A light shone from his very own window, and Gilbert admired it while picking out change in the dark for the taxi. He let himself in with his key and opened the door to see Buddy sitting, in Gilbert's very own bathrobe, drawing a picture.

Gilbert froze. "What are you doing in my house?" he whispered.

"Hi," said Buddy. "Have a seat."

"*What are you doing here?*"

"Now, look, old man, you sublet this apartment."

"Not to you, I didn't. Get out."

"For God's sake, Gilbert, what's bugging you? Margy'll be home soon. You can stay to dinner. I made meatballs."

"Oh, you did, did you?"

"Take it easy, Gilbert. I can understand your being upset, that's perfectly natural and normal, but you don't have to be unpleasant about it. Hey, look at this. I'm taking art lessons. Want to see?"

Gilbert looked at him in amazement and then beyond him. He saw that the bed had a bedspread on it. He looked back at Buddy, who was holding out his sketch pad.

In a ferocious gesture, Gilbert ripped off the bedspread, threw it over the cat's box, and lay down on the bed, turning his back to the room. Buddy sat down where he had been and went on with his drawing. When Margery came in, twenty minutes later, it was all quiet, and she called out, "Honey, I'm home!" before she saw the figure on the bed and screamed.

"It's okay," said Buddy. "Just sit down. It'll be okay."

A voice called out weakly from the bed, "Margery! Margery! I've come home!"

Margery screamed again, but at a more controlled volume.

"Everybody keep calm," said Buddy. "We need to talk this out. Margery, sit down."

"Margery! Margery! Come, give me your hand!"

Margery ran to the bed, but she put a hand on Gilbert's forehead and one on her own. "Gilbert, are you all right? Forgive me! Gilbert! Please say you forgive me! I didn't mean it!"

"Give me your hand."

She did, and he suddenly sprang to life. "Now," he cried, "give me the rest!" He snatched at her skirt, and Margery screamed again and pulled away.

"Everybody keep calm," said Buddy, hopping up and down on one foot. "This is a delicate situation, but we can talk about it. Everything'll be fine if we can just talk about it. Okay? I'll start. Gilbert, I'll tell you how Margery has come to feel about you, and then you can tell us what you feel. Okay?"

Margery was looking at Gilbert, and Gilbert was looking at Margery, so Buddy continued without an answer to his question. "Margery and you had what was a very unhealthy relationship. You were both very unhappy, which you may not have realized. When I explain it to you, you'll see that."

While Buddy was talking, Gilbert beckoned to Margery, luring her with a crooked finger onto the farthest corner of the bed. Buddy saw them but did not deign to let present events interrupt his interesting commentary on the past.

"Whatcha been doing, toots?" Gilbert asked Margery in a low voice. "Want to show me?"

Margery shook her head haughtily, but stayed leaning over him, ready to catch his whispers. "We're all friends, and there's no reason we can't remain so if everybody is reasonable," Buddy was saying.

"You don't love me." Margery pouted to Gilbert.

"Oh, sure I do," said Gilbert nastily. "Want to see?" He showed her.

"Wait a minute!" said Buddy.

"Okay," said Gilbert. "Come on in."

"I hate you!" screamed Margery.

Gilbert had adopted Buddy's tone of voice and asked, "Who? Me? Him? Both at once? How about both at once? Shall we try it?" and Margery started to cry.

This time, Buddy swung into action. "It's okay," he said. "It's okay. He's just sick. There's nothing to worry about. I know how to handle this sort of thing."

And before Gilbert knew it, Buddy had his arm locked around Gilbert's neck, pushed him down, and madly tucked in all the bedclothes around him. Gilbert still had his shoes on. "My God, my God," Margery kept saying, and Buddy repeated, "It's all right, *it's all right*."

Gilbert's problem was that Buddy was a lot stronger than he, and it wasn't possible to move with Buddy's arm like a stake on his chest. He closed his eyes and consciously went limp.

"Perfectly natural episode," Buddy announced. "He'll be all right. He needs to talk it out."

"Bentley," said Margery, "stop behaving like a fool."

"A fool? Me? I'm behaving like a fool?" Buddy was spluttering and looked as if he were going to cry. Gilbert opened his eyes and winked at Buddy behind Margery's back.

"That's not fair!" cried Buddy. "I'm trying to help. I am helping. I got everything under control. I'm willing to talk about this. That's not fair!"

"I think you should realize how this looks to Gilbert," said Margery.

"That's right," said Gilbert, seconding her from the bed. "You're the only one who's ever cared about how I felt."

"Shut up," said Margery. "Both of you. Bentley, you go out for a while. I want to talk to Gilbert. You can come back in an hour."

"I? Why should I go out? Why doesn't he have to?"

"I can't move," said Gilbert.

"Damn right. I don't trust you," said Buddy.

"I trusted you. You were my best friend. My best friend and my girl."

"Shut up," said Margery. "Go on, Bentley, now. I'm going to talk to Gilbert, and then Gilbert is going to leave."

"It's my house."

"Don't you let him push you around, Margery. He sublet it to you. You have your rights."

"Make it an hour and a half," said Margery. "Go. Now."

"Or stay." Gilbert leered.

"Well, we could settle this," said Buddy, but he caught Margery's fierce eye, disappeared into the closet, emerged dressed, and left.

After the footsteps had gone from the porch, Gilbert clasped Margery, laughing, and said, "You're a girl after my own heart."

"No, I'm not, either. I mean it about your leaving. Bentley has been good and decent and kind to me, and I really like him a lot, even if he is the way he is. Nobody's ever been that nice to me since I came to this rotten place."

"I didn't know that was what you wanted. Why didn't you tell me?"

She sat down wearily on the bed next to him. He had wriggled free, and she let him take her hand and then park their clasped hands on her leg. "You didn't know I wanted you to be nice to me? Oh, Gilbert, that's just what I mean. Why can't people ever love people back? I wish I loved Bentley, I really do."

"But you don't. You love me." The hand was traveling up.

"Don't do that. I don't love anybody. I didn't even miss you. You never wrote or anything."

"Margery, I went to see my poor mother. I thought I could trust you."

A smile played on her face. "I thought so, too," she said with some pleasure.

"Funny, your thinking I wasn't good to you. I meant to be." He pulled her back to lean against him.

"I know you did," she said absently. "Maybe it's me."

"Didn't I do anything right?" He caught her eye with this, and they both started to laugh. They giggled and rolled about before they started playing seriously. Gilbert was going to stop and ask her if she really meant it, but her eyes still looked merry, so he didn't dare. They were laughing again when Gilbert said, "Hey, Bentley's coming."

"Oh, my God." She was out of bed and throwing clothes around wildly. "What am I going to say? Gilbert, for God's sake, help me. Shall I tell him? I can't."

"Don't let him in. Let him knock."

"He has a key." She was pawing her clothes and his, unable to figure out which was which. "Help me!"

"A key? To my house? Margery, you are a slut, you know that? You really are a slut."

"I know! Come on, help me!" She was jumping up and down, with her hand through a stocking, and Gilbert authoritatively grabbed all the clothes and rolled them in a bundle and shoved them under the bed. He threw her his bathrobe, which Buddy had vacated, and climbed into the bed, primly tucking the sheets around himself, as Buddy had done to pin him in. "Shall I make him move out?" Margery whispered, and Gilbert whispered, "No, no, you can both stay until school starts, hush," as Buddy walked in the door.

"Hi," they said in unison.

"Oh, no," said Buddy.

"No, no," said Gilbert.

"It's not what you think," said Margery.

"I guess I know when I'm not wanted," said Buddy.

"Oh, no you don't," said Gilbert. "Wait. We were talking things out, you see. We got everything all talked out."

"I can tell."

"We had to use visual aids," said Gilbert apologetically.

"I'm sorry, Bentley," said Margery, and Gilbert was disappointed at the look of shame on her face, which had just been mirroring his own excitement.

"I'll explain," he said. "Bentley, there's nothing wrong. Margery and I are old friends. She cares about you, but she feels a responsibility for me, too. I had a shock, you know. You two are the people I trusted most. Margery thinks we all ought to stay until I can get used to it, so I'm going to sleep in the chair and not bother anyone. I think you owe me that. You two can go on and not pay any attention to me. The lease ends next week."

"Believe me, Gilbert, I didn't plan to cut you out. I mean, before you got here."

"Okay, okay. Meatballs for supper, did you say? What're we waiting for?"

"Wait just a minute," said Margery. "We're going to tell him exactly how things stand."

"Now, Margery, I did tell him. No more games now. Daddy's tired."

That night, they all three lay on the bed, Buddy keeping alert, Margery in a motionless despair, and Gilbert soundly asleep. When Buddy left for work the next day, after volunteering to stay if it would help clear things up, Margery said, "Gilbert, I want to ask you something. Tell me the truth. Did you ever sleep with anyone else since we started going together? Please tell me. Don't worry about my feelings."

"Are you sure?"

"I'm sure."

"All right, you asked for it. Margery, the answer is: I can't do what you've been doing. It's not in my nature. I really trusted you. I'm sorry, but you asked me to be honest."

She buried her face against his knees. "Forgive me, Gilbert. What shall I do with Bentley? Let's just tell him how it is. He'll get over it."

"No," said Gilbert, "I'm not going to do to him what he did to me. You can still be friends, but you don't have to sleep with him."

"I won't," she said. "I promise."

MARGERY REFUSED to clean Gilbert's apartment before she moved out, claiming that clean was relative and it was a lot cleaner than when she had moved in.

"Two wrongs don't make a right," said Gilbert, who noted sullenly that there were a remarkable number of boys' shirts in the wardrobe she was packing, and they weren't his. "Two dirties don't make a clean. Where's my cat?"

"That's right, I'll get her. I gave her a name, by the way. It wasn't right for her not to have one. Bentley thinks so, too."

"Margery," he said, "you can't name someone else's cat. That's not right, either. I mean that's not right."

"All right, I won't tell you what I named her."

"You don't have to. Gertrude Stein. Cleopatra. Cattullus. Am I right?"

Margery extracted a pair of men's bathing trunks from a drawer and nonchalantly threw them on the pile in her suitcase.

"Okay, Margery. Tell me. What is it? Come on, Margery, if you tell me, I'll tell you her real name."

"I don't believe you. You always said she didn't have one."

"She does. Maybe you've hit on it. Wouldn't that be amazing? Maybe you just naturally called her by her real name. You think so, Margery? What did you call her?"

"Margery."

"What?"

"I called her Margery. Like me."

"You called the cat Margery?"

"Yes. How many times do you want me to tell you?"

"Oh, boy. Does Buddy know about this?"

"Yes, he knows. What's the matter with you? I just happen to like the name, that's all."

"What does he say? This ought to be good. Old Buddy

knows a weird one when he sees one. You mean to say you called the cat Margery, Margery?"

"Bentley didn't care. He just wanted her out of the house. He's allergic to cats. I got a receipt for her—I sent her to the cat hospital. You owe about forty dollars."

Gilbert stared at her. "I guess I'll go halves," she conceded. "But I didn't rent the cat from you."

"For your information," said Gilbert, "the cat's name is Diane. Not Margery. Diane. And she only eats the good cat food, with the kidneys and fish in it. With the picture of the Siamese on the label. *Are you listening to me?*"

"Hi," said Buddy, the only person in the college still in summer Bermudas. "I'll take Margery's stuff."

IT OCCURRED to Gilbert that college was an excellent opportunity to learn. (He had some regrets about the previous year, but decided that he had probably wasted it less than if he had spent his junior year abroad.) He started taking the daily, as well as the Sunday, newspaper from the floor across the hall.

For the first few weeks, he couldn't understand the stories because they presupposed information from previous newspaper reading, but after a while he got used to the gaps in his understanding and read around them. He could take the pulse of a threat-to-world-peace perfectly well without knowing or wondering why it was a threat. He even got the suburban stranglings sorted out and began to recognize the names of the police spokesmen and the methods of killings.

Then he got a Harvard catalogue and started changing his courses, dropping Problems in Romantic Style for

The History of Political Thought, and squeezing in Party Government in the United States. If he had time, he would audit Civil-Military Relations in Western Society.

There was little to distract him from his newspapers and textbooks. Margery and Buddy visited him only on Sundays. Either Margery would arrive an hour early, or she would send Buddy home an hour early, hardly bothering to see him out the door before peeling her clothes. But it was not the same for Gilbert now that Margery never fussed or whined or made love speeches or wheedled or otherwise embellished the plain act.

He had gotten the hang of the new courses, and was turning out twenty-page papers on "Thomas Jefferson: Radical Conservative" and "Alexander Hamilton's Liberal Legacy." He wrote a paper on "Political Theory in Robert Frost" for the Government Department and one on "The Metaphor in the Public Utterances of Vice President Nixon" for the English Department. The grades were good.

One day, he greeted a long-forgotten friend on the street and noticed that she behaved as if she had a grievance. Had Erna expected him to call her during the fall? He certainly would have if he had thought of it. Why hadn't she called him, then? But he remembered that shame covered the girls who called boys. That must have been why, long ago when he had had nothing better on his mind, he had made girls do it. Erna may have had her reckless moments, but in her right mind, she knew how to behave.

"What do you hear from home?" he asked over a conciliatory cup of coffee at the Mozart Café.

"Ha," said Erna. "They're going on a cruise. Can you imagine? A Caribbean cruise. They were going to go to

Cuba last winter, but they got scared, so now they're going on some stupid ship at Thanksgiving and they expect me to take off and go along. Ha."

Gilbert, who had meant the house in Georgetown when he had said "home" wasn't sure what she was talking about. He accepted it, however, as conventional small talk. Bad-mouthing your parents was always polite conversation.

"What's wrong with that?" asked Gilbert, who would sulk if his parents so much as went to the movies when he was home.

"Where am I supposed to go for vacation? I'm certainly not going with them—they can get that out of their heads right now." Erna now had short curls, and she pulled them as she talked and let them spring back. She leaned over the table and blew the whipped cream poof across her coffee as if it were a toy sailboat on a pond. When he asked her again why not, she had an unusual burst of unbecoming frankness. "Who am I going to meet on a stupid cruise?"

Gilbert didn't like it. Meeting was, of course, the prime business of everyone in their world. In a community composed of thousands of teen-agers of both sexes, similar backgrounds, and related achievements, where the mere fact of being there constituted an introduction and even a recommendation, the biggest problem for everyone was how to meet anyone else. Sometimes seniors who were getting married confessed to friends of their own sex that a major factor in their decision to do so was the relief at never having to try again to meet anyone else in their whole lives. "I'll always have a date for New Year's Eve" was a favorite way of putting it. Yet for an unengaged girl to tell a boy that she was looking was a breach of decency.

"Why don't you stand on a street corner and lift your skirt?" he asked, as if everyone he had met in the course of his entire social life had been presented to him at dancing class. "Try Inman Square, why don't you?"

Erna's eyes had wandered, and Gilbert followed her gaze to a tall, flush-faced couple in matching ratty furs, making loud remarks and guffaws about strangers within hearing distance. To be tipsy at three o'clock in the afternoon, to have a raccoon coat that your parent wore to Harvard (that year, second-hand raccoon coats were being sold in New York department stores at high prices) —the hard-edged self-satisfaction it indicated still impressed Gilbert.

He recognized the tall, large-boned man with the beefy face and big teeth as Christian somebody, a British student who had been in his freshman corridor and about whom legendary stories had later been told. He had fallen out of his club's ground-floor window when drunk, and not spilled a drop from the glass in his hand. He had been invited to dinner at a famous professor's, had thrown up in the man's library, and had calmly returned to the dinner table and resumed propositioning the professor's wife. According to one version, she had accepted and suggested they disappear into the library.

Gilbert was surprised when this hero started making rude faces at Erna and she hardly paused in her conversation to stick out her tongue in return. "God, I'm a senior," she was droning to Gilbert. "It's not so funny. What am I supposed to do next year, go to Katie Gibbs? Get a master's in teaching?" The last word was said with such loathing that Gilbert did not understand why, if Erna had a secret connection to the aristocracy. He jerked his head toward the furry drunks and raised his eyebrows at Erna.

"My brother," she said.

"No, he's not," said Gilbert. "I know who he is."

"Okay, he's not," said Erna. "Maybe you'd better tell my mother. He doesn't have much to do with me here. He's a year older; it just took longer to get him through high school."

Gilbert's head was swiveling between the two. "His name's Christian something," he insisted.

"Boothe. Frank Boothe. He made up Christian."

Gilbert stared at her in wonderment. In her family stories there had always been only the child-star. "Then how come," he said as a final, crushing argument, "how come you're not English?"

"How come he is?" Erna asked.

IT HAPPENED that just a week later, Gilbert had a chance to solve the problem of Erna's future. He had passed Margery walking down the street arm in arm—not even with Buddy, but with someone new—and he called Liane for comfort. Not about Margery, of course; Liane was bored with boy-girl games, she said, and had never credited him with the success of his tactics with George. So he told her, instead, about Christian Boothe and the pose, apparently fully developed at the beginning of freshman year, that had entirely fooled Gilbert himself and, apparently, the set at which it was aimed.

Liane shared his interest and admiration, but was doubtful about its post-college possibilities. "Especially for a man," she said. "A girl could marry and abandon her real background, but a man of that age ought to be going into his family interests, or something." Gilbert had called her in a pique at Christian's having cut into his own business, the do-it-yourself character & background trade, but Liane had a generous spirit, and he soon found himself wishing Christian well as a colleague.

"Erna reminds me," she said. "I've got something hilariously funny to tell you. Only it isn't funny, of course."

"Go ahead."

"No, this is too funny. It's about Walter Oliphant. The one Erna was after this summer?"

"That's not quite fair," he said under the new benevolence. "He used to be after her. But go on."

"Poor old Walter was in an accident. He smashed his Triumph."

"Oh," said Gilbert, finding the gossip paltry. "Was he hurt?"

"That's the point. Not physically, that was nothing, but he put a few dents into his career and a few other things. His boss's wife was with him."

"Was it three o'clock in the morning? Was she naked?"

"No, it was ten in the morning, and they say he was driving her shopping. She was supposed to be out of town."

"Does anybody really care?"

"He does, for one. He's scared silly. He bought a Volkswagen."

That was how Gilbert realized that Erna could have Walter back. He generously told her that she should spend Thanksgiving in Washington, and he even got Liane to agree to put her up.

LOCALLY, he turned to Buddy. Margery had, in effect, betrayed them both, and Gilbert had a vague idea that he and Buddy could take some male comfort together, of the sort that they had never shared in the old days when they didn't know any girls well enough to be jilted.

"How are you, old Buddy?"

"Depressed as hell," said Buddy. It was his conventional reply, Buddy's equivalent of "Fine, thank you, how are you?" but Gilbert used it as an opening.

"Margery problems?"

"No, she's fine. I'll tell you a secret. We're going to get married. Your old bachelor buddy is finally going to tie the knot. I'd ask you to be best man, but my father would kill me. He always wants to be the best everything."

It was not in Gilbert's nature—no one would believe it, but it never had been—to be gratuitously nasty, but he was suffering a sense of not being able to catch anyone's attention. "I saw her with someone else today."

"Yeah, I know," said Buddy. "She's dating a lot. She wants to be sure."

"You mean to tell me you're engaged to her and you're letting her see other people? What are you, crazy?" He didn't count himself because he had priority rights.

"What can I do?" whimpered Buddy. "If I do anything, maybe she won't marry me at all. She's kind of tricky, you know, and—hard. Didn't she used to drive you crazy? I think she doesn't mean to, but she can't help it. She just has a hard nature. Probably to protect herself."

"So why are you marrying her? Especially if she isn't sure about you, either?"

"Look here, Gilbert," said Buddy, loudly in spite of the quaver in his voice. "Don't be so smart. Margery is a girl in a million. You couldn't hold on to her. Besides, you don't know everything. We want to be sure this is right. We don't want to go getting a broken home. If it

doesn't bother me, I don't see what business it is of yours."
Gilbert could hear the teariness, and he stopped.

"Forget it, Bentley," he said. "She's a great girl. Let's
go to the movies."

"I can't. Lolly's here."

"Lolly's your sidelight? Jesus, Bentley, that's some
engagement you've got going there. Allow me to congratulate you." His sympathy had vanished.

"You know Lolly. My sister Louella. My father's at a
meeting here and there's a banquet tonight and I promised
to look after Lolly."

"How old is she?"

"Nineteen."

"Is she a looker?" As Gilbert said it, he remembered
about Lolly. Lolly was legally blind, although she could
distinguish some light. To cover his remorse, he quickly
added, "You and me'll take Lolly out."

"Uh, Gilbert. Lolly, uh."

"Never mind, I'll take you both. We'll all go eat at
Henri Quatre, my treat. I'll be there in fifteen minutes.
Put on a tie, will you?"

"Uh, Gilbert. Lolly's, uh, not your type, know what I
mean?"

"Shut up, Bentley. Everybody's my type. You just don't
want your sister to marry one. Don't go away."

"Gilbert! Lolly is—"

"Shut up," said Gilbert. "I'll be right over."

SHE WASN'T a looker. She looked like Buddy, except more wavy-eyed, and her clothes had obviously
been chosen by someone older.

"I'm not hungry," she said to Gilbert, and to Buddy, "You promised Mommy and Daddy you'd stay with me here."

"Look, honey," said Gilbert, after a lot of this, which Buddy tried sociably to cover over so that Gilbert wouldn't understand that his sister talked back to him, "it's my invitation. Unless you want me to give baby brother a quarter to go to the movies and you and I'll go to my place. Or here, if you prefer. Frankly, I think you ought to thank me for inviting you and your relative here out to dinner. Doesn't anybody have any manners in your family?"

They both colored, and got their coats. Lolly fixed on a little flat hat, and took her collapsible cane and Buddy's arm for the walk over, leaving Gilbert circling around behind them. At the table, he did all the talking, and put his hand in Lolly's lap. Both she and Buddy, who saw it, choked, but neither moved. When the pastry tray came, Lolly asked Gilbert to choose her a squishy one, and began to talk. It seemed that she was musical and the family intended her for a career in music therapy. She was not unwilling to listen to Gilbert's opinion, no less positive for his not having heard her play, that she should try for a concert career, instead.

It was Buddy's arm she took again in the street, but Gilbert firmly tucked her other arm in his, and after a while, she dropped Buddy's.

The next day Gilbert got a polite telephone call from the family of no manners. "You were terrific," said Buddy. "Boy, I'll never say anything bad about you again. Lolly had the time of her life. That was really a nice thing to do. You must have a blind person in your family."

"No," said Gilbert, "and stop apologizing. I had a good

time—I mean compared to spending the evening just with you, which was what I was going to do. Why don't you just let her be?"

"Are you kidding? I've practically dedicated my life to her."

"Well, don't. It must be a real pain for her."

"Thank you," said Buddy, but there was no sarcasm in his voice. He was still giving his original thanks for Gilbert's social charity.

Gilbert had really gone out with them because he was lonely, but now he began to think of himself as munificent. But why? He knew he didn't pity her. Lolly would do all right. He saw her sailing onto a concert stage, cane pointed like a rapier, with all the Loomises waiting anxiously in the wings for her to come offstage and snap at them. If anyone was to be pitied, it was he, Gilbert, who had no career planned.

He decided that he had enjoyed taking her on because Lolly was tough, as who would not be, living in a nest of guilty Loomises. So many of the people he knew seemed to be spiritless in their normal state, and unhappy when they were forced to be strong. Surely Margery wasn't having as good a time torturing Buddy as she had in being subservient to him.

ONE DAY he picked a new girl in the Bick. He needed his energies to deal with the panic he felt about launching himself into politics, so he didn't try for a challenge. The new girl had brown braids and brown eyes and wore cameras crisscrossed on her chest and had altered her name from Sally to Shelley, with a Sherry period in between.

When he awoke from a nap and found her in his bed, he had to force himself to realize that she was there because he had apparently slept with her. It seemed to him that he asked fewer questions, and yet got the same amount of life story, with all the decorative character judgments and philosophic conclusions, as if he had been pretending to be interested.

Had the role of lover become superfluous in all but physical presence, in the great drama of the college girl? Had all his anxiety and strategy and tactics been employed only so that he could appear in their midst as that comic stock figure, the boy friend? Gilbert looked at her, leaning over his face with a panting smile. He rolled over and said, "Go away," knowing that he would find her there, if he needed company, when he awoke.

H E   T O O K to going out when she, by habit rather than invitation, was expected, and found himself wandering a lot, kicking crumpled city leaves on the sidewalk. It was boring, but so was the idea of an enthusiastic Shelley, waiting to drag him through the routine.

On one of those afternoons, when the whipping edge of the wind warned him that he would soon be deprived of even the meager refuge of the streets, he walked into Sanders Theatre, thinking he might hear the end of a choir practice or rehearsal. He didn't care what, any more than a winter wino cared what pornographic movie was showing. He was seeking warmth and walls.

The something turned out to be a lecture by a large, squarish man whose salt-and-pepper hair was falling in his eyes and had to be swept impatiently away with a strong hand, and whose tie was loosened in the effort of athletic rhetoric.

"I don't take that . . . stuff," said the lecturer. The pause was to let the students know what he meant instead of *stuff*.

"Who is it?" Gilbert asked a girl leaning against the back wall. "Shhhh," she replied.

There were not many people in the audience, but the stage was well populated. Six men, some of whom Gilbert had seen around Cambridge, and one woman sat on wooden chairs behind the lectern. Gilbert had seen the speaker, in the same attractively disheveled pose, pictured in the newspapers. Groton, his name was. He was a governor or an ex-governor from some neighboring state.

"Frankly, being young doesn't seem that much to me, one way or the other," he was saying to the slouching students. "I'm called young even now, if you believe it, and if you don't, you should see some of my colleagues, especially the ones who call me that. They don't mean it as a compliment. Neither do the people who keep talking about you as youth. They mean go and have fun and don't bother us grownups. Well, let me tell you frankly, you'd better start looking into what the so-called grownups are doing, what they're doing with your future. And you might want to decide that you don't want them messing around with it anymore. People are getting younger in this country, and a lot is going to be expected of you. You're not 'preparing for life' here, as I was told when I was an undergraduate—you're living it. And if not, then when are you going to start? I've got a lot of young people working for me now because, frankly, I'm interested in the future. And I want it now."

He paused at the scattered applause, wiping his brow

and mighty forelock at the same time with the back of his hand.

I can do that, Gilbert thought. That's easier than a term paper.

A DEAN, who had been leaning over to talk to the governor's wife at the end of the speech, wiped his glasses with his handkerchief, held them to the light, and restored them to his round face before getting up and clasping an arm on the shoulders of the speaker. "Governor," he said, "you still look as young to me as you did when you left here. If that's an insult, I wish someone would insult me."

Or I could be a dean, thought Gilbert.

"Governor Groton has consented to answer questions for ten minutes." The dean pulled out a pocket watch.

"Yes," said the governor, pointing at a student in such a way that the young photographer on the stage apron bent and shot upwards to the governor's upraised arm.

"Governor, are you running for President?"

"No, sir. Yes?"

"Sir, do you foresee the possibility of war in Asia, and if so, how do you feel about it?"

"No more easy ones, huh?" Laughter. "Possibility, yes. Probability, no. We have to keep in mind the interplay of factors that make up that delicate fabric we call peace. Peace is not the absence of war, a simple thing; peace is a combination of hundreds of fragile, vulnerable bits of machinery, and one of them goes out, the whole machine blows up. Then it's got to be fixed. That, frankly, that is what nobody wants to do. So we—you, I hope, and I, all of us—are going to try to keep it oiled, in running order, so that, creaky as it is, it doesn't break down, and then—maybe then—one day one of us will invent a new machine that really works."

God, thought Gilbert, nothing to it. He practiced, in his lap, a short move of the hand intended to represent the governor's motion of drawing his hand back along his forehead. That would be the hard part—standing in the dock while everyone judged you. What if I just wrote the speech and directed the policy? he asked himself.

"Governor, are you interested in the vice presidency?"

"Noooo, ma'am." Laughter at the delivery. "Yes?"

To Gilbert's surprise, it was Gilbert standing up. He had only half raised his hand, and now drew it back on his forehead. "How old is the youngest member of your staff, and are you really serious about hiring people of, uh, our age?"

"It's my wife, Cindy, who's not a day over twenty-one, and—oh, oh, look; see what a serious look she's giving me? Later, dear. No, really, yes, of course I'm serious. See me after the lecture."

The dean stepped forward, and the two stood with their arms about each other. Gilbert felt feverish. He had never before asked a legitimate question in public, his classroom participation having been limited to the hand-grenade type of question. He felt disgraced, but fated to go on with his appeal, and moved against the audience to the stage. A man of about thirty years of age stopped him from approaching the governor. "No more questions," he said, spreading his arms wide, police style.

"I'm the one he asked to see."

"Sorry. Write him a letter."

The governor came up and as Gilbert began to open his mouth, said, "Neil, what hotel're we at?" He noticed

Gilbert and nodded. "Good to see you." Then he went back to the dean and Neil smiled at Gilbert. "Some other time. He's got a hectic schedule; I'm sure you understand. Give me your name, why don't you?"

Gilbert just stood there, because it seemed a touch less humiliating. The conversation onstage was breaking up, and the wife came down the steps.

"Cindy, go rest up," the governor said. "I'll be by in an hour."

"I thought I'd go walk around for a while, maybe look at the bookstores."

"No, I might need you. Just sit tight till you hear from me."

"Do I go to the dinner tonight?"

"Better not. I'd like to do some serious talking. Say you're too tired."

"All right. If it's really necessary."

The group was moving up the aisle, and Gilbert was not exactly moving with them, but being shoved by Neil. At the street, the governor kissed his wife's brow, and she went off in a car with Neil, just as Gilbert was about to propose himself for a walking tour of Cambridge featuring the choicest second-hand bookstores.

GILBERT ran to the hotel because he couldn't help it. It was like running after the last train. He watched her go up, waited ten minutes, and followed.

She answered the knock herself—had he expected ladies-in-waiting? There was a dingy sitting room, a minuscule bedroom visible beyond. Mrs. Groton smiled at him non-committally.

"Neil told me to wait here, but if I'm disturbing you, maybe I should sit in the lobby."

"No," she said, "if he said come up, you'd better come in. I thought they were going to be gone for some time."

"Nobody told me nothing," said Gilbert. "I just do what I'm told."

It drew a smile. Mrs. Groton was not glamorous, like her husband, but comfortable-looking, with untidy hair and a dress with a pussy-cat bow under her chin. She stepped back and picked up stray newspapers on her way to the sofa. "I don't think I've seen you before," she ventured hospitably.

"I'm local. Gilbert Fairchild. I hope I'll be with you in the campaign. That's what I'm supposed to be here about. What do you think? Do I have a chance?"

She shrugged. "How'd you think it went?" she asked, putting on a pair of gold-rimmed glasses and pushing the fruit bowl on the coffee table toward Gilbert.

"Not bad," said Gilbert. "What'd you think?"

"Oh, I don't know. That youth business—that doesn't quite come off, does it? You're a student, aren't you? What do you think? Isn't it offensive for him to make jokes about my age?"

An hour and a half later, Gilbert knew that Cynthia Groton had been a member of the state legislature when they married, that they had three adopted children, and that the staff didn't want her to give her husband advice. It was said in a friendly, joking way over the tea tray she had ordered from room service, and she also said how lucky she was, and how rewarding and exciting she found being in politics. They both were startled when the door was opened.

The governor walked briskly, and he almost made it

into the bedroom, pulling his tie out as he went along, before he caught his wife's signal that the visitor was for him, not her. Gilbert was prepared for trouble, but the governor didn't seem to doubt his right to be there; he was a man whose petty arrangements were made by others.

"I want to talk to you about your speech," said Gilbert, winging it, at twice the speed of normal thought. He hadn't even heard most of the speech. Mrs. Groton left the room, shutting the bedroom door behind her.

"Did you eat the grapes?" the governor asked. Gilbert didn't understand the metaphor. "The grapes. My wife leaves me the grapes. *She* didn't eat them." He pointed to the ashtray Gilbert had filled with the skeletons of grapes.

"Your youth bit needs a lot of work," said Gilbert. "It doesn't come off."

"I'm not interested in bits, youth or otherwise. I say what I think. If there's anything else bothering you, I have five minutes." He looked at his watch.

"Yes," said Gilbert. "You need more substance. It was good, especially the ad-libbing, but there's nothing anyone can go around repeating, or write home with your name attached. You need some little point that can be repeated."

"I'm sorry, I didn't realize you were a political analyst. I haven't seen my wife all day. Do you mind?"

"You need an honorary degree here, and maybe the commencement speech. It gives you a kind of solid backing."

"I've got that honorary degree. They told me this afternoon. So you can stop worrying. Nice of you to drop by."

"The committee hasn't met yet," said Gilbert.

"What committee?" The governor was feeling around

the bottom of the fruit bowl for a last grape and had stopped listening.

"For honorary degrees. Funny if they already told you when they haven't met yet. It doesn't seem fair. Also, it's supposed to be kept secret."

"What are you accusing me of? Oh, never mind." He laughed. "I think I like you."

"I can do better," said Gilbert. "Give me a job in your campaign."

"When do you graduate—May? Write me in, say, April. We'll see."

"When are you opening your Washington office?"

"Never. I'm not running for President. You forget. What are you offering me, besides your nuisance value?"

"The fact that you'd better stop telling jokes about your wife being young—middle-aged stuff like that. Kids think it's dumb. It makes you sound so old."

"Give me your name. You sound like my wife."

Gilbert wrote it on the margin of the newspaper the governor handed him. "What are you going to do with it?"

"What would you do? Burn it, just as soon as you get the hell out of here. Anything else before you go?"

"I thought I'd tell you I like the long hair. That's really good."

"Oh, good. The long hair. You like the long hair." He laughed again, and put Gilbert's name in his pocket.

WEEKS LATER, Gilbert was still embarrassed every time he thought of that afternoon, but months later, he remembered it as one of the only two vivid episodes in the whole academic winter. The other was when Margery threw Shelley out of his apartment.

EVERYONE WAS announcing plans. Margery had been accepted at Columbia Physicians and Surgeons, and Buddy at Boston University Medical School. Their parents had met during spring vacation, and agreed to treat them to marriage. Buddy's parents said it would steady him, and Margery's parents hoped it would put some romance into her life. They all were looking for an apartment on the railway map.

Erna kept announcing that she would have an announcement any minute now. Gilbert asked Shelley what she was going to do next year, and she said, "Go to school, of course." Gilbert hadn't realized that she was only a junior.

Liane called up and said, "Guess what?"

"You had an accident with Walter."

"Close."

"You've come to your senses and decided you loved me."

"Wrong. I love you, yes, but I've lost my senses."

"Liane, listen. Can I come live with you next year? With or without. Help me find a job."

"Listen to me, will you? You know where I'll be living next year? McLean, Virginia!"

"You joined the CIA."

"Better! George and I are getting married. Actually, I've already moved in. Not officially, of course."

"Liane, you're not serious. Please tell me you're not serious."

"You can come to the wedding."

"Liane, let me tell you something. Married men don't

leave their wives for their girl friends. Everybody knows that. What'd he do, move you into the maid's room? Are you posing as the governess?"

"Gilbert, you're supposed to be nice to me. You're my best friend, and I'm getting married. You ought to be giving me a shower. Aren't you glad I'm happy?"

"I guess so."

"All right. I'll tell you a secret. It's not funny, and don't tell anybody. It is sort of funny, though. She left him."

"Who? What?"

"George. He didn't leave his wife. She left him. Remember the admiral? Well, it's been going on for years, it seems, and when she found out he had someone, too, she told him and left. She's getting married before we do. He was really upset. I guess it's funny. But you see, married men do marry their girl friends. Isn't that terrific?"

"Yes. Terrific."

"It's so funny, but I can't tell anyone but you. We're getting married in June, so everybody'll think it was on the rebound. June third. I can't invite anybody, but will you come?"

"No. I mean, we have graduation then. Why don't you come to commencement, instead?"

"Well, anyway, you'll be working in Washington, and we'll see each other all the time. Won't that be great?"

"Terrific," said Gilbert.

GILBERT WAS typing earnestly when Margery and Buddy walked in without knocking, and he waved them away. The floor was covered with crumpled sheets of paper with the Harvard seal; the final version in the typewriter said:

Dear Sir,

You're doing much better. I read the Princeton speech in the papers, and I was proud of you.

I thought you might be interested in a student poll I did here, very informally. I'm not sure whether it means that you did better here last fall than I had thought, or that everybody else is so bad on student issues, or that you are just generally coming into prominence.

Anyway, here it is. Of 128 students polled (all over 21, but some juniors as well as seniors), I found a 74 percent response to . . .

The next day, he walked down Harvard Street with his upstairs neighbor, Mrs. Pergino, carrying the letter, and playing with it while he asked her what she thought the issues would be in the next election. (She thought they would be: wages, prices, and cost of living, in that order.) Somewhere along the way, he mailed it.

THE GOVERNOR was not the only candidate who received an honorary degree at Gilbert's commencement. The double appearance was considered something of an event, and the Commander lobby was crowded the morning of the graduation. Gilbert, in his cap and gown, pushed through and caught the eye of Cynthia Groton, who congratulated him; Gilbert kept talking to her long enough to slip back into their room with her.

Neil Rutherford was there, too, and although Gilbert couldn't get the attention of the governor, who was listening to three other young men at once, Rutherford handed Gilbert a press release about the honorary degree which mentioned, at the end, the "informal student poll" with the figures Gilbert had made up.

"Do I have a job?"

"Sure. We don't know yet if we can pay anyone, but call me tomorrow. No, I won't be here. Call me—I don't know where I'll be."

Gilbert looked at him. He had heard of corporations flying Harvard seniors to New York for job interviews and laying out their plush futures over sumptuous restaurant dinners.

"Okay, okay. Can you go to Washington?"

"Can I go to Washington? Sure!"

"Joe!" A young man detached himself from the governor's orbit. "Mr. Gilbert here—he'll be in Washington next Monday." He turned to Gilbert. "We're on—I forget. Look it up. Groton Headquarters, not in the phone book yet, but information should have it by now."

"Right," said Gilbert crisply, all but saluting.

"Put him to work—youth program, whatever."

Grinning, Gilbert rushed out of the room, holding the skirts of his academic robe, and raced to line up with Dunster House for the parade to graduation.

HE HAD put off giving his parents their semi-annual tour of Cambridge until that afternoon, hoping that everyone else would have gone home. It was less of a visit than a photo opportunity. Both of his parents had cameras, from which they never detached their eyes to look at anything first-hand, and Shelley followed them around, taking pictures of them taking pictures of Gilbert.

"Nice girl," his mother had stage-whispered. "A little common-looking, but good. You can see that."

At another time, his father stage-whispered, "Has she got a last name?"

"Search me," said Gilbert. "You can ask her."

In front of Memorial Hall, they ran into Margery and Buddy holding hands for the benefit of their sponsors, all four parents. The happy couple was leading a tour, also, and Gilbert called his group off before they could merge and something awful would happen. Margery was already looking haughtily at Shelley.

As Gilbert veered off, he ran smack into Neil Rutherford, arm in arm with, oh, God, S. B. Brewster. Gilbert waved and quickened his pace, but Small Boy called out, "Gilbert Fairchild!"

It stopped the rest of his party. "Your friends are calling you, Gilbert," said his mother.

"Come say hello," called his father to the young men in identical cord suits.

The two marched up and stood there, smiling, while Gilbert introduced them to his parents. "And Shelley Uh," said his father, Gilbert having pretended she was merely photographing the family. He did not mention that Neil was his new boss, or something like it.

"You boys just graduate?" asked Gilbert's father. "No, I guess you're too old."

"My boss is here getting an honorary degree," said Brewster.

Gilbert's mother took a close look at him and said, "Why, you're . . . you're . . . you're . . ." accompanying each "you're" with a pointed finger.

"I'm afraid I am, ma'am. They used to call me Small Boy. It was a great incentive to grow."

Gilbert's parents thought about that for a while, and after a moment or two of silence they started laughing uproariously, each saying to the other, "Get it?"

Horror was assailing Gilbert from all sides, and he hardly knew which aspect to deal with first. "You working for Groton?" he asked Brewster. "I mean the governor?"

"Me? Oh, no. Wrong party. There was more than one degree handed out today. I bet you got one yourself. Smart boy you got there," he added to the Fairchilds, who beamed and thanked him profusely.

"Yes, indeed," said Rutherford. "Sam and I are in different parties, but we're old friends. Friendly rivals. We went to Yale together. We were just talking about Gilbert's class. My man heard there was a poll showing they supported him, and Sam here doesn't believe it. He doesn't even think there was any poll taken."

"Oh, now, Neil, Mr. and Mrs. Fairchild aren't interested in our squabbles," said Brewster. "They're real proud of their son today. Good day, ma'am, sir. We'll be on our way. Good luck, Gilbert. Maybe we'll run into you again."

"Nice boys," said Gilbert's father. "Nice boys."

"Charming," said his mother. "Kind of gives me a lift to think about Gilbert going into politics. That Small Boy, I remember seeing pictures of him romping on the White House lawn. My, he's certainly made something of himself since then, hasn't he?"

She gave Gilbert a squeeze to indicate her faith that he could, too.

PART TWO

Chapter VII

I T I S T R U L Y amazing what you can learn in four years if you apply yourself, Gilbert reflected as he set out the tea things. This inauguration would be a decided improvement over the last, as, indeed, the five previous ones had been from one another. At each of these, he had sought and achieved an increasing amount of public exposure and participation in what he had been pleased to call history; this time, his concern was for a minimum of exposure to the weather and of standing around on marble steps and floors between ceremonial events.

Teatime at his own fireside, lounging on the tufted wine velvet loveseat in his beautiful evening clothes, to watch

Wanda complete her toilette for the balls, was, on his private Inauguration Day schedule, the choice activity of the day.

Undoubtedly, it helped to have your own President. Gilbert was one of very few people in town that day who had no urge whatsoever to strain for a look at the new President, either outdoors in the throngs or through the democratic eye of television. Having spent the last fifteen years scrutinizing the man's every gesture and word, Gilbert felt that, this being a national holiday, he had a right to take the day off.

He had accumulated his own everything in the last four years. He had his own White House title, Special Assistant to the President, and his own choice seats at the wind-swept ceremony and the chaotic official luncheon afterwards in the Capitol. At the last inauguration, he had attended events on the extra tickets of his chief, then a senator, and had watched a new White House Appointments Secretary once known as Small Boy Brewster sweep by to a place of honor.

He had his own elegant wife this time, instead of a date with an excited junior movie star. He had his own parents with him, everywhere. That he might have had in any previous inauguration, even the first one after college. They would have loved to help him stand around in the cold. But only now that he had arrived could he afford to flaunt his not-very-chic origins.

He had his own faultless clothes for the white-tie in-augural balls. Like the new President, he had concluded, only after the election was conceded, that the time had come for him to buy tails. The Vice President, 98 percent of the United States Congress, newly appointed cabinet secretaries, heads of independent agencies, and lobbyists who foresaw their social fortunes rising had nevertheless come to the opposite conclusion: Black tie, or the proper outfit from one of the harried rental firms, would do. They would also probably show up wearing daytime shoes and wristwatches. Gilbert would not. He did not expect to be much noticed at this mass social event, unfortunately shared with thousands of old and new donors, voters, and other nobodies, where brand-new leaders of the free world would be trampled, unrecognized, and required to produce their tickets by their own administration's guards who had not yet memorized the latest appointments, but Gilbert himself would know that he was correct in every detail, from his patent leather shoes to his pocket watch.

Gilbert was careful about his appearance. Both the symbolic and the aesthetic effects had to be considered, and he remembered with horror the shock of observing, while shaving one morning in 1969, that a failure to achieve the proper balance had turned him into a carica-ture of his former self. As the employee of a rich and liberal senator, whose social climb downwards into the hearts of the masses Gilbert was directing, Gilbert had naturally allowed his hair to cavort freely over the back of his pin-striped suits. What he had failed to notice, until that morning, was that his hairline was receding at the same rate that he had been allowing his back hair to grow, so that the romantic headful of curls of his college days just seemed to have slipped backwards. That was when he realized, after a quick review of his love life over the last few years—carried out under the erroneous assump-tion that he was beautiful—that looks, in a Washington man, apparently didn't count. Nevertheless, the backward slide had been ruthlessly stopped that morning at the barber's, and the head was now firmly balanced in front by a pair of gold-rimmed round eyeglasses that had be-longed to his maternal grandfather. When Gilbert peeled off the glasses at a dinner party, revealing his fine eyes in a bold look at his dinner partner, the effect was almost similar to the effect on Margery, back in his college days, when he had peeled off his pants.

Still, one never stopped learning. The lace tea cloth he spread under the sprigged china and cut-glass sherry decanter and glasses was not as satisfactory to him as when he had found it at a charity bazaar stand and noticed that it was embroidered with an *F*. Perhaps it was a *J;* one couldn't quite tell. But he hadn't felt the same about it since Wanda told him that one had to have more than one initial on one's things, or people would suspect they were bought ready-marked. The other items on the table were fine. Wanda and he had chosen their silver and crystal and china together after turning in a wealth of Scandinavian steel, wood, glass and electronic wedding presents.

All four Fairchilds had tickets that were good for all five simultaneous inaugural balls, which would enable them to spend the night following the Presidential party through the icy streets (but without his siren escort) instead of waiting at one ball for him to come to them. Being a Special Assistant did not entitle Gilbert to his five tickets. You had to be the lifelong best friend and working partner of the First Lady's new social secretary, Liane Beaufort.

Wanda, with a mouthful of hairpins she occasionally parked to sip the sherry, was anxious to go. Gilbert's father announced the time from upstairs every fifteen minutes. Gilbert had not been able to make them understand that this was simply not the day or the night on which they could see him served his wedge of the limelight pie. The inauguration was too crowded and too full of the rigorous demands of the television schedule to dwell on such details as Gilbert Fairchild's rise to relative power. All the way home, Gilbert's parents had grumbled about his making them leave the parade stand before the last high school band had appeared, believing that if they had hung around long enough, surely the President would have found time to make them a private speech about what a great day it was for their son.

Wanda had backed him up then, but he saw now that she cherished impossible notions of shining at the ball. Just looking at her, glowing from the firelight, he could penetrate to the cliché she was manufacturing in her head —crowds of newsmen and jealous women scrambling to find out the name of the young beauty whom the President of the United States had selected to be his dance partner. Wanda was new to Washington.

Her ball dress was heavy, bias-cut silk taffeta, and it had turned a gentle pearl gray some decades before she had discovered it at one of her favorite London antiques-boutiques. That had been a year ago, when Gilbert was performing the ritual of accompanying her in her shopping, in the role of fiancé. Gilbert was amused and charmed by the strange clothes that had been the despair of her father, William Clay, Counselor of the Embassy of the United States at the Court of St. James's.

SINCE SHE HAD dropped out of Vassar, or rather wandered aimlessly away from it, Wanda had been supposed to act as her father's hostess. He was gallantly prepared to share with his slip of a motherless girl the social success he had achieved as a handsome widower (Mr. Clay looked like Thomas Jefferson but without the dark, clever sparkle in the eyes) with beautiful manners (he was continental in America and American when in Europe) who served only at the best posts (Foreign Service talk for Western European capitals).

But instead of paying attention to being launched into British society, Wanda still wandered about purposelessly, off to the Continent with unknown Americans, or foraging in London's attic shops. Among the junk she brought home, her father looked in vain for something that could be renovated, such as the rebel son of a peer. He had had one high moment, when he distinctly saw Prince Charles, then still in his prolonged bachelorhood, look at Wanda at a garden party. After all, he had rationalized, the prince might have psychological family reasons for admiring a Victorian look, and he might find Wanda's aloof stance and limp hair and limper clothes a pleasant contrast with all those glossy English and international young ladies who kept re-crossing his path. But Mr. Clay was too worldly not to know that he was being a fool even to hope that the prince's notice would make her interesting to the next level or so down. Before a week had gone by, devoid of any diplomatic hint from anyone remotely connected to the palace, Mr. Clay had his hopes back down to younger sons and junior diplomats.

When Gilbert Fairchild appeared at the American Embassy, traveling with a famous senator as his trusted adviser, and obviously possessed of several good suits and enough wit to capture even Wanda's attention, the old American diplomat felt that his country had at last rewarded him for a lifetime of service.

The counselor prayed that Gilbert nevertheless lacked the wit to notice that Wanda was hopelessly different from sleek young women with expensive handbags and heavy blond hair. He calculated that a fortyish bachelor might consider a twenty-six-year-old young enough so

that her lack of either a husband or a career or, in spite
of the deceptive good living that went with his job, what
used to be called a girl's fortune, might not seem peculiar.
He had so much fixed on Gilbert as his last hope that
even while casually warning him of her "distinction"—
so much more diplomatic a term than the one Mr. Clay
used to his daughter's face—he noticed that she was not
coming down to do her hostess duties, and he resolved to
kill her as soon as the guests had left or, if that weren't
harsh enough, to ship her off permanently to his sister in
St. Louis.

It was at that point that Gilbert, noting the look of
failure on a maid who had been sent upstairs to tell Miss
Clay that her guests had arrived (half an hour ago), decided to fetch her. He had been expecting an oddball
child, perhaps an amusing antidote to her father's impec-
cably driveling conversation, but what he saw was a thin
woman in a crocheted shawl, her hair theoretically up-
swept but with as many sweepings hanging down as
pinned up, giving her, in the window-seat light, a reddish
halo. When she could have been exerting herself to cap-
tivate a handsome, if married, senator, his distinguished
entourage, and all kinds of stage Englishmen, she was
sitting, smiling to herself, and writing in a leather book.

She blew a stray lock of hair out of her face. She
looked up. She looked back at her book. Gilbert's heart
stopped.

In a second, he had himself under control and said, "Get
the hell down there. Do you realize that you are keeping
Gilbert Fairchild waiting?"

It was more or less what her father would have said if
he had made the trip upstairs, except that he would have
used the senator's name, but in this case it worked. Gilbert

coldly offered her his arm, and she tossed her head con-
temptuously and took it.

It was not long before he acquired her hand. For some
time, Gilbert had no longer been finding it dashing to be
an eligible bachelor. He was being told too many women's
life stories, and he was beginning to be approached by
men. When he wasn't being bullied by hostesses, he was
being cross-examined by his parents. One wife, even a
frail one, would still all this clamor.

Any number of potential wives for rising politicians
had displayed themselves to him with show-window flair.
This one he had found by chance, and even had had to
dust off.

Gilbert had discovered, before the finger bowls appeared at that first luncheon, that Wanda's originality was
not unstudied. She had not intended to reveal so much,
and she felt unmasked, but Gilbert was satisfied. He did
not want a static ornament, any more than he had wanted
a utilitarian appliance. Besides, she reminded him of himself, when he had been beautiful and had practiced on
himself the arts he now taught to politicians.

For a wedding present, Gilbert had given Wanda an
old necklace of tiny diamonds in a setting so intricate that
it could never be thoroughly cleaned. She was just now
fastening the grimy treasure around her neck for the
inaugural ball, as Gilbert looked with approval over his
fragile teacup at the graceful gesture.

ONE FLOOR UP, Albert Fairchild was fastening
Ginerva into her new four-hundred-dollar jersey print
dress with the matching costume necklace. They had
been alternately puffing and giggling ever since they had

managed to climb to the fourth floor of their son's house and to fall onto the mahogany sleigh bed with its frayed patchwork quilt. Albert did not allow his heart thumps to be mentioned.

"Antiques I can understand," Ginerva was saying. "People have antiques. French, Italian, Early American. But my mother's old furniture? Albert, you remember Mother's parlor before she had it done. How many people do you think got a mark-up on this stuff between now and then? If only I'd known, I could have asked her to save it."

"Hold still," said Albert. "You want the horse and buggy to leave without us?"

Mr. and Mrs. Gilbert Fairchild's house was built in 1897, gutted and remodeled in 1966, and restored to its original form by the present owners. It cost them thousands of dollars to re-create the original bathrooms and to put in interior walls, making each narrow level into tiny rooms instead of the modern "living areas" that had cost the previous owners thousands of dollars to create.

It was not in Georgetown, to the disappointment of the senior Fairchilds, that being the only Washington neighborhood of which they and their friends in New York had heard. It was on a leafy street of late Victorian row houses in Kalorama Triangle, an area that came later than Georgetown to the typical V-shaped success of in-town Washington, and was therefore slightly cheaper. What had been built as *haut bourgeois* respectability had gone plummeting to boarding house level and worse, and then, with the help of the builder who had put in those improvements the Fairchilds replaced, back up to *haut bourgeois*.

The senior Fairchilds, who were familiar, through the *New York Times*, with airy renovated brownstones, all furnished in white and plants, were appalled by their son's cramped, dark quarters on a block that had had its own murder. They took care to point out that for the same price, the children could have had a horizontal house—one day they would be older and sorry about the stairs—with a palace of a kitchen. Their supposedly bright son had sunk a great deal of money into a house which boasted neither beauty nor security nor efficiency. On the ground floor, the house had nothing useful. You could leave a dripping umbrella there, but that was all you could do there. One flight up were the drawing room, dining room, and kitchen, all dark and furnished in dark woods with lots of what Ginerva called fussies about—lace doilies, velvet hangings that didn't stop when they got to the floor, massive but purposeless articles of silver or disappearing silver plate, and senile clocks. The third floor had the master bedroom, its great carved bed outfitted in heavy layers, including laces at the head and a fur robe at the foot, like an invalid dowager. It also contained the room in which Gilbert had laid out tea, which Gilbert referred to as Wanda's dressing room, Wanda called Gilbert's dressing room, and which they used as a sitting room, the second-floor parlor being opened only when they entertained. On the top floor were Mr. and Mrs. Albert Fairchild visiting their important son. No chair in the guest room could hold their Val-a-Pak open, so it was spread out on the floor of the adjacent room, which was being temporarily used as an attic, containing all the unwanted pieces of new furniture the owners had somehow acquired before their taste was formed.

When the elder couple descended to the third floor, they were dismayed to find Wanda and Gilbert dawdling, although the ball tickets plainly said nine o'clock and it was a few minutes past that hour.

"My," said Ginerva, "where did you find such an un-usual dress?"

"My grandmother wore it to Woodrow Wilson's in-augural ball," said Wanda. "I love you in those bright prints, Ginerva."

"Wanda, I don't like that," said Gilbert. His mother thought he was referring to her own plea against moder-nity (God knows these children weren't guilty of any other modern practices), which was wanting her daughter-in-law to call her Mother. But Wanda, feeling that her tone had been careful enough to protect her from charges of sarcasm, knew Gilbert meant the funny lie about the origin of her dress, and she turned away so that he couldn't annoy her about it further. He looked so solid, so middle-aged, in his evening clothes, and his stuffiness about her decorative fantasies, as she called her small mis-statements of strict truth, was pedantic.

She turned to Ginerva instead, but Ginerva's way of showing affection was to grab one of Wanda's carefully curled wispy locks and to try to stuff it back into the top knot from which it had presumably fallen. It was unfair because Wanda's style had been refined since she had learned to carry the social weight of a well-married woman, and the careful disorder that remained could be considered random by no one but Ginerva. The evolution of Wanda's wardrobe so that she looked timelessly above fashion, rather than stuck in a period that had passed, was noticed with satisfaction by Gilbert, but it escaped Gi-nerva entirely.

She retreated when her daughter-in-law pulled away from her neatening touch, and whispered to Albert, "I think the wedding dress finally came." It was a family joke that their charter flight to London for Gilbert's wedding had been canceled, so that they just managed to get to the reception from Heathrow, and Ginerva had spent several maternal hugs on a young lady in peach satin before she realized that the thin girl in the navy panne velvet suit, the one who had promised to find her an ashtray, was the bride.

The plan was to go to at least two of the inaugural balls. The Fairchild party was to meet Liane and George Beaufort at the Mayflower Hotel for a conference on logistics. Albert said once more that the President and First Lady would probably be busy, so that Gilbert was not to bother them by dragging over his parents, who would be just as happy to watch them from the distance. Wanda adjusted her white foxes, Ginerva slipped carefully into the evening coat that matched her dress, Gilbert got his Chesterfield, and Albert put on his lined trenchcoat.

BY THE TIME Gilbert had herded his little party into the crowded hotel, he knew he had been only too right about the evening. The crowd was rough and edgy and wearing, with an air of defiance, lavish but awful evening clothes of the sort favored by people blowing everything on one fancy wedding at which they would start feuds lasting years to come. Gilbert, who noted the contrast with the true Washington style, in which evening clothes were as dowdy as the equivalent daytime dress, either because the important people weren't rich or were politically motivated to look frazzled, was sorry his own clothes were perfect and new. He knew that for people of position in Washington, evening clothes were working clothes, and therefore, both the men's and the women's tended to be sensible, unmemorable, and slightly worn.

Perhaps he could get them frayed artificially, like jeans.

The ball guests' facial expressions weren't local, either—Gilbert had seen them on airport crowds all over the country, when he had had to announce that the candidate was running late but would be there any minute.

He was now an advance man to find Liane and report back to his group, waiting their turn in the coat check line. He pushed his way quickly down the block-long hotel corridor, occasionally looking down to see the red and gold pattern of the carpet rushing by under his feet. He searched for her in the blurs of fancy dress reflected in wall-sized gilded mirrors—the mirror image looked more festive than the original crowd—and on side trips to the even more tightly packed ballrooms, but had to report back unsuccessfully to his impatient charges.

For a frail waif of his own discovery, Wanda was running a remarkably eager eye over the crowd. "Oh, I'll find Liane," she said, and disappeared. "Don't worry about us," Ginerva told Gilbert, "you go and have a good time." They, too, drifted off, leaving their Washington guide standing there with his credentials.

Where or how Gilbert was supposed to accomplish his good time alone, he didn't know. The dance floors were jammed with people just standing there, with their backs toward him, shoving against one another as they waited for the President to appear. Then there was a huge surge forward, and Gilbert, in spite of himself, strained to see and hear.

A huge wave of laughter rolled through the crowd when the President called out, "Why aren't you all dancing?" Except for the shoving, they didn't move, though; they just waited for him to get off another comical line.

The Presidential face had grown as large as a poster, and the smile which had been telecast to every corner of the nation seemed to stretch across the room. Other famous people, as many of these dressed-up tourists were remarking to one another, looked smaller "in person"; the new President, standing on a platform with his hands above his head—in victory formation? as a request for silence?—was larger. Perhaps it was because people were scanning the Presidential face so carefully, searching for any tiny blemish or tic that could be taken home in the form of an anecdote, as a souvenir. Also, the wedge formation behind the great man had grown unwieldy. Time was when only Gilbert and one other senatorial aide walked slightly to the side and behind the man to form a triangle. Now the triangle, even without Gilbert in his usual place upstage left, was immense. So was the tangle of microphones that sprang up in front of the President's mouth like a Hydra every time he paused. Gilbert remembered when the presence of a single microphone had been enough to turn the man sweet-voiced, like a Forties crooner. Now he nodded nonchalantly to the menacing cluster of metal snakes, hardly bothering to placate them with individual comments. He had also mastered unfurling the smile under the strobe-light unreality of television lights going on and off, and for the undulating formation of photographers, moving in a close circle in front of him like a Chinese dragon costume with all the many pairs of feet showing.

Another history-making remark was coming up. "I order you all to dance, do you hear?" There was another great laugh and some applause. During the campaign, Gilbert had given up writing witty lines for him, because the man was never able to extract a chuckle. At best, people asked one another, "He's joking, isn't he?" Suddenly, he was the world's greatest comedian. Gilbert shook his head in wonder.

He actually found himself standing on tiptoe to see the President, but his reward was that he spotted Liane, standing back against a damask-and-gilt wall. He laboriously threaded his way to her, and they exchanged an amused look of bashful pride, like the parents of a debutante who has emerged from difficult adolescence into triumphant womanhood.

"Look what we did," he said. He was the most senior surviving member of the staff, and Liane, whom he had introduced at the office six weeks after his arrival, was second. She looked tidy and reliable now, with her plain-combed daytime bun and her good bony face.

"I told Her not to wear those shoes," said Liane. "She didn't think anyone would dare trample Her, but She forgot about having to dance with Him." Ever since the election, Gilbert and Liane had stopped calling their respective bosses by their first names and referred to them only as Him and Her. The combat talk of the campaign had been replaced by a White House style of talk that nobody had been taught but everyone knew.

"Stop fussing, Mother. They're doing great."

"You should have seen them at the Hilton. They're a sensation."

"Terrific. Aren't you proud? They do us credit."

"Maybe they won't need us any more."

"Where's George?"

"He was having dinner with some people and was going to meet me here. I'll never find him."

"Come on, we'll look," said Gilbert. "I've lost Wanda, too."

"I can't leave. I've got Her purse," she said, waving a golden apple at him.

Gilbert grabbed the chain. "Hand it over. Let's see what She's got."

Liane gave him her first sparkling smile of the evening— the others had been wistful. "Gilbert, let go. That's not funny."

"Oh, come on, don't you be a poop, too. I'm having a rotten evening. Maybe She's got Her American Express card in there. We could just take off."

"And I thought you'd grown up." But she watched as he extracted a wad of Kleenex, lipstick, chipped plastic compact, Lucite pillbox, and an index card with the first names and departments of the cabinet and their wives. "Are you satisfied, Gilbert?" A burly man nearby had been watching them tensely, but he was, so far, allowing Liane to control the situation. He and Liane were old, old comrades, dating back together ten weeks, to election night. They both had been among the first fifty people to think of calling the newly elected one Mr. President, and had the satisfaction that people have in a wedding reception line when they think they are surprising the bride by addressing her as Mrs. Whatever. But, unlike a wedding, the division between His people and Hers had come afterwards, and this man, having gone with Hers, didn't know Gilbert. Gilbert didn't know him, either, but he had learned by now that anybody in a crowd who wasn't staring at the President must be in the Secret Service. It spoiled the fun to be supervised at play and be approved.

"What did you mean, a rotten evening?" Liane asked, re-packing the purse.

Gilbert kissed the air toward her face and plunged

back into the crowd. He spotted Wanda, arm in arm with a professionally dapper bachelor of several administrations' standing, who was known as one of the three sexiest men in Washington. Gilbert had once seen him talking at a party with the other two, also divorced fifty-five-year-old veterans of more than one cabinet position, and the impassioned hush from onlookers had been so profound that you could listen, in the silence, to the sound of their hair thinning.

Gilbert waved discreetly at Wanda and was on the way to round up his parents when he came across a handsome white-haired man in his sixties, snuggled on some balcony steps with a very young girl. "Hello, George!" he called loudly as a warning.

"C'mere, Gilbert," said George, reaching out for him. "Miss Dillon, this is *the* Gilbert Fairchild, the bright young man you've been hearing so much about. See him on 'Meet the Press'? Ought to cultivate him. Very good friend of my wife's, I might add. Very good friend." Miss Dillon looked blank, or maybe it was Miz Dilly. George tended to revert to southern when he was feeling charming.

Gilbert shook himself free, fetched his parents, and guided them back into the mirrored freeway that separated the ballrooms. He had warned them not to expect a scene from a historical movie, with waltzing and strolling young couples in brocades and jewels. Nevertheless, the herds of unhappy people disappointed even him.

"Had enough?" he asked with false hope in his voice when Wanda joined them. "Anybody for home?" Three shocked faces stared at him. "You two take the tickets and Wanda and I'll go home?" he tried again.

Nobody said anything; they just looked at him. "Never

mind," said Gilbert, "forget it." He felt in his inside pocket for the four other large cardboard red-white-and-blue tickets.

Gilbert got his party to the Museum of American History, the next ball site, by opening the door of a strange Cadillac and telling the owner to take them there. "I'm waiting for my wife," the man protested, but when that lady appeared, bundled in Autumn Haze, he drove them there, and he and his wife called to them to have a good time. They were going to a post-ball motel party, they said; they were having a wonderful time, and they thought the new President and First Lady looked like very down-to-earth people. The wife was not quite satisfied even with that high praise. "They're so—so—so human!" she finally brought out, triumphant at having located the exact word.

THE MUSEUM seemed sparsely populated, in comparison to the hotel ball, with only a few couples in evening clothes wandering listlessly among the tractors and timepieces and steam engines. "Come on, I'll show you something," said Gilbert, and he led them into the replica of an old country store and post office, where his family again just stood there and looked at him as if he were crazy, until Mr. Fairchild peered behind the counter and said, "Will you look at that?" They all leaned over as a couple picked themselves off the floor and stalked out.

Everyone was on the second floor, crowded together near the wall-sized, battle-scarred Star-Spangled Banner and the half-naked statue of George Washington that had been rejected by the Capitol, over the pendulum that was already beginning to hypnotize some of them. Their shovings made a wavy pattern, such as the banner might have done if it hadn't been pinned down, and they were reacting angrily to a rumor that the Presidential plans had changed, and this would be the last stop of the evening, not the next.

Some dispersed, others decided that this was a ruse to make them forfeit their places, and stayed put. After much debate—Wanda had the bright idea of their using their connections to call the White House command post to find out where the President actually was, and going there—the Fairchilds, reprimanded by their leader, decided to look at the museum. To the senior Fairchilds, one of whose all-time favorite vacations had been taking Gilbert to Washington when he was ten to see the Smithsonian museums, and to Wanda, who had kept saying she couldn't wait to finish fixing up the house so she could enjoy Washington's great cultural riches, this was a colossal disappointment.

The three of them perked up whenever another wanderer nodded to Gilbert, but no one stopped to talk. As they walked by Everyday Life in the American Past, from which flashing lights and disco music glared and blared, Mrs. Fairchild gave her husband a significant look and said, "Darling, we'll just rest here a bit. You two young people go and have a good time."

They strolled hand in hand over the slippery floors, pretending to look at covered wagons and old uniforms when Wanda, hearing commotion back at the Star-Spangled Banner, dropped his hand and ran off. Gilbert walked to the edge of the crowd into which she had disappeared, heard a familiar voice calling, "Why isn't anybody dancing? I thought this was supposed to be a ball!" and slunk away during the laughter.

Upstairs, he found a few couples dancing in corners without benefit of music, and Liane Beaufort, relieved of the First Purse. They sat on the edge of a diorama, with two life-sized plaster Japanese printmakers in kimonos kneeling behind them, frozen into the working position, and rested quietly.

"You've got post-partum depression," said Liane. "It happens after elections."

"No," he said, taking her hand. "I'm in love."

Liane flushed. "Yes? May I ask who it is this time?"

"The belle of this stupid ball. The about-to-be toast of Washington. Wanda Fairchild. Surprised?"

"Why, I think that's very nice."

"No, it isn't," said Gilbert. "She doesn't like me."

"Oh, for God's sake."

"Liane, you know how these things go. It's the same old story. I dazzled her, we came here and bought the house right away, and there was all that work, and on top of everything the campaign, and you know what that was like."

"So, now you'll have a normal life."

"That's the trouble. Everything was fine until it was normal. We had a fabulous time. Late-night phone calls, surprise visits—remember she used to show up on campaign stops with a bottle?—letters. She writes a wonderful letter. And we kept diaries for each other, so we wouldn't lose a minute by being apart. Then I took December off, just to be with her, which is something I'm going to have to pay for at the office, and there we were, with the house all finished and cozy. I didn't think there'd be any harm in falling in love with her. She's really a riot, with her real silk underwear and high-necked nightgowns you wouldn't believe. Anyway, we're married, aren't we? I'm tired of kicking around, playing games. I come from a happy home—you can see that, can't you?"

"Yes, they're sweet," said Liane. Gilbert was holding and stroking her hand.

"So I did things like buying her presents and tagging along wherever she wanted to go, and brushing her hair for her, and taking her out to lunch and telling her about my childhood, and taking pictures of her. I bored the living daylights out of her."

"I don't believe that. Of course she loves you."

"Liane, dear, you're not paying attention."

"Well, even if it's true, you don't have to worry. You're one of the most attractive men in this town, married or not. You've never had any trouble before—and now you're in the White House, for heaven's sake. Do you know what that does for you? She's the one who should be worrying."

"I told you, I'm not going to play games any more."

"Sure you are," she said. "That's part of life."

"I saw big George making time at the Mayflower."

"We're not talking about me," she said stiffly.

"Okay. Sorry."

"George'll be home when I get there." She drew back her hand. "That's the only way he's going to find out if I get there," she said with a grim smile.

"All right, Liane. I said I'm sorry."

They both watched as Wanda slid toward them in her stocking feet, giggling. "Everybody's going to Clyde's for a drink!" she announced.

"Oh, good," said Gilbert. "Where're your shoes?"

"I'll get them. We've all been on the merry-go-round animals downstairs! I was on the sea horse, and then someone put me up on the ostrich!"

She hopped down on the escalator, and Liane took

Gilbert's hand. He smiled kindly. "She's only twenty-seven," he said. "Do you suppose my insurance covers it?"

ALL THE Fairchilds ended up at somebody's private catered omelet party, lured by cries of spontaneous hospitality from people Gilbert thought he had seen before but couldn't place. He saw his beaming mother being pumped for the family's ethnic background by a charming diplomat, who would cable it all home in the morning, and thus write off his pre-ball dinner for six at the Lion d'Or.

Wanda was feverish with success, and the volume of her musical-scale laughter was getting alarming. She perched on the arm of someone's chair, throwing back her head with such abandon that Gilbert pictured her spending the remaining social season in a neck brace. It was her first Washington superbash—she refused to believe that the quiet dinners they had attended were more important—and the first he had gone to in years without a specific working purpose. At least on inaugural night, there were no secrets or pacts or goodwill to be gathered. Gilbert declared himself off-duty and sank back on an empty sofa, prepared to enjoy restful wallflowerdom.

The cushions had hardly exhaled from his weight when the two seats on either side of him were filled. A woman with a silver streak in her hair and matching silver fox sleeves on her black dress smiled at him insolently. On the other side, the son of local art patrons snapped a cigarette case under Gilbert's nose. Expectant faces were turned towards him from across the room. He noticed that he was suddenly ahead of Wanda, who had culled only two or three gallants after an hour of determined gaiety.

In the car, on the way home, she reported that she had had a marvelous time. They didn't know whose car it was, another unknown having pressed it upon them, but the chauffeur apparently knew their address. Wanda was busy taking down her hair, kicking off her shoes, turning her furs backwards to serve as a blanket, and otherwise settling into the car cushions for the night. "Everybody seemed impressed by you," she said in a tone that was part graciousness and part curiosity.

"Yup." He accommodated his arm to her snuggling, but stared out the window at the blocks of houses going by. The chauffeur pushed silent buttons, and the window raised and lowered itself until it stopped just at the level of Gilbert's nostrils, apparently the correct position for a gentleman's intake of night air, as they cut through the park.

"I can't believe it," said Ginerva in a low voice intended to elude the driver. "Everybody's so friendly. It's just like a small town, isn't it? I got invited to the—wait a minute—the Heads of Independent Agencies' Wives' Club tea next week—do you think I should come back for it?—and the ambassador of Thailand or Malaysia—I don't know, I talked to them both—said if we wanted to vacation there, we could use his family palace, and he gave me his card. I hope I didn't lose it. Oh, and the best thing was I had the most fascinating talk with the Secretary of Commerce. All about the economy. What a nice man."

"That's it," said Albert. "You learn more here in one night than a lifetime of reading the newspapers. Am I right? I suppose you know more about these things than I do, Bert, but that's my judgment. What's the name of that congressman who used to be an alcoholic? You know the one I mean. He's on all the shows. I just straight off asked him what he thought was our biggest problem. You know what he said? Food! That's right, food. We got a farm problem, we got people starving all over the world, we got food wasting, we got kids going to bed hungry, we got farm kids don't want to stay on the farm—food. Every single country, every race, white, black, brown, green—its deepest emotions are about food. Ever notice that? Ethnic food, soul food, Mamma's cooking. I must admit, I never thought of it like that. He was fascinating.

"Wars are fought because some people like rice and others don't. World War Two: Rice against potatoes. Potatoes versus spaghetti. Korea. Vietnam. You name it. Rice! It goes deep into the grain. Get it? That man is really onto something." He seemed to ignore his wife's rolling eyes, which warned that the chauffeur might be offended by the mention of ethnic food, but when they arrived, he gave the man a five-dollar tip.

When the bedroom doors were closed, Wanda yanked off the crewel bedspread and smacked the pillows in their eyelet cases. "You looked down on everyone tonight, including me," she said.

"Yup," said Gilbert. He was punching the gold studs out of his shirt.

It deflated her annoyance. "Why can't you have a good time?" she asked more kindly. "Don't you see that there's a marvelous life opening up for us? There were some really terrific people there tonight. I had a lot of fun. I thought you'd be pleased. My father always complained I wasn't being charming enough, and now I am. Gilbert? Are you just embarrassed because your parents are being so—so touristy? Is that it?"

"No, I like that," said Gilbert.

"I don't mind, of course, but I suppose it does give people an odd impression."

"Actually, I like it better than trying to give people a good impression," said Gilbert. He had given up on his cuff links and tossed them, still clinging to his shirt, into the antique trunk they used as a hamper.

"What does that mean? Me?"

"You're hustling, Wanda," he said. "You were hustling tonight, and you're full of hustling plans for the future. You're even worried about my artless little parents. Of course, I happen to be the one with the White House job."

"Which you got by hustling. Which consists of hustling."

"True enough," said Gilbert. "True enough." He patted the bed for her to sit beside him, and took both her hands. "But let me tell you a couple of things. First, I'm bored with hustling. Bored. That place tonight was like a salesmen's convention. You're damn right, I hustled my way up here, but now I'm there, and I'd like to stop. That's number one.

"Number two is helpful hints for you young hustlers coming along. Don't do it so it shows. Anybody laying it on as thick as you did tonight is not going to make it. People get suspicious and wary. Don't be hurt, Wanda. I love you. But I remember you in London. You were the only American in town who didn't have an English accent."

Wanda had looked troubled, but she smiled at the compliment. "Are you jealous, Gilbert? I really felt people liked me tonight. Don't be like my father, watching me all the time. I still love you, even if you're a sour-puss. You can't help it if you have a popular young wife.

Anyway, it's probably just because I'm so much younger than anyone else."

Gilbert got up, taking no notice of the playful arm she was trying to put around his neck, and fished through the pockets of the pants he had taken off. "That's probably my problem, too," he said, throwing a small pasteboard card into her lap. On it was engraved the name of the new wife of a famous Congressman, with a telephone number written in lip pencil.

"What's that supposed to mean?" Wanda asked soberly.

"I'm trying to tell you, but you're not listening. I'm trying to say that making it isn't that hard. It's all done with mirrors."

"You always told me you were the champion."

"That's right, I am. Did you hear my Inaugural Address today? Best speech I ever wrote, or half wrote."

"I was proud of you."

"Didn't say a damn thing. Be proud of me because I know what I'm doing. I'm so far ahead of those people you admire, it isn't even funny. You want me to teach you the game, I can teach you better than anybody. But let's not us hustle, Wanda. Let's not us plot and spar and carry on. I'm really through, and I picked you because I thought you were smart enough to see through all that. Wanda, I really love you. Wanda? Wanda, can you hear me?"

Wanda had left the room in mid-speech and was back with her hairbrush, bent over in front of him, brushing the back of her long hair downwards. It was all hanging upside down, over her face.

"Wanda, are you there?" he inquired, getting down on the carpet on his knees, and looking up.

She straightened and flung the hair back so he could see her smiling face, but she was looking away from him.

"Wanda? Did you hear anything I said?"

She kissed the beach of forehead his receding curls had left. "You're such an egoist I can't believe it," she said fondly. "How come everybody else in the world is such a fraud and you're the only one who knows it? How is it that you have such exquisite taste that there is nothing for you to do but sit above the clamor and sneer at it, and that you can anoint me to do that, too?"

"Because I'm the champion, and I'm retiring from the ring."

"Before you get beaten? Gilbert, you don't mean that. Champions can't retire. And look at me, I've barely started. Look, Gilbert, I'm not a social climber. You know that. You're the one who's a snob, if you're trying to tell me that being in the White House—just being in the give-and-take of politics—isn't good enough for you. What is this moral indignation? You've never had to do anything dishonest, have you? Gilbert, there are interesting things going on in this city. I want to be a part of the excitement, and I suggest you find a part for yourself, too."

"I can't, Wanda. There's nowhere to go. You know I can't run for office myself—I couldn't keep a straight face—and anyway, what for? I'm in a position now where I can do whatever I like. The question is what."

She climbed the little steps to her side of the bed. "Be sure and wake me when you find out."

Chapter VIII

SITTING opposite each other at the English table, each with an old English silver plate butter knife in one hand and a warm English muffin in the other, they slowly spread bitter marmalade and simultaneously read the society news. This extraordinary feat, sparing them the usual marital vulgarity of impatiently sharing one newspaper, was made possible by the simple luxury of having two subscriptions.

Wanda had discovered a post-post-inaugural party whose existence she had not suspected, and was making the worse discovery that the guests there were all the same guests as at the post-inaugural party they had attended. The President had made a surprise 3:00 A.M. appearance at the later party, fooling the Secret Service, who had seen him home (but not actually tucked in) at the White House at two. Wanda remembered ruefully that she had, at that very hour, been sinking into the satisfied sleep of the socially sated.

That was merely the first of the weekend parties about which they were reading on Monday. It seems that for two days, straight, the President had been all over town for breakfast, lunch, and dinner, enlivening the entire city with his famous wit. What struck Wanda to the heart was that one stop had been to the table of an old friend of her father's, with whom Willard Clay had proposed to stay when Wanda explained that she couldn't put him up during the inauguration. She had managed to discourage the entire paternal visit, the desire to do so being connected with her inability to discourage the visit from Ginerva and Albert Fairchild—but if he had been in Washington, duty might have placed her at those very steps when the President arrived.

Having spurned her father's patronage, she naturally turned to the man with whom she had replaced him. He looked up when her butter knife went through the newspaper account as she strove to point out the subject of her question.

Gilbert gazed at her mildly over the tops of his spectacles, and admitted that he had, indeed, led her to believe that all of Washington went to bed early and that this President, in particular, had to be prodded to attend even crucial parties. Perhaps he had omitted warning her of the brief burst of activity that occurred when a brand-new President took office. It was not the festivities of the inauguration that produced it, but the discovery, by the new Chief Executive, of the mechanical joys of being President of the United States.

The cars and guards and telephones and buttons were all his now, at his command, to enjoy without the nerve-straining demands of campaigning. Each President spent about a month trying out all the White House toys. They always hid from their guards and then popped up all over town, just to watch the turmoil. For the next three and a half weeks, no one who asked three friends for pot-luck supper within ten miles of Washington, D.C., would be safe from a surprise visit from Guess Who.

It didn't mean anything, Gilbert assured his wife. Right on schedule, the President would tire of playing, the little boyishness would drain from his face, leaving new lines and ridges, his talk would dwell morosely on the oppressiveness of the White House, and his only escapes would be to even more isolated fortress-retreats.

In this superior knowledge, Gilbert had skipped the freshman frolics, giving himself the distinction of being the only staff member who had resisted going in over the weekend to try out the White House. He had, instead, given courteous attention to his parents, driving them on a tour around town, or at least around the forty-five-degree wedge consisting of half of northwest Washington, plus a few blocks on Capitol Hill, in which he had confined himself for more than two decades. They knew only of Georgetown because of its association with the Kennedy Administration; he also knew the neighbor-hoods in which senior officials had inflated the real estate in each of the succeeding administrations. When he drove across the bridge to Virginia, in response to a request for "country," he got lost in the tangle of motels and had to ask his way back of a native.

He had also spent the weekend, especially after his

parents left on Sunday, paying intense attention to his wife. It was a bad habit, he reflected; it made her feel that he was neglecting her interests.

"It's like not coming down to lunch when you're expected," he said, because she still looked doubtful about his explanation. "People get curious and go up after you."

"Will you ever believe that I was just engrossed and forgot? Honestly, Gilbert, haven't you ever made an unstudied gesture in your life?"

"Not until recently. How about you?"

"You certainly don't expect me to answer a question like that honestly, do you?" she said, blowing him a kiss across the table.

Gilbert felt good again. The sun shone on his English teapot, his mahogany table, and his wife's tousled auburn hair. He was glad she had omitted the cap that no doubt came with the antique confection of laces and pink ribbons she wore to breakfast. The dressing gown, too long, like their velvet curtains, trailed after her as she took the empty silver toast rack on the way to the kitchen. She stopped and squealed, "Gilbert! It's here!"

He restrained himself from running to the window and instead picked up his leather case and let her hold it while she helped him into his coat.

It really was. He had imperially requested that a White House car be assigned to take him to work, and there it was, a discreet gray car with ostentatious telephone and lamp, right on time. He composed his face with difficulty on the short walk across the sidewalk and opened a newspaper the minute he had been handed into the back seat. Gilbert had never been comfortable driving, and he found sitting in the back, holding, if not actually reading, the paper, easy to get used to. While he waited in this posture for the iron gates of the White House to be opened, a family of tourists peered unabashedly into his car. Gilbert did not flinch when the Daddy tourist reported that it didn't seem to be anybody. That was what made them tourists.

G ILBERT 'S OFFICE was in the White House itself, not big, but covered with the overgrown gold carpeting that spread itself over the entire West Wing. He had fought for this little space, around two corners and down the little staircase from the Oval Office, rejecting a corner suite in the Executive Office Building next door that had a working fireplace, working bathroom, and three windows overlooking helicopter landings and other pageantry on the South Lawn. That such an office had even been suggested to him was his first sign that a tangle of other loyalties had grown up while Gilbert had had three weeks off with his bride.

In the closet-sized outer office, also done in the bland cream tones of official luxury, Toby, who was on the telephone, waved a wide silken tie at him, and when Gilbert came over to inspect this wonder, proof that Toby recognized on his person the dignity of working in the White House, he saw that the little ducks on it weren't ducks at all, but were ferocious gold eagles chomping on olive branches. Toby waved him to stop laughing, and when he got off the telephone said, "Morning, dear, you missed a good breakfast. Tut, tut. Should have been here." Toby affected homosexual overtones when addressing Gilbert, hoping to add some raciness to what he felt was Gilbert's unfortunately dull reputation. He had known his boss for only six months, as a high-key worker too engrossed in the crisis of the moment to be individualistic or humorous.

There had been rumors when Gilbert had hired a male secretary, particularly one who blossomed before everyone's eyes from an urchin campaign style of T-shirts and jeans into a showcase of custom-made male finery. But the women who had worked for him had all been unhappy, personally or professionally, and Gilbert, who had not been able to erase the habit of looking sympathetic, kept being offered their confidences and affection, instead of accurate telephone messages. He knew that Toby cherished hopes of making a friend and a dashing figure out of his poor old work-ridden self, but he found he could tell Toby to shut up, and besides, Gilbert's appointments and comforts of office life had never been handled so beautifully.

Truthfully, Gilbert was mildly curious about his secretary's sexual preferences, since he had found him in the campaign hotel rooms with girls of increasing quality and once in a Senate hideaway office that didn't even belong to their senator. But he figured that if he opened the floodgates of personal confession, he would never be able to get them shut again, and so encouraged the notion that he was prudish, and suffered Toby's teasing him.

"Are we going to start that?" asked Gilbert. "I'm sorry, but I have breakfast with my wife, and I don't change that for anybody."

"Too bad," said Toby, wiping off a silver picture frame with his handkerchief and placing it on Gilbert's desk. "Prez had everybody upstairs for his very own fresh-baked popovers."

"Don't call him Prez," said Gilbert. "Let's have a little dignity around here for a change."

"Whatever you say, Mr. Fairchild. I tell you, though, I've been scouting around, as is my wont, and 'Prez' is about the best. You know what They call him?"

"They," between Toby and Gilbert, stood for new-comers hired during and after the election. When the campaign had first gone national, Gilbert had been begging for extra help. For years, he and Liane had been seeing to all the details themselves, but it was no longer possible. So what he had done from intuition had quickly passed into the hands of experts, with their trends and surveys. Gilbert, who had been out of whack with his contemporaries all his life, impatient with their taste and impervious to their criticisms, had simply invented what he needed—the Disenfranchised Voter, for example, who was a worker who couldn't get into a union, or a consumer who couldn't get services, or a professional whom regulations hampered from working as he saw fit—and had always been successful. Now he had to work with those who claimed to know scientifically what the voters wanted, and who were often wrong.

Gilbert used to complain to Liane that the candidate had turned into the logo of a vast corporation, and a true photograph of him would be a group picture, one of those long ones that roll up, with the man who had given his name to the enterprise frolicking in front of the rows of workers like their mascot. And Gilbert had found it increasingly hard to find his own face.

Knowing better than to encourage Toby, but also knowing that scouting was one of the most valuable services he provided, Gilbert examined the silver frame. Inside it, in Toby's special calligraphy, was his own schedule for the day. There was nothing on it except lunch and an afternoon staff meeting.

"The creep says 'The Old Man,' " Toby went on.

"You know Lipscomb, the tough one with the squint who talks about Men of Good Faith? He says 'The Old Man.' And then the younger ones, the ones that get their suits in Baltimore, and their wives, too, from the looks of them, they say 'The Boss' or 'Boss.' "

"Did you find out what happened at the breakfast?"

"Find out? My dear, I was invited. Personally. Prez came through the halls and stuck his face in everywhere and invited everyone his very self. 'Come on upstairs, there's a French chef, and we've been baking together.' Those were his exact words. Everyone was there. Don't worry, I told him your father'd been rushed to the hospital with a heart attack from all the excitement. I'm supposed to send flowers. Why don't we have them sent here? It'll brighten the place up."

"Toby, let me ask you something. This is important. What are we supposed to do?"

"About what?"

"All day. Until lunch. What am I in charge of around here? What's my assignment?"

"Dunno," said Toby. "My goodness, don't you?"

"No idea?"

"You could help me with the decorating. *I* have only too much to do. We need some pictures, and that table stinks. By the way, there's some mail on it, but that stinks, too."

It was another batch of you-remember-me letters. Since the election, Gilbert had heard from everyone he had ever known, back to his high school girl friend Paula, who insinuated that her marriage wasn't so fulfilling that he couldn't court her again, if he hadn't altogether forgotten who she was. All of these letters contained the rhetorical statement that Gilbert had probably forgotten the letter writer, and the implication that confirmation would be proof of bad character.

Gilbert had even written one such letter himself, before he had discovered how standard they were, to congratulate Cindy Groton on her election to Congress. Covering as many pages as Paula did—but not including a snapshot—he had summarized their first meeting on the presumption that she had forgotten, and had, humorously, he thought (Paula probably thought her tone humorous, too), told her of his own nervous hope at the time that her husband's apparently uncertain rise would carry him into a modest career in politics. In a way it had. Fearful of finding his name blacklisted at Groton headquarters, Gilbert arrived to find that nobody there could find any lists of any kind in the chaos. He needn't have worried, though, about getting a job. They were taking on anybody. Some months later, they were putting everybody out, without providing them with the fare back from New Hampshire to Washington. Gilbert hitched a ride back with some of the senior Groton staff, and kept hitching as they joined the staff of their late rival, a campaign that took somewhat longer to die.

By that time, Gilbert had learned to pay full attention to the business at hand, of making contacts. He hopscotched from one small Capitol Hill office to another, until his masterful suppression of a scandal long overdue to an old lion of a congressman had, on that gentleman's death, possibly from shame at having been saved by a Harvard smart-ass, left Gilbert as that marketable item, a young man on the way up.

He began to approach election years with an experienced eye. Instead of watching candidates, he trained that eye on the politicians to whom those candidates went for support. He finally decided to make a long-term investment in a Presidential campaign. That way, he wouldn't have to watch some unknown figurehead get up and smash his, Gilbert's, career with a blunder that Gilbert could have anticipated.

He could not say, even now, that his man would not have become President without him. But for fifteen years, Gilbert had patiently re-fashioned every aspect of the man, from his wardrobe to his timing to his children's education—everything, in fact, but his political philosophy, which had never come up.

In summarizing this to Cindy Groton, Gilbert merely went from his inspiration in New Hampshire to his modestly realized ambition of the present. He wrote chiefly of the satisfaction with which he had followed her career from school board to mayor to Congress. After that, the Grotons had looked up Gilbert and Wanda, and had a merry evening during which they both confessed to having not had the slightest recollection of ever having seen him before. Gilbert noticed, however, that Governor Groton had recently taken his advice about joining the Congressional Wives' Club.

The top letter on his desk now was on the stationery of the Mullinger-Kraft Clinic, and when Gilbert ran a finger down the long list of names printed down the left-hand margin, he found Dr. Bentley Loomis.

Hey, Gilbert! [it began]
My old roomie in the White House? If I said I couldn't believe it, it wouldn't sound very nice, but I'm sure you'd rather I be sincere. Seriously, congratulations. My wife and I saw you on television today. You looked cold out there on the Capitol steps, and we couldn't help feeling glad we were indoors and warm, although we envied you your place in history, truly. We saw a girl next to you, the one in the fur hat, and

wondered if that's your wife. We would love getting together and meeting your wife, and having you meet
mine, and talking over old times.

So, anyway. Here we are—you in the White House,
and me here. Perhaps you don't know about what we
do here—I'd like to sit down with you sometime soon
and tell you. I'm sure you've heard of PG—Positive
Growth. I and a few of my colleagues originated the
technique, and we have a book coming out in May,
paperback, of which I'll send you one, or several if you'd
like to distribute them around your office. We think it's
just about the most exciting thing that's happened in this
country since the sensitivity boom. Maybe since Sig-
mund Freud in person. (Just kidding.) It's catching on
like wildfire. You may have heard of Farley Smith at
Harvard—he was after our time, but he became something of a cult figure. He's shown a lot of real interest
in PG, practices it himself, religiously. What I thought
was, maybe he and I could fly down to Washington and
tell you all about it. Believe me, when I say it would be
quite a thing for you to introduce PG into government
training. You're in the right place at the right time. We
feel it's the answer to the essential, underlying problems of discontent and strife, not only on a personal
but an international level. How about I call you next
week to set up a date?

Your old
BUDDY

Gilbert drew out a sheet of White House stationery
from the perfect drawers Toby had arranged in his desk.
He noticed that there was an elaborate ship model he
had never seen before, decorating the top of a mahogany
sideboard he had never seen before, either.

"Dear Old Buddy," he wrote.

"Actually, your wife may remember me. I am the one who—"

He crumpled the paper. "I'm going to go wander for a while," he said to Toby.

"Miz Beaufort's been in, why don't you go visit her? Up the stairs, down the hall, through the Cabinet Room, preferably if the cabinet isn't sitting in it, and out the French doors, walk along the porch there and through the house, and it gets you right to the East Wing; she's on the second floor."

Gilbert was going over this in his mind, standing in the doorway, when an unannounced visitor backed him in again, shaking his head at the sight of Toby, as so many of Gilbert's visitors did.

"How's it going?" asked Gilbert. "Still think it was worth it?"

"Sorry to hear about your father. Enjoyed meeting him."

"That was a false alarm, Mr. President. I'm sorry I missed your breakfast. I hear it was delicious."

"Right." Lately, the President had developed a habit of talking telegram-ese in private, as if to compensate for his public verbosity. "See you," he said, moving on down the hall.

"That's a comfort," Gilbert said to Toby.

"I told you I fixed it. Count on me."

"No, I mean that he doesn't know what to do with himself, either. See you."

LIANE'S OFFICE was much bigger and airier than Gilbert's, and beautiful young women were rushing in and out of it. Liane, on a white telephone, a pencil in her mouth, another in her hand, and a third in her hair, waved Gilbert into a deep chair, part of a living room area at the end of her office, with two sofas, four easy chairs, and a coffee table.

She had thoroughly moved in. Her long wall was decorated with mural-sized photographs: Liane and the First Lady weeping happily at the victory announcement; Liane disembarking from an airplane with the First Lady's cosmetic case; and, incredibly, Liane the previous Friday night, already frozen into popular history, standing next to the First Family at the White House before they left for the inaugural balls. Behind her desk were small frames of china, inlaid wood, and flowered cloth, displaying letters from the President, the First Lady, their daughter, their son, the Vice President and the Second Lady. Gilbert's easy chair and its mates had pillows in stripes of navy and cream to brighten up the ubiquitous White House Off-White.

In contrast with the studied décor and the bevy of sleek young women who served her, Liane looked undone, with the faint lines on her face and her hair coming out of her bun. She rolled her eyes upwards at Gilbert several times to indicate impatience, but when she hung up the telephone, she turned her attention to a Lucite clapboard before she turned it to him.

"What on earth are you doing? We're all bored stiff over on the men's side. Including Old Man Prez The Boss."

"Are you kidding? We haven't been able to breathe. Janet! Bring us some coffee, will you? I tell you, Gilbert, if you think it was bad on the road—" Her special telephone line rang, and she shrugged toward Gilbert.

He took the clipboard out of her hands.

Dear ——— [it said]

Thank you for taking the trouble to write to us at the White House. It's always fun to hear from another dog lover.

Terry is adjusting just fine to life here at the White House, although sometimes we think she wishes she could get out just for an hour or two to chase rabbits again in our old backyard, with none of the fuss and attention.

Don't worry about her diet. She's eating very well, although, like so many of us, she is learning to go without the most expensive cuts of meat these days. . . .

"*No*," said Gilbert as Liane hung up.

She laughed.

"It's not funny, Liane. No. Absolutely not. I forbid it. You tear this up right now, or I will."

"That's my re-write. You should see the original. It was from Terry, signed with a paw print. How'd you like that?"

"Liane, we're just not going to go in for this kind of thing. I don't believe in much, but I do believe in a little minimum taste. There's no reason in the world why we should have to do this kind of thing now. No strippers at state dinners, and no puppy dogs in the mailbags. Understand?"

"Don't you snap at me, Gilbert Fairchild. This is not my department. I did a try at it, only because She asked me to. She didn't like the Terry one. But all this comes out of Family Press, and you'll just have to yell at them. Next office down. Some high-powered advertising type from New York. Go ahead."

"We have them, too," said Gilbert. "I don't know where they all came from. Some of them I actually hired myself, I think. Oh, God, Liane, I can't take it anymore. Did I start this business about image and clever little tricks and those, uh, deliberate scenarios?"

"Oh, I think it was just one of those ideas that a lot of people came up with at the same time. I first heard all that from you, yes, even before you were out of college. You were certainly a pioneer on the Hill."

"Of what? I was just fooling around. These people have taken over politics with their trends and surveys and media expertise. There aren't any issues any more—that's why we're all hanging around with nothing to do until something happens we can react to; then it'll be a madhouse. That's all anybody knows how to do any more—try to make things look better in a crisis than they are, or make people look responsible or not responsible or strong enough to lead us out. Nothing happens any more. All I was doing was manipulating things a little so that voters could see in some tangible way what a candidate was—and what's more, I never meant any harm. These people are so grim; they scare me."

"Well," said Liane, "I don't know. What was the name of that man who killed himself on television? I've blocked it out."

"Liane! That was not our fault!"

Liane's assistant, one of the legion of White House beauties, appeared with a tray.

"I remember that, Mrs. Beaufort. I was in high school then, and I watched it and I remember my parents telling me not to worry about it, he would have been shot for treason anyway. Was that you, Mr. Fairchild?"

Gilbert looked up, "No, as it happens, he was innocent," he said. "We didn't know that. It's too complicated
to explain. Mrs. Beaufort had nothing to do with it, and
I was only peripherally involved."

"I'll pour the coffee," said Liane. "Just leave it, Janet,
and shut the door." When that had been done, she said,
"Are you going to commit suicide in public now, too?"

"I might as well, before I die of boredom."

"You're mistaken. It's not going to be dull around here.
The job in the White House, in case you haven't heard,
is to stay in the White House. That means everybody,
from the President on down. Maybe you don't think it's
a job. Just for starters, have you heard the rumor about
your old friend S. B. Brewster coming on board?"

"Don't be silly. He's not even the right party."

"So what? I think he's switched. Anyway, we're bi-
partisan now. The President of All the People."

"God! Bi-partisanship! Are there no principles left?"

"It's true, because I had a request to have him to the
state dinner."

"Liane! You're not going to."

"Oh, yes, I think I will. The request came from the
hostess."

"That's all I needed. Liane, why is my life such a
struggle? Why do I always have to fight just to hold on
to the simple, basic things? What did I ever ask for but a
decent job and a quiet home life?"

"That reminds me," she said gently, as he was leaving.
"There's a certain Mrs. Fairchild who keeps hinting that
she'd like to go to that dinner, too. What do you think?
The senior staff are going to have to take turns, you
know."

"You better put us down."

"Oh, Gilbert, I already did. I was just teasing you. Tell Wanda it's fine."

"You mean, I can let her think it was my masculine prowess that did it? Oh, boy."

TOBY PRODUCED what he claimed was a genuine President McKinley desk for Gilbert from the bowels of the General Services Administration, and what he called a Vice President Barkley one for himself. The day Toby heard about borrowing from museums, though, Gilbert began to worry. Toby decided to skip the White House curator; the telephone call to the gallery sounded distinctly as if Toby were speaking from the President's bedroom, or rather as if the First Lady's decorator were: "I don't think we can say exactly where it will hang. Let's just say where it will be richly appreciated in private by the person whom it will do the most good." Toby excused his behavior to Gilbert by proclaiming that he had gotten him a Manet or a Monet, and promised never to do it again.

"Well. Which is it?"

"Whichever is better," said Toby. "Look, dear, if I had a Harvard education, would I be just a secretary?"

STRANGE PEOPLE rushed by his open door all afternoon, that army of political experts grown from sowing dragon's teeth in White House corridors. Toby was dashing about on errands he had no time to explain, and the staff meeting was canceled. At four-thirty, when it was already getting dark, Gilbert wandered into the

Oval Office because he saw others streaming there. It seemed that the President had gone into the press lounge and invited everyone to his office for a drink. But he must have been overruled by his secretary, because what she ordered for the instant crowd was not cocktails, but coffee, with silver bowls of potato chips to be placed on the end tables.

The President crouched on a footstool in front of his fireplace and lit the perfect arrangement of logs himself, while a butler nervously watched; veteran reporters occupied the matching sofas on either side of him; and everyone else crowded around, standing with heads bent as if for a burial. Gilbert stood on the edge of the Presidential Seal rug, watching a beaming President in a glowing room responding happily and openly to respectful questions politely put.

How did he find his first three days in office, what were his top priorities, was he going to see the press regularly like this, what role would the Vice President play? People who had called him by his first name for years, who had treated him on the campaign as if he were their creature, were now studiously calling him Mr. President; and Mr. President was just as studiously remembering to call them Bill and Jo and Mike and Dana.

Apparently, though, he was anxious. There was nothing to fear out of a first-day story, but the President had turned too hospitable, too eager to please. Gilbert heard him offer to be godfather to a substitute wire service reporter's new baby. Smiles were being exchanged among the reporters not new to the White House, calculating what they could grab before the door shut in their faces.

Gilbert, moving to his old position just behind the President, from where he was used to supplying names, facts, and signals, exchanged a glance with Roxanne, the

President's bulwark of a secretary. She nodded, perhaps just a quarter of an inch.

"We appreciate your coming," said Gilbert, leaning into the hairy ear of an old man who had gotten the potato chip bowl on his lap. The man arose, giving two novices the quick illusion that one of the precious sofa seats was becoming available, and said, "Mr. President, we thank you for your hospitality, and your, ah, drinks." Everyone laughed and filed by the new President to get a souvenir handshake and perhaps word of recognition on the way out.

Gilbert tried to stay, thirsting for one of the old confidential critiques and thinking to bring up the question of his future, but the President, though he grabbed Gilbert's shoulders in view of whatever parting reporters cared to notice—a gesture now diluted into being nearly worthless—retreated formally to his desk, and Gilbert left before he would have to observe him and Roxanne exchanging that same look.

"Have fun?" Toby asked him.

"Oh, terrific. I got to meet the President."

"Listen, dear, I've got lots for you to do, so don't fret. Just look at the invitations!" Toby had the cheer of a mother producing an improvised diversion for a convalescent child. "I've been talking to Mrs. Fairchild, and we've marked the things we ought to accept. The flowers came; aren't they nice? Let's not forget to write our thank-you note. You can't use that transition ID any more, so you have to go get yourself photographed. Everyone else got theirs on Saturday. I decided not to ask for a parking space because it might jeopardize getting portal-to-portal car service, and anyway, Wanda's learning to drive, so she'll need the car. Did you know you can get a haircut here? And there's an exercise room with showers. You can have a heart attack, too—there's always a doctor. It's like the Pentagon Mall, this place, or Leisure World. A little city, all in itself. We're going to be very happy here."

Toby was walking around the office as he talked, adjusting books and furniture lovingly, like a woman brushing nothing from the shoulders of a man, just because he's hers. As he went by Gilbert to draw the curtains, he lowered his voice and said, "Lipscomb. Corner office upstairs. Watch out."

Gilbert's heart leapt, and he swerved, feeling small in his leather judge's chair. "What do you know about him?"

Toby sat on the edge of his desk. "Shhhh. These partitions are like paper. You've seen him—the big one with the beard? Real toughie. The worst is, he went to Yale Law School with Small Boy, and that's where that's coming from. You can't trust anyone any more. He's drawing up the game plan or the flow chart or whatever—I can't talk White House yet, but I'm learning. Nobody asked him for it, mind, but he's got this big sheet with boxes all over the place and chain-of-command lines. Looks like Queen Victoria's family tree. Let me tell you, we didn't even have a box at first. I heard him say, 'Fairchild? What do we do with Fairchild?' and he had us on the side, with the people they don't know where they're going to fit. I fixed that."

"Toby! What'd you do? How'd you find out about this, anyway?"

"Don't ask. I sicced Liane on him. They're all just terrified of Liane Beaufort. Just trembling in their little cowboy boots. We have a good friend there, Mr. Fairchild, sir, a very good friend."

"Are you kidding? I took her into this stupid outfit

and every other good job she's ever had. She was a nothing State Department wife with a dumb job someplace addressing envelopes."

"Yes, yes, and I was just an ignorant orphan, and we're all so terribly grateful to you for letting us serve our country, we just don't know what to do. Mrs. Beaufort adores you, and I don't think it's helpful for you to make nasty about your best friend. Pick on me, if you're such a bully. I'm just a servant. I can't fight back."

"Okay, Toby. Tell me what you did."

"Never you mind what I did. You just remember that Miz Beaufort is the only true friend our President and First Lady have, and you be good to her."

Gilbert laughed. He was thinking of the time he and Liane had drawn up a list of the now-President and his wife's friends they wanted fired—a soggy and hilarious prep school roommate who played practical jokes on foreign dignitaries; the television hostess from back home who was getting them photographed with too many people one knew nothing about; the old Marines buddy who had taken to threatening people he didn't like in the candidate's name, a version of "My big brother will beat you up if you don't do what I say"; and the girl next door, whose law practice specialty was getting to be defending organized crime. The couple had protested, but Gilbert told them they were lucky they didn't put her brother the liquor dealer on the list and, as a matter of fact, they weren't too crazy about his sister the amateur astrologer, either.

"You have to work late, so I kindly offered to give Mrs. Fairchild dinner. Cheer up, it's all so decadent around here, you'll soon be your old self. No, no, you have to work late. There's a directory in your middle drawer with everyone's picture in it; you can study that. Or

there're some comic books in my desk, if you get desperate. But this is your first day on the job, and it wouldn't
look right if you didn't work late. Appearances are everything around here. Ta-ta."

Chapter IX

THE HAND of a fine valet could be seen in the details of the sleeping quarters. Fresh flowers, cut very short, floated in an etched bowl on the bedtable, next to a clean notepad stamped "The White House" in navy, and a navy blue pencil stamped "The White House" in gold. Oriental ashtrays, hand-painted in individual designs of navy and cinnamon, were strategically placed on the many little tables, and each had a matchbook with the Presidential Seal in gold and, in small letters, "The President's House." A lacquer tray contained writing paper, one size with only the Presidential Seal and another with "The White House" centered on it, and several bill-signing pens with the President's signature reproduced on the barrels.

But Toby was, in fact, his own valet. It was he who had arranged the flowers and perfected the arrangement of table objects in this quiet room, high off Pennsylvania Avenue. The effect was unique. The other apartments in his downtown high-rise building were still decorated with Christmas cards stuck in the Venetian blinds.

Toby delighted in choosing presents for himself, and also in receiving them from himself. Sometimes a friend comprehended the spirit of the place enough to bring an offering that was passable, but most presents he was given by others were unusable. If Toby were feeling low, he would nip into a china shop and emerge with a gift-wrapped surprise for himself. He often brought people home, too, but he didn't like them to stay long. A girl who gave the furniture ignorant compliments, randomly calling it Queen Anne or Mexican, had to be watched, or she'd go around pocketing all the Presidential matchbooks Toby had put so much care into collecting. He didn't even feel safe with visiting colleagues from the White House, should they notice that *his* matchbooks were not from the offices but from the living quarters of the executive mansion.

But today's guest was someone he adored. He had lovingly smoothed the navy blanket cover, now lying crumpled on the floor, and had patted, with excited expectation, the flounced pillow which now had Liane's hair carelessly spread on it.

Liane had been too agitated to notice anything. She cursed when she had had trouble unlocking the door, she had thrown her lynx coat on the sofa without considering that its melting snow might leave a wet mark on the upholstery, and she had sworn again as she pulled off her boots and her sweater dress and her matching underwear and her tiny diamond chain necklace. The other gold chains she left, not wanting to take the time to undo all their clasps, but it was a point of honor with her not to wear George's keepsake to bed with someone else.

She had now been forty-five minutes in Toby's apartment, and was plotting her escape. The monarch who would be the President's first state visitor had attended so many more White House dinners than Liane and her First Lady combined that the two of them felt at an unfair disadvantage. Liane's mind was wandering back to seating charts and guest flow maps when Eric distracted her by taking her nipple in his mouth.

It was annoying almost to the point of being offensive— the nibbling, the time robbed from her day, the awkward trip to ask Toby for his keys, the sentimental talk that would be required before she could get away from Eric for another week. Toby had stopped probing to find out who her mysterious lover was, which meant that he knew. He would tell her tomorrow how divine the bed had smelled afterwards; that indicated that he was adding the debt to her tab.

It wasn't at all the way it used to be when she and George had run away from their duties so many years before. Then she had adored the squishy state in which she had gone back to work. Now she knew she would feel irritable until she had a bath and found an excuse to press her body, perhaps in a passing hug, against George's. Yet she had no kindly feelings towards him. Eric was his fault. If George did not insist on being the old beau-about-town, incapable of meeting a too-fat or too-thin woman at a party without reassuring her of her beauty; if he did not listen to the recitals of unfaithful husbands, demanding mothers, ugly divorces, hostile children, and the rest of the litany of female woes; if he did not send flowers on the birthdays of every woman he had ever flirted with, there would be no Eric, and no Jeremy, either. While she was protecting herself, Liane had figured, she might as well protect herself against the emotional ebbs and flows of any one lover, as well as against George's meanderings, whatever they were. She suspected that they didn't go beyond all that public gallantry, but the constant thinking about others made fidelity a technicality. So there was also, concurrently, Jeremy, a curator of medieval history, who didn't have the money to fly to Washington and disrupt Liane's schedule, and then add to the outrage by expecting her to be pleased. He was more convenient by being in New York when she needed an escort to a party or company in a hotel room too luxurious to waste.

Eric was slightly more trouble because he lived in Washington, but fortunately he had marvelously active guilt feelings that engrossed the major portion of his emotions. He also had extraordinary good looks, Liane realized, but they were of no value to her, as she didn't need an escort in Washington, where George was always happy to attend anything interesting.

Eric's hair was dark blond, and his thick mustache a coordinated shade of pale brown. He wore his three-piece suits like a model, and had large but smooth hands accented by the thinnest of gold watches and wedding bands. If Liane was often annoyed by him—she found it an imposition, for instance, that he expected her to recognize his unidentified voice on the telephone—she remembered some of the others she had let annoy her before she acquired Eric.

Besides, it had been getting increasingly difficult to find replacements. It wasn't just the thought that, approaching fifty, she might startle, rather than delight, someone to whom she signaled her availability—but her job. She had turned down a political reporter, a military aide on White House social duty, a lobbyist for the cotton industry, and a congressman, this year alone. Eric Royce was a lawyer who did some government-related business, but not much. His wife was a historic preservationist who had gone to school with Wanda Fairchild, and they had met at one of the Fairchilds' five-course dinners for eight. It had not been one of Wanda's "A" dinners, what with old friends and worse. Liane had watched George carry a napkinful of canapés and a heartful of sympathy to a shy legal assistant who everybody in the office knew had been searching all summer for someone to tell her grievances.

It was hard to say who had been more riveted, Eric or Gilbert, when Liane turned on a beacon of charm and directed it mercilessly towards that guest, who was innocently trying to pry election secrets out of his host. But Liane was unperturbed, knowing that her routine was perfected by use, and it was not long after the dinner that Eric found himself taking her to lunch, and not many lunches before he was telling her that he had never been unfaithful to his wife except once that didn't count; that he couldn't risk exposing himself to a hotel clerk or anyone who might wander through a public lobby; that he was a new partner and shouldn't take time off from work; that his wife opened all the bills and would know if he had used his credit card illicitly; and that he couldn't do this to George, who had seemed like such a nice man. He was still babbling like that the first time she led him to Toby's apartment, and Liane was still listening graciously.

Eric prided himself on being a terrifically thoughtful

lover. Liane wished he weren't quite so terrific and thoughtful, because his inventive attentions kept calling attention to the fact that he was there, this stranger in whom she had no interest, thrusting himself into her recognition. Jeremy was better. Jeremy would turn out all the lights and pound away until she forgot her identity, her location, her husband, and her career. Eric wanted to look at her and tell her what he wanted her to do, and kiss her and come at her from different directions. There was this silly man, lapping about her, all over the place, and she had to pretend to be charmed, or else she would have to begin the weary search for someone else.

There were moments of rebellion or hope, when she thought she could kiss Eric on his handsome forehead and send him packing. Times when she and George were alone at dinner, or on airplanes, or serving themselves breakfast in bed, she would whisper into his wisp-filled ear, "We don't need anyone but us, do we?" and George would return her smiles and kisses and pressures and agree. Then Liane would happily plan the dismissal of whoever was the current Eric, until the day or week or two later, when George would mention with elaborate casualness that some nuisance had called or dropped by his office and was unhappy and seemed to think of him as a father figure, and since Liane would be late at the White House anyway, he thought maybe he'd take her to dinner, and didn't Liane think that was the kind thing to do? She always said yes, she did, indeed.

So Eric Royce found himself in Toby's bed at eleven-fifteen in the morning. Liane tried to think of something to distract him from worrying her nipple, but couldn't, so she just pulled it away from his too-rosy lips.

"Darling? What's the matter? Tell me."

"Nothing," said Liane. "Work. I had no right to run

out today. But," she added hastily, "I couldn't resist." She
tried to look guilty; guilt was something he respected.

"Tell me."

"Tell me what?"

"About your work. About how you feel about it. I
want to know all about what it's like, working at the
White House. Did you ever dream that—"

Oh, God, she thought. But she told him about the state
visit, trying to make it amusing, and throwing in some
gossip, to stretch it, about people angling for invitations.

"And there you are in the middle, dispensing or with-
holding favors, and everyone clamoring at your feet."

"Eric, I'm not the First Lady. I'm just the social secretary, you know. I send out the invitations, I don't decide
on the guests."

"You have some leeway, don't you?"

"Why? Would you like to go to the White House?"

"Me? Good heavens, no. My God, what would she
think? You know I can't do anything like that. Liane, you
know how much I love Josephine. I've always said so,
right from the beginning, haven't I? We have a really
terrific marriage. She'd sniff out something like that in a
minute. She'd have it out of me before I knew what I was
saying."

To calm him down, Liane stroked his hair the way he
had explained that he liked, and even kissed him on the
mouth. It signaled to him that it was time to start again,
and Liane only wished he wouldn't try to lock her eyes
with his and smile soulfully at the same time. She broke
it off by closing her eyes, counting on his assuming they
were shuttered in ecstasy. And soon it was what is technically considered ecstasy. That is, the mechanism of her
body went off properly as a result of his activity. She just
didn't take any personal interest in this phenomenon. It

was like having her knee react when the doctor's mallet hit it—amazing, reassuring, but hardly thrilling. In a society where everyone talked about orgasms, and no one ever seemed to have enough, Liane had never heard of anyone else with the complaint of having boring ones.

They smiled at each other. It was a courtesy each had always extended at such moments.

"Wouldn't your husband be upset?"

Liane stiffened. At what? At how often Eric was boring her? She was filled with wifely resentment. There was nothing wrong with old George, except his wandering eye.

"If Josephine and I were at the state dinner."

Liane sighed. "Eric, dear, I don't have that kind of power. I was thinking maybe when they have a couple of hundred extra people in after a dinner, for the entertainment and dancing. But I can't on the first dinner. It's too conspicuous."

"Do you want me to lick you? I want to lick you."

Liane wished he wouldn't announce it like that. She wished he didn't have the whisk-broom mustache. She wished he wouldn't look up, from down at the bottom of the bed, so that she could just see his big eyes surface between her legs and look at her, confidently expecting approval. Then she closed her eyes and decided that if she had to spend twenty more minutes here, before being allowed to escape to work, this was not the worst way to spend it.

SHE EMERGED ALONE on Pennsylvania Avenue, having convinced Eric that the entire world was out there at lunchtime, looking at building entrances to see who was going to come out with whom. She felt braced by the cold wind and cleansed by the oversized wet snowflakes that settled on her hair and coat. She looked back automatically for a taxi, but put her hand down in midhailing. It was better to walk and have all that sticky intimacy frozen out of her before she got safely back to her desk. People would think, by now, that she had gone to lunch. She walked briskly, forcing her thoughts back into work—it had been so easy to drift into thinking about work when she was with Eric—to rid herself of Eric's closely looming, self-satisfied face, as it had looked when he had emerged from what he obviously considered administrating a special treat.

Turning in at the Northwest Gate, so she could deliver the keys to Toby, she met Gilbert coming out, his head down against the storm, so that he didn't see her until she tugged at his sleeve. He gave her a kiss on her cold nose, and went on. Liane wondered if he had found her distasteful. Perhaps something of Eric clung about her, and was costing her her friend. Then she remembered, with shame, that she had picked up Eric at Gilbert's house, while Gilbert watched. Was that so dreadful? Before Gilbert was married, Liane had often invited women to her house for him to meet. He had once seen her holding hands with a previous lover in a restaurant, and had sent over drinks with the message that they were a token of admiration from a stranger. He certainly had no sympathies with George. He loved her, she told herself, feeling, miserably, that the kiss was perfunctory and that he had rushed too quickly away. It was no use asking herself what she expected from him in a snowy driveway, next to the open guardhouse; she felt terrible. And she still had to see Toby's insinuating smile and listen to his amplified sniffing.

GILBERT'S MIND had been occupied with nothing more nor less than his chances of getting a taxi in the snow. There was nothing wrong with being late to a lunch with Buddy Loomis; in fact, there would have been something wrong with being on time. But the snow was smearing his glasses, and when he took them off, it clung to his eyelashes.

He considered going back and ordering a car. Only delicacy had prevented his doing this before—he didn't want to overwhelm Buddy with his success. Gilbert had every intention of complimenting Buddy on his own success, but it would have to be done skillfully, or it might be taken for sarcasm.

While he was standing helplessly, a taxi stopped of its own accord, to disgorge a reporter whose perfectly good press credentials were going to be examined by the guards in their warm guardhouse for a very long time, while the reporter stood outside being snowed on. Gilbert knew this, because he had made the suggestion himself. While the guard was asking the reporter's middle name and date of birth, Gilbert snapped up his cab.

The snow worsened noticeably as they went along, and the taxi radio reported that the government was being dismissed early. The driver grumbled that he had been intending to go home, too, when Gilbert had jumped in without asking—there would be too many people trying to get home, and he didn't want to get stuck in that mess. It was Washington's southern panic in the face of what Massachusetts would have described as a flurry. Gilbert knew that Special Assistants to the President were not being let out of school for any emergency, and he felt that was unfair, though it was true that they might have privileges that ordinary civil servants did not.

At the Cosmos Club driveway, a knot of people waved and jumped at him and all but cheered him as a deliverer. They had despaired of ever attracting a taxi. But Gilbert's driver was too quick for them and sped off empty and triumphant.

Gilbert found Buddy in the front hallway, reading a newspaper on which the club had stamped its name, to protect its investment against unscrupulous guests. Buddy kissed him. "Hey, you look terrific," he said. "Really terrific. No kidding. What happened to your hair?"

"So do you," said Gilbert, disengaging himself and nodding at an elderly gentleman, a former Under Secretary of State whom he had met at a club session to discuss admitting women to membership. The gentleman had raged that it would ruin the contemplative atmosphere; when he had sat down, he had had to be helped to take a pill.

"Farley's in the gents."

"We'll go have a drink, and he'll find us," said Gilbert. A relatively new member, he felt how wrong Buddy looked, even with the excuse of the storm, wearing a turtleneck sweater with his plaid suit. He was annoyed that the club didn't catch him. He was annoyed at himself for caring, but he did. He was, in point of fact, a great deal less tolerant of Buddy's wearing a sweater while he wore a suit and tie, than Buddy had been in college, when he had always worn ties and Gilbert had taken to wearing turtleneck sweaters.

Gilbert led Buddy past the walls of photographs of club members who had won Nobel or Pulitzer prizes, trying hard not to look like a proud parent. "Twenty years, hey? More!" Buddy said several times, but when Gilbert asked him about Margery, he said, "Oh, boy," and refused to tell him until later because "Farley's time is important, so we'll do that first and chat afterwards."

Another wrong person loped into view—a bundle of assorted woolens, worsteds, tied up in long scarves, and with thin strands of gray hair hanging over the back. Gilbert wanted to hang a sign on him explaining that he really was a genuine professor from Harvard.

"Farley's really into PG," he said. Gilbert made an instant decision to skip drinks and get them in and out of the dining room as quickly as possible. At the table, Buddy alternated between enthusiastic statements in gibberish and grand declarations of "Don't forget, this is all on me," while Gilbert tried to elicit their lunch orders.

"You don't have horsemeat here," was Farley's contribution. "At the faculty club, we have horsemeat."

Finally, Gilbert had had enough. He explained to Buddy that a guest cannot pay for the food in a private club, no matter how grandiose he had become since he had last seen the club member; he told Farley Smith that nobody ever called him Gil, and addressed him as Mr. Smith as he did so; he explained to them both that he did not abuse his position by selling the gimmicks of friends to the President or the Civil Service or the American public, and that he still didn't know what PG stood for besides Prince Georges County, Maryland. He further stated that he was not unhappy, that he did not intend to improve his life, and that if he did, he wouldn't pick his old friend Buddy to re-design it. And if they didn't tell him what they wanted to eat, they weren't going to be fed.

Farley Smith shifted uncomfortably in his chair, as if

he were preparing to react honorably to insult, but Buddy
looked pleased. The warm glow of old friendship overcame him, and the warmth of Gilbert's reprimands had
re-established their relationship.

"Hey, Gilbert," he said, "take it easy. You must be
getting too much pressure in that job. I'm not trying to
sell you any gimmick. I'll have the fish du jour. Farley
only eats vegetables. We have scientific proof for the
value of PG—Positive Growth, remember? I wrote you
that; are you sure you're all right?—and we have an appointment tomorrow with a very important person I can't
name who is highly interested in trying it in a very major
government department, so don't think I'm asking you
for influence. I've got more than I can handle as it is.

"Look, I don't know, maybe you are happy. Frankly,
I doubt it. This is a pretty hectic life nowadays, and
we're all under a strain, which your outburst just proved,
and it would be pretty hard for me to believe that you're
functioning successfully in the White House, in the nerve
center of the free world, without some of this getting to
you where it counts. I'll tell you, too, marriage isn't easy
these days, either, with all this flux in roles people are
juggling. I haven't even asked you about that yet. Everybody needs help. I did, too. I admit it. I'll leave some of
my stuff with you; you'll see what real people, people like
us, say about PG. It's no magic or anything. No mystical
thing. Just a simple technique for making life work.
Jesus, you don't need to knock me, Gilbert, just because
we were kids together. Are you using your butter? These
popovers are terrific. Look, Gilbert, Farley and I aren't
faddists. We wouldn't be here if we didn't have something real to offer. Frankly, we're doing you a favor, old
friend. Never mind the fish, I'll have the short ribs with
the tomato juice first and the coleslaw and the peas and

carrots, creamed potatoes, and I'll think about the dessert later. What's with you, Gilbert? You can't tell me you don't need help."

"Salad for you?" Gilbert asked Farley Smith, who nodded. Then he asked him what he had published, and found that Farley and Buddy had collaborated on a book called *The Self Looks at Itself*. Gilbert also found out that Smith had been in Asian Studies before Psychology, held two doctorates but was untenured. Whether he was actually, currently employed by the university was never made clear.

"Listen to me, Gilbert," Buddy broke in. "Jesus, I got all this from you."

Gilbert did listen. "Got what?"

"PG. My whole philosophy. See, I was your average downtrodden miserable kid in college, and I noticed you were a success. You always had a girl; even my sister liked you, and she doesn't like anybody. So I asked myself, 'What is it with this guy?' And I thought, boy, he is so together that he doesn't insist on continuity in others, or in the different parts of his life outside himself."

"What?" said Gilbert. "You didn't get this from me."

"I got it from Margery. She told me that at first she thought you were just a liar and a manipulator, but later she saw that you had a kind of unifying truth in yourself, and treated the different parts of your life as separate episodes, making each one as perfect as you could, without trying to relate them or make them consistent with each other. See?"

"Yes, I see," said Gilbert. "You're peddling snake oil, and you're trying to claim I'm the snake."

"Oh, no, pal. I must not be telling it well. Margery said you were ahead of your time. That you have a sense of fragmentation that is the true rhythm of the modern world. Everybody has it now from watching too much television. There's not a deep sense of right and wrong, for instance, but what works, and what works one moment doesn't necessarily work the next. That's why everybody's crazy. But not you, maybe, because you're one of those people who doesn't have to connect, because you're all connected up inside. Or at least you were before this job got to you."

"Where is Margery? I'll kill her."

Farley was looking out the window and humming. "Later," said Buddy. "Right now I've got to tell you how PG works, and what our plans are."

And so he did, while Gilbert played with his watch chain, drank coffee he didn't want, and gloomily chalked up the number of acquaintances who, in spite of the storm, had managed to see him with these salesmen.

Nevertheless, he invited them for dinner, his natural horror of having barbarians invade his velvet house overcome by his desire to see Margery and have it out with her. Buddy's parting shot was to volunteer that he understood Kalorama was a very dangerous neighborhood. Then he slipped two one-dollar bills under the napkin with the club's name sewed on it in red. Gilbert removed them and handed them back to Buddy in the vestibule, but Buddy just left them on the counter. No one being in attendance, they took their own wet coats from the hangers.

GILBERT HAD EXPECTED his wife to be legitimately annoyed at this importation of old rejects, but she giggled over the telephone and said she could hardly wait. Gilbert, who had invited them for eight o'clock, offered to cut his day short and be serviceable, either in

picking up supplies or in cooking, but Wanda told him it
wasn't necessary. He got there at six-thirty, anyway, not
without Toby's disapproval at his leaving the office early
—any time before eleven was early to leave the White
House—and found the table set for six. "I got your old
girl friend," Wanda said merrily, transferring the catered
meal from its foil pans into her own copper pots. Gilbert
looked blank. "The love of your life!" He still looked
puzzled. "Erna Elephant! Erna Oliphant."

"Oh, no."

"I thought it would be fun. Her husband's in Afghanistan, and she calls Liane all the time, so I told Liane I'd
take her off her hands. Liane's so busy, I thought I'd do
her a favor. Anyway, Erna's just delighted. She and
Buddy can fall in love all over again."

"Wanda," he said patiently, "she and Buddy never even
knew each other at college. I don't think. Wait a minute.
I'm not sure."

"She and Margery must have known about each other.
Don't you think it'll be a scream?"

"Oh, a scream," conceded Gilbert. He did not admire
the way Wanda looked, as she bent over the table, carefully rolling the large damask napkins on top of each
pewter service plate. There was something that bothered
him about the way she relished the stories of his old
adventures. She had never really told him anything revealing, but had coaxed the most complicated details out
of him, never showing any emotion except amusement.
He hoped it was confidence in the idea that he had loved
her faithfully from the time they met, which was true.
He suspected it was a lack of possessiveness, something
modern, which he had not experienced in previous attach-
ments. Female tugging and securing had always been part
of courtship, and for a man to get married was, in the

sexual world Gilbert had known, a magnificent concession. That Wanda might live in a world where these
things didn't count unsettled him.

"You know," he said cautiously, "I've been thinking
about Margery. I'm looking forward to seeing her again.
There was a sort of voluptuousness about her that one
rarely sees in young women."

Wanda didn't comment. She was narrow all over. Gilbert had no way of telling if she had noticed his experiment, and her dignity, if she had, made him a little
ashamed.

"What did Erna make of your calling her?" he asked
neutrally.

"If she never knew your Buddy, she certainly faked
it. And she knew all about me. I think her husband is a
jerk I met once in London. They're just back from a
tour of duty, or rather, she's back early with the children,
to start the new semester."

When Gilbert opened the front door on Erna Oliphant,
he didn't find the good Foreign Service wife who dutifully follows a husband around the world at an ever-
widening gap—arriving at a post a month later, when the
new baby can travel; two months later at the next post,
because the house had to be rented; three months at the
third post, to coordinate with school schedules—and serves
him and her country in the remarkably ill-paying job of
ambassador of goodwill.

Erna seemed to have gotten stuck in about 1968. Her
hair was too high, and too many colors of ash. Her leather
skirt was too short, and her lips were too pale. It wasn't
from looking at Erna that Gilbert noticed all this—it was
from watching Wanda sweep by to welcome her. Wanda
was dressed in a high-necked woven robe the color of
mulberries, with her limp locks of hair caught in orna-

mental bone hairpins. Erna, who had been the smartest-looking wife at the embassy Christmas party in Kabul in the outfit she was now wearing, took one look at Wanda and knew she had had it. The wildly flirtatious glance she had given Gilbert at the door was not repeated. Whatever lame charm she was able to muster, she directed at Wanda.

It was the next knock at the door that interested Gilbert. From the moment he had said it to his wife, he had been thinking of Margery's body. Three people stood on his doorstep: Farley Smith, Buddy Loomis, and a small brown girl in a large plaid coat. Gilbert stared past them, looking for Margery in the darkness, until Wanda sailed forward again and admitted them.

"Meet Immaculata," said Buddy. "My old roomie Gilbert you heard so much about."

The little woman put out a small paw and a look so timid that Gilbert almost didn't have the heart to demand, "Where's Margery?" Almost, but not quite. Buddy had been putting him off all day. "Where's Margery?" he demanded.

"In New York, I expect," said Buddy.

"Oh?" No games were going to prevent Gilbert's finding out how he had been cheated, but the possibility that Buddy was now cheating maritally did not occur to him.

Immaculata was apparently not programmed to say anything, but she nevertheless registered Gilbert's disappointment at finding her in the place of the powerful and glamorous Margery, and she spoke up. "She and my husband divorce. She is married with Gower Dale. The famous personality?"

"With what?" Gilbert peered at Immaculata to see what she was—Puerto Rican? Thai? Bolivian? Filipina?

He was about to dismiss her as one of those pliant sub-
stitutes for wives whom American servicemen acquire
abroad at PXs, but there was a strain of dignity about her.
He charitably decided that cultural barriers had prevented
her from assessing Buddy's true lack of value.

"With Gower Dale," Buddy repeated proudly. "The
news personality. On TV. Margery married him after
we were divorced. I had already met Immaculata, of
course, and I knew I'd never be satisfied until I made her
mine. Immaculata is a pediatric surgeon. And, frankly, a
terrific mother. We have three children, and if you beg
me, I'll show you their pictures. Bentley, Junior, Immaculata, Junior, and Amelito. Amelito's by her first marriage,
which was a disaster. He's in medical school. I always
knew Margery could fend for herself. You wouldn't have
recognized her after we'd been married a few years. She
really blossomed." Buddy put his arm around his wife's
sloping shoulders as he said this. "We see each other all
the time. It's a real friendly divorce. When did we last
see them, honey?" Immaculata smiled and looked at the
floor. "Anyway, we get together whenever we can, but
we're all real busy. Did I tell you, Immaculata's a surgeon?"

"I met that man Dale at the convention. He's an idiot.
What does she do? Does she still practice?"

"Are you kidding, Gilbert? She has an office on Park
Avenue, she's on all the best staffs, and she's the founder
of Disabled Marchers. You must know them—they get a
lot of media coverage. It's a civil rights thing for patients.
Handicapped. She's big on that. Gower wants her to do
a regular program, taking questions from a live audience
or mail, but she says it's not real medicine. She's funny.
She won't even study PG, because she says it's her job to
make people healthy, and then they can afford to be

neurotic if they want to. Frankly, she's crazy, but I love her. I mean in a platonic way, of course."

Wanda was pouring sherry and charm all around. She moved about the cozy room, sitting on the arms of people's chairs, asking Immaculata about the children, Farley Smith about his rivals, Erna about the new administration, and Buddy about PG and his famous sort-of-relative the network newscaster.

The dinner went smoothly, because she orchestrated it as if it were an "A" party, and not Gilbert's chumpy college friends coming around to spoil their legends. At the end, she even saved Gilbert from having to ask for Margery's address by requesting it herself.

''WHAT DO YOU THINK?'' Gilbert asked, as she tossed the ruffled elbow-pillows off their bed for the night.

"I think they're all just darling."

"Oh, stop it. So I remembered the past as being racier than it was. I'm sorry."

"Don't be sorry, Gilbert. I thought it was fascinating. Erna Elephant and I are having lunch on Tuesday."

"That's going too far."

"No, I want to. She's brought back a lot of stuff from the Middle East, and she wants to open a boutique. She has a friend in Kabul who will send supplies. With her loot and my contacts, we should do splendidly."

"Wanda, you're not serious."

"Why not? Don't be so grumpy, Gilbert. I'm sorry Miss Margery jilted you, but that's not my fault. We'll have her over, and you can take another look at her. Also," she said, laughing and petting his forehead, "it's not my fault you made it sound as if you'd led a ruthless life in your youth, among all sorts of glamorous people. Anyway, you're not to snip at me if I want to have lunch with a lady. Tell you the truth, Erna reminds me of the embassy ladies my mother used to go around with. In the early days, when I was a little girl. They were always trying to cook up something to make life interesting— for the American community, of course. Nothing else counted. Of course, we hadn't been to London then. But I remember, there was always one who was the heavy flirt, and all the rest were scandalized, or pretended to be, and said she smoked too much and drank and neglected her children. It was all very mild, and the other wives kept her around all the time, on their committees, so they'd know where she was, and also to get new material to talk about. Erna amuses me. And the shop idea really does interest me. I've got to do something, you know."

"Until we have children."

"After, too. Why couldn't I do both?"

"Of course you could." Gilbert was delighted. He had never even spoken to a child since he had been one, and not much liked it then, but part of his getting married had been a sudden yearning for progeny. The risk, he figured, was that they would appear as he had been before he had spent so many painful years renovating himself, but such a child would have his guidance and be able to transform itself more quickly. Wanda's remark was the first concession that she was no longer maintaining she wasn't ready for children. "When?" he asked with a reverent tone.

"Oh, Gilbert, you know I'm not ready for children. You wouldn't want me to lose my girlish figure, would you?"

"Why, what're you saving it for?"

"What?"

"What're you saving it for? In my day, girls used to say they were saving their bodies for their husbands. They could hope to get better husbands that way. Fresh goods went for a higher price. My understanding is that you're already married. So would you mind telling me what you're saving it for?"

"Oh, Gilbert, let's not quarrel. I will, all in good time. Women my age aren't having children yet. Besides, I've seen it spoil too many marriages."

"All right," said Gilbert, "we'll talk about it another year." He felt he was spoiling his marriage quite enough by himself.

Some weeks later, Gilbert got two pieces of mail from the former Doctors Loomis.

Buddy wrote that Immaculata and he had had a marvelous time with him and his gracious and charming wife, Wendy. He hoped they would all keep in touch, now that they had found each other, and enclosed some reading matter he thought might interest Gilbert or maybe his lovely wife. He said a certain government department had given him the go ahead on a PG course for civil servants on a voluntary basis, and he was very excited about it. He also mentioned that he had slipped a word to Margery and Gower about Gilbert and Wendy, and wouldn't be surprised if they let him know the next time they hit Washington.

Margery's letter was brief. It said she would love to see Gilbert, and he should call her when he went to New York. It was signed, but not in her old rolling handwriting, and a secretary had scrupulously noted, "Dictated by Dr. Dale, signed in her absence."

Chapter X

ERNA TRIED AGAIN when she met Wanda Fairchild for lunch. She wore an ankle-length skirt with two Western shirts, one open to reveal the other, and $180 boots; Wanda showed up in a sweater-suit of nubby, natural-color wool, with a knitted beret to match and spectator shoes. Erna ordered a Lillet, instead of a Martini, which was what she usually drank; Wanda asked for Saratoga vichy water. Then Erna got cautious and ordered the pike soufflé, after Wanda had pointedly recommended it—but Wanda explained to the waiter that she wanted to have a broiled rockfish without any butter used in the cooking, and a fresh lemon with it.

When Erna bragged of her husband's career, Wanda pointed out that Gilbert's job threw her into dull company. Erna switched and complained that she was bored with her roles as wife and mother and anxious to find deeper fulfillment; Wanda confided that she loved nothing better than to lounge at home, doing nothing. They ended by agreeing to become partners.

As Wanda explained it later to Gilbert, Erna was willing to put up the capital and do the work, but she lacked entrée and what Wanda had to call dash. "What do you know about commerce?" Gilbert asked.

"Why, nothing. You know that."

"Wanda, how can you run a business? People go to business school for years. They go into executive training programs at stores to learn merchandising, advertising, I don't even know what. You can't just open a shop. With a Georgetown rent? You're crazy."

"Aren't you? Did you study political science? If you are lucky enough to be born with style and nerve, you sell that. You just have to put a high price on it."

"Okay. Try. My grandparents didn't know anything about it, either, I suppose, and they made a success of it."

"That's right," she said. "I forgot your family was in trade. Nobody in my family ever was, as far as I know. Sometimes I think that's why we have trouble understanding each other."

"No doubt," said Gilbert. "No doubt." But he conceded that she had as much right as he to barge her way into a field she knew nothing about, and he was glad for her to be doing something besides assaulting the town socially. Erna was at least not a less wholesome companion for her than Toby, with whom she had been hitting the embassy national day circuit until Gilbert asked her what she would have thought if he had been going about socially with a secretary. She seemed calmer now, sitting by the fire with scissors in one hand and magazine clippings all over her crocheted lap rug. He swallowed her telling people that she had been "involved in the boutique scene in London" by reminding himself that it was true if you counted involvement as a shopper.

Erna's function in the scheme seemed to be to annoy him. Every time he noticed how badly her face matched the color of her neck, he felt his teen-age triumphs being mocked. Erna's anxiety about what Wanda thought of her was stronger than any emotion she had shown in the short time she had been under Gilbert's spell. The more Wanda showed that she outranked Erna, the more Erna tried to prove that she could learn, if given the chance.

It seemed unlikely that she could, and Gilbert failed to understand what Wanda was getting out of the association. She at least had the grace to look apologetic when she informed Gilbert that they absolutely had to go to Erna's to dinner.

They had heard a great deal about the house, none of it specific. Erna had put her small inheritance into it, and was unveiling it at this dinner, completely furnished after months of work, for Wanda's discriminating eyes.

They knew from the Cleveland Park address that it was expensive. It turned out to be one of an attached cluster of three brand-new Federal town houses, on the lot where one large dilapidated estate had finally relaxed beyond all repair. Erna's set, of which her house was the center, was an oddity among the seedy sprawling clapboard houses of the old Democratic neighborhood, long the pride of high officials whose liberality was expressed in the magnanimity of having children, bicycles, dogs, and block parties.

Erna had unfailingly hit the wrong note again. The style of the house was correct Washington, and the neighborhood was right, but the two didn't go together. Almost anyplace else in the city, such a house would be more than respectable, with its reproduction Colonial lighting fixtures at the front door and over the dining area; in Cleveland Park, any shack would have done. The combination was a disaster, like Erna in her hostess costume of tartan skirt and tank T-shirt.

It was furnished in basic Foreign Service. The sofa and three chairs were upholstered in hemp, and there were bright pillows on them in primitive tapestries, some sprinkled with bits of mirror. There were Thai stone rubbings, African masks, and Finnish weavings on the walls, along with scenes of modern Haitian rural life. On the Indian rug were several Indonesian tables, on which were Japanese lamps, Mexican ashtrays and an international collection of clay figurines of donkeys.

Erna's husband was not yet back from Afghanistan, and she had as host her brother, Christian, who said he dealt in commodities, and who treated Gilbert as an equal, even an old school friend. Gilbert was at first flattered to be recognized by one of the lords of his class at Harvard. He momentarily forgot that in the crush of the outside world, any Harvard graduate at all, even so unlikely a one as he, was endowed with all the attributes of the New England aristocracy—by those who hated them. He had also forgotten that Christian was not the genuine article. But his errors of the moment vanished when he saw how grudgingly and apologetically Erna watched her brother. Indeed, the pose did not wear well. Gilbert considered it lucky now that the hopelessness of his ever passing had prevented him from trying and had made him seek an original pose. Wear always took the shine off the dross, and even Erna, who was married to a version of the real thing, showed her true metal now.

Christian, who had a hearty laugh, told hilarious stories about his wife, from whom he was separated, and his daughter, who was in love with a horse, and not even a horse from a decent family, but a hack from a rental stable.

The other couple, from the World Bank, were recently arrived from Afghanistan, and the man seemed to be heavily involved with Erna, who was ignoring him for Gilbert, at whom she directed clearly non-sexual deference. She kept dumping little piles of unidentifiable chopped foodstuffs on Gilbert's plate, in spite of his attempts to guard it as he picked away at the curry. The World Bank wife pressed her knee against his; he moved it, she advanced to meet it, and finally, he crossed his other leg so that the foot stuck out in her direction, giving her the choice of nuzzling against the sole of his shoe or giving up. The Oliphant children kept coming downstairs and demanding things, and had to be shouted back up by their uncle, whose nostrils flared when he addressed them. There were three wines with dinner, a cheese course apparently consisting of samples that Erna had brought back in her luggage, and two different mousses for dessert: raspberry with vanilla sauce, and chocolate with brandy sauce. Christian occasionally picked a piece of fruit from the centerpiece, but after examining each one, he put it back.

Gilbert was queasy by the time they pushed back from the crowded round table and filed back into the main part of the same room for Turkish coffee and sweets. When Wanda and Christian returned from a tour of the house, innocently hand in hand, Gilbert took her other hand and smilingly tugged her along until he had her coated and out the door.

"Oh, cheer up," she said in the car, tipsily putting her hand on his knee. "A business dinner once in a while won't kill you."

"I don't know where you find such people," he commented.

THE SORT of social event he offered Wanda, in contrast, was a full-fledged state dinner at the White House, the first of the new administration. Gilbert was stunned when he found it was to be only black tie, and complained bitterly to Liane. He had regarded the candidate's wife's statement that she wanted "to bring back the old-fashioned dignity of the White House" as a sacred pledge to have white-tie dinners and, having invested accordingly, felt as duped as any other citizen who had counted on a campaign promise.

Wanda was frankly excited from the moment the invitation arrived, and Gilbert took pleasure in her anxious consultations, although it was, in fact, his first White House dinner, too. "Oh, I reckon it won't be much different from an evening with our own friends," he told her. "We'll all just sit around on camel saddles, giving each other the eye, and eating till we throw up. You'll love it."

"Gil-bert!"

"Then the President usually tells obscene stories about his wife and daughter. You'll die laughing."

"Gilbert! Now stop." She was covering her face with her hands and peeping out with merry eyes. Things were basically good between them, Gilbert decided.

One thing about the dinner he didn't tell Wanda was that it spoiled things for him to find Margery's name—"Mr. and Mrs. Gower Dale, N.Y. (Mrs. is Dr.)"—on Liane's clipboard dinner list. Since the day with Buddy, he had pictured Margery coming to his splendid office or elegant house, but she was now coming as a guest where he would be a hired hand. His wife would be lucky to be acknowledged by his boss; Margery's husband was being courted. He tried to put some faith in the fact that he would carry official rank, which even television personalities did not, and that as out-of-towners, the Dales might be awed by the occasion.

"I can't help it if that's your old girl friend," Liane said when he complained in general about the quality of the list. "Practically everybody was, it seems. But we need Gower Dale. He's one of the most powerful personalities on television."

"Are you kidding? He doesn't even cover the news— he reads it. What's powerful about that? We make the news. Anyway, personality is right. When's he going to work his way up to being a person?"

"My, my, aren't we particular. Tell me again who you are?" Liane put her hands on Gilbert's shoulders as she said that, but he turned and walked away.

H e   s p o t t e d Margery the moment he and Wanda walked into the Diplomatic Reception Room, while he waited for the card that had come with their invitation to be X-rayed by a military social aide against possible forgery. Wanda was shaking her dress to freshen it after the ride, although the burgundy taffeta, with its old-fashioned rosettes, was pressed flat, like something from the Smithsonian's First Ladies' Dresses exhibit.

Margery was across the room, wearing her daytime eyeglasses with a long gray wool dress decorated with a big rhinestone belt buckle, but her cheeks were flushed, and she looked confident and healthy. She made her way to Gilbert and heartily pumped his hand. "I knew it," she said. "I told Gower you'd be here. And there you are!"

"Here I am," said Gilbert, putting everything he had into his eyes. "And there you are," he added, insinuatingly.

"Imagine! Here we are." Margery gave him a wide grin.

"Don't let me interrupt this," said Wanda. And when Margery turned her booming enthusiasm on her, Gilbert was afraid his wife would crumble into valuable dust. Many years before, he had wincingly watched the President, then a new senator, give Haile Selassie a real American handshake. Gilbert had composed a letter in his mind at the time, to be addressed "To the People of Ethiopia" in accompaniment of a box of powdery bones and linen remnants, such as you find in the Egyptian sections of museums that can't afford mummies. "Here's your Emperor back. We're terribly sorry about what happened to him. We were just trying to be friendly. You know how it is."

"Hey, Gower," said Margery, tugging her husband away from two self-declared fans, one of whom was a cabinet wife and the other the Director of the United States Mint. "Hey, this is Gilbert Fairchild. I told you! And his wife—Wanda? Is that right? Wanda? What's your last name, Wanda?"

"Fairchild," said Wanda, growing smaller as Margery beamed at her. "I mean Clay." She threw an apologetic look back at Gilbert, and then turned to Gower Dale, with whom she exchanged a radiant look. At least, she had thought it was an exchange until a moment later, when she saw the great personality, with his famous dimpled chin and seriously concerned eyebrows, smile at his own wife. Wanda then understood that what she had gotten was his public smile.

"Gilbert, I have things to say to you," said Margery, ignoring the light in which her husband's fondness was publicly bathing her. "Can we have lunch tomorrow? You're welcome, too, of course, Mrs.—Wanda. We're at the Madison. Can you come up? It's easier than going out."

Wanda stood gaping, and Gower gave her his attention for the polite purpose of allowing their spouses to talk privately. "It surely is an honor to be in This House," he said. "No matter how many times I come here, I always feel it's a privilege. Don't you?" He deftly snatched her a glass from a passing tray and told the waiter to bring him an orange juice. "Don't you find yourself thinking of all the history that has passed under this roof?" he asked, after having given his private orders to the help.

"I like your wife," said Wanda.

"Thank you, kind lady. I like her myself."

"I like you, too," said Wanda. She didn't, though.

"Thank you, again," said Gower, flashing the public smile. His eyes, however, were on a tour of the room, and they came back not to Wanda, but to Margery. He waited for a break, dancing attention, and whispered, "I got your juice coming, honey."

Wanda moved over to Gilbert, who noticed that she

held his arm particularly tightly. He smiled, trying to give her a fresh infusion of the reckless glory she had exhibited when she had swept into their drawing room to show him her look for the evening. She lifted her head and smiled back, but she was still clinging as they moved through the receiving line.

In the Blue Room, their names were announced and the President put out his hand. "We're extremely happy to see you in This House," he said, as Gilbert's hand met his.

"I work here," said Gilbert.

"Hey, Gilbert," said the President, looking up and shaking his hand as if the first time didn't count. "And The Bride. May I kiss The Bride? Always love to kiss a bride." Each time the President had met Wanda, over the last year, he had called her The Bride, and it was beginning to annoy Gilbert, who took it as public proclamation that the President didn't know his wife's name.

"*Wanda* and I are happy to be here," he said clearly. "Aren't we, *Wanda*?" Oh, what did he care? Wanda was too flustered to notice, as a battery of cameras had gone off on the kiss, and a group of women reporters had leaned over the velvet rope that corralled them to ask her who she was. Oh, well, he thought, it's better than the jokes about his being a bachelor. No matter how many times he had told the man that the word was no longer innocent, the then-senator had insisted on innocently teasing him about being a gay bachelor.

At the end of the receiving line, some goaty senator had committed the rudeness of addressing words of conversation to the visiting Queen. She was willing to acknowledge having met him before, anyplace he said, but he wouldn't let her off until he had also told her what they had said to each other before, so the receiving line was stuck. Gilbert and the King stared at each other with fixed smiles until the breakdown farther along the line could be repaired, and the train moved on its way. Wanda asked him in a whisper, as they disembarked safely at last in the Red Room, why he had frozen like that. "Because that's the way it's done," said Gilbert.

She smiled at him the way Erna smiled at her when she dropped a useful social tidbit. "You're handsomer than a king," she whispered.

"Yes, but not as rich."

He took her to her assigned table-for-ten, and then threaded his way across the State Dining Room to his place. Each of them, he noticed, had a foreign visitor on one side and a celebrity on the other. His celebrity was a retired movie actress who ran a wigs and cosmetics firm; Wanda's was Gower Dale. Thanks a lot, Liane, he thought.

A small merry-go-round horse looked at him from the center of the table, and his napkin was rolled in a minia-ture stirrup. He smiled at the foreign visitor. "No English," she said pleasantly.

"*Français?*" he asked, afraid of a *oui* that would require him to expose his French. She shook her head, smiling.

"*Español?*" Another shake, with a giggle this time.

"*Italiano? Deutsch?* Come on, give me a hint."

"No English," she said triumphantly. It was final.

"Oh, I get it," said Gilbert.

From the other side, the former actress leaned over and said, "Now, who might you be?" She took his place card, and read, "Mr. Fairchild."

"Got it on the first guess," said Gilbert, wondering why that nifty "Honorable" that preceded his name on letters wasn't used here. "I'm the President's hairdresser," he said. She looked up. "Oh, don't worry. It's an honorary position, sort of like being a Knight Commander of the Bath—you don't really give them a bath anymore. I wouldn't touch a hair on his head. Now—who might you be?"

But all he saw was a back, criss-crossed with silken cords. The table was quiet now, except for the shuffling of paper. Everyone was grabbing menus, placecards, and matchbooks and stuffing them into evening purses and pockets.

All right, thought Gilbert, enough. This is the night I'm going to fight back.

GILBERT'S SOUP PLATE had just disappeared over his right shoulder, and he gave himself until the end of dinner to plot his comeback. He needed a subject. The whole administration needed a subject, and he needed to be the one who chose it. Things were busy enough in the West Wing now, and there were frequent meetings, to many of which Gilbert was not invited. But he knew, through Toby, that they were discussing people, not ideas. People in the Administration, including himself, people in rival organizations, such as the departments of State and Defense, people in the media—it was all about who was with them and who was against them. Campaign stuff, still.

A glazed salmon appeared at his left elbow. A theme, he thought, I need a theme. If I had a cause, I could lead it and defend it and work out strategies for it, the same as when the cause was to elect the President. "*Sauce verte*," said the butler, to whom Gilbert had addressed a quizzical look. *Sauce verte*, he thought. Salmon. Fishing rights. The Law of the Sea. No, they're all lawyers.

Think. Wildlife. Preservation of resources. Exploitation of resources. Development of resources. Energy. No. Think!

He looked around the candlelit room at the alternating black and bare backs against the gilt chairs. Gold. Money. The rich. No. The poor. Been done. Cost of living. Labor. Management. Industry. Imports. Exports. World trade. Let's see—world trade, world trade, world trade. World Bank! Development. Developing countries, Third World, alignment. Balance. Balance of trade, balance of power, balance of— Another set of plates had come and gone, and he looked at his menu card, which he had anchored with his water goblet to protect it from scavengers. Saddle of veal. West. Frontier. New Frontier. No. New—new what? Think!

His foreign dinner partner flashed another smile at him, to indicate her satisfaction with the progress of the meal. He flashed one back, to keep up the appearance of talking that would protect them both and give him the privacy to run a flashlight around the inside of his brain.

He frowned at his mimosa salad and Brie for being no help. Nor was the murmuring room. The trouble was that all of these issues were so hackneyed. He had dealt at length with each one of them in speeches. There weren't any new angles that he could think of, especially as others had supplied the points of the speeches for him to shape, and he had never bothered to find out what any of these traditional subjects really meant. He looked up his ice cream on the menu: *Bombe Glacé la Reine.* Terrorism! he thought. Great issue. Glamorous, exciting, lots of coverage. Dangerous. Okay—might as well save marriage with same effort. Terrorism!

". . . kidnap you and your gracious lady," he suddenly heard someone say. It was the visiting King, who was standing up. A dozen skinny young people in gaudy clothes were arising from different tables and slipping out, against the walls, and re-gathering in the foyer.

". . . how else to lure you to my country," the King continued. They had apparently been toasting for some time. A man sitting across from Gilbert hailed a waiter as if he were a taxi, and indicated, by describing a circle in the air with the same pointed finger, that the supply of goodwill around the table had overtaken that of champagne.

Gilbert stood with everyone else and smiled suspiciously at the throng moving out of the dining room and into groups of two and three to take coffee and liqueurs. They all looked like disguised hijackers; he recognized them from airports, where he had scrutinized them uneasily before what turned out to be uneventful flights. He eyed a man who was standing much too close to the President's daughter. Would we pay to get her back? he thought. We'd probably have to; question of national prestige. Have to negotiate.

An even slimier-looking man was leaning over Wanda. You, we just go in and blast, he thought. And then: This is some issue. Beat up the bad guys and impress the girl. Wanda introduced him. "Gilbert!" she chastised after he said only "How do you do?"

"You don't know what it's like to be married to a workaholic," she said apologetically to the stranger. "My husband never goes to the movies. But you've heard of him," she prompted Gilbert, who said, "Oh, yes," and added, in his thoughts, Let them keep her.

He steered her into the East Room, and, estimating his rank in the crowd, into the sixth row of the roomful of little gold chairs facing the temporary stage. The President went visiting up and down the rows before settling in the middle of the first row, and some of the bolder guests went up to him there with breathless social statements. Gilbert saw the young terrorists from the dining room, now having thrown off their cheap finery and wearing all black, slither into the room from the far opening. Suddenly they all ran out and faced the President with stony faces.

The arts! thought Gilbert. That's it! Support for the arts!

He looked at Wanda, who stared with a cultured half-smile at the dancers, lips turned up but eyes very serious. In London, she said, everybody always went to the ballet and concerts and theater. In Washington, nobody did, Gilbert had told her. Only lawyers from the Justice Department and scientists from the National Institutes of Health. A politician was supposed to be doing important things.

But why not change that? He knew something about painting and sculpture, and Wanda, who had gone a lot to the Kennedy Center when he was off on the campaign, could help him with the performing arts.

"What'd you think?" he asked under cover of the applause, requesting her opinion as a staff report.

"They did this naked in New York," she said.

Gilbert was unabashed. He took Wanda up to the stage afterwards and reached up and shook hands with the leading woman dancer and thanked her for having come. "Was I awful?" she said. "I ate too much before. Not to mention drank."

"You were marvelous to grace these halls," said Gilbert, practicing.

With his new enthusiasm, he introduced Wanda to the Attorney General, the President's press secretary, an Olympic swimmer, a network president, and a Supreme

Court Justice, only the first two of whom he had met before himself, although they all faked knowing him. The Justice seemed to take, and Wanda was soon whispering to him and making him smile, so Gilbert backed away and found an old friend from Congress and asked her to dance. They had to step aside to avoid being mowed down by the state party's leave-taking. The King and Queen were at the door with the President and First Lady, and the entire foreign contingent was funneling out the door behind them.

Another, more relaxed party began. The President stood around, leaning politely to catch the questions of reporters in evening dress, who formed a semi-circle around him. The military aides of both sexes marched out to grab stragglers and draft them as their dance partners. Several men were standing around the First Lady, smiling at her, but none of them asked her to dance, so Gilbert broke through and did.

He saw Wanda's face as he whirled by. Her Justice was still with her, but he was ninety-two and didn't dance. Gilbert considered asking the First Lady to ask the President to ask Wanda to dance, but decided to keep the balance in his favor. Instead, he told his partner that she looked, in her one-shouldered chiffon dress, like a Muse, and that he saw the evening as the beginning of a new Age of Pericles.

"Gilbert's telling me we have to keep the house full of these people all the time," she told Samuel Brewster as she and Gilbert glided to a halt and Brewster handed her a glass of champagne.

"That so? Not if you have to keep them clothed, I would say. They lost the only interest they had, didn't you think?"

"That's not really the point," said Gilbert. "The point

is, why should we be the only capital in the world in all of history, really, where the leaders aren't the greatest patrons of the arts?"

"Didn't know you cared," said Brewster. "I thought you were all work and no play. Say—some of us have a little chamber orchestra going. Sundays at my house. You would be most welcome. What do you play?"

"I'm usually working on Sunday," snapped Gilbert, but they didn't notice his embarrassment after he had said that, because the First Lady was busy quizzing Brewster about the membership of the group, and laughing over who played what.

The President was beckoning to her, and they quickly waved at the guests and headed for the elevators so that everyone would feel free to go home or to stay and relax. Wanda's Justice was standing there in his coat, holding his wife's coat for her and telling her to never mind but come on.

Gilbert rescued Wanda from watching this scene by asking her to dance, and then they left, passing Liane, who had a long strand of hair hanging down the middle of her face and was tossing down a glass of champagne.

"Swell party," he said.

"It wasn't supposed to be fun," she retorted. "I thought it went off very well."

G ILBERT OFFERED Margery lunch at the White House Mess, and still, she insisted that he come to her hotel room. She was carrying on a conversation with her husband while Gilbert was trying to make the arrangements. Normally, he hung up on people like that. Now he just held the telephone and listened to her tell Gower to take her dress bag back with him and have the dress sent to the cleaners.

"Why am I doing this?" he asked himself on the chilly walk over. He had been curious to see Margery; he had seen her. He had registered the fact that she had married someone famous, and she had registered the fact that he had been the only man to dance with the First Lady. If she had bothered to stay for that. Gilbert hadn't been able to find her or her husband after dinner, and had the awful feeling they had left. Out-of-towners, who are thrilled to be in This House, where so much history has been made, are not supposed to hightail it out of there the first chance they get.

He reflected that for all her blustering glow and brand-name husband, Margery was still Margery. Of course, she had married—she had married Buddy, too, hadn't she?—but she had also insisted that he come to her hotel room, and she made sure that he heard her say good-bye to her husband. Gilbert was uncertain how to deal with her. He had settled happily into marriage, not necessarily committed to the principle of fidelity, but contented with the practice of it.

Margery had the advantage of living in New York, where she was unlikely to waylay him in his daily life. The husband might welcome some excuse for diversions of his own. Gilbert felt kindly towards her, and he recognized that she had risen enough in life to be able to claim him as an old friend in a way that in Buddy was a liberty, but he wasn't promising anything.

The desk clerk asked which of the Dales' rooms he wanted. They had taken a suite and two extra rooms. Gilbert had to go to the house telephone and ask Margery. It was not in her favor that she was causing bother. When he knocked, some kind of stewardess showed him in and told him to sit down.

"No, thank you," said Gilbert. Margery's case was getting worse.

"I'm Derry. Gower's secretary?" She put it as a question.

Gilbert said nothing, but looked at his pocket watch.

"You work in the White House?"

"Yes."

"That must be exciting?"

"History in the making," said Gilbert.

"Oh, I know," she said. "But not every day?"

"Oh, yes. We already did some today."

"You've met," said Margery as she entered the scene. "Gilbert, I really appreciate your coming. I know you must be busy, so I've ordered lunch."

He walked over and kissed her. "I have a little time, but not much."

"I have so much to tell you. How many years has it been? You look terrific. Your hair's different, isn't it? I'm so happy to see you again. I've got some notes around here someplace about what I want to say."

"Shall we, uh, go someplace where we can talk?" But as soon as he said it, the door was flung open, and two men wheeled in a table and began setting up its leaves.

"It's all right," said Margery. "Derry doesn't work for me. She's just filling in because my secretary didn't come down. Gower's gone back, and he said to tell you he's sorry. He ordered lunch, so I don't know what we're eating. I can get something else if you don't like it. Here's what I wanted to talk to you about." She put on her glasses, and read to him about discrimination against the handicapped in education, public accommodations, and transportation. The secretary walked in and out, and so did a waiter and bartender.

"All right," said Gilbert after a while. "You," he said to Derry, "go get your own lunch downstairs. I don't want to see you back here for an hour. Make that an hour and a half. You," he told the hotel employee who stood with a coffeepot poised, "clear this mess away right now and shut the door." It took fifteen minutes and more questions, but then Gilbert put the chain across the door, motioned Margery to the sofa, and sat down next to her. She took off her glasses. He took off his.

"Gilbert, you know how I feel about you. Will you help me?"

Gilbert only paused for a moment. "Yes," he said, putting his hand out for hers.

Margery was looking shyly the other way. "I don't like to ask—I know how many people must be after you. But, you know, if the President really made a point of this, if federal codes and regulations were enforced, if children saw people in high offices who had disabilities and saw them as people like everyone else, it would make such a difference. Gower knows about public relations, I don't pretend to. He says it would be wonderful if you would help. Visibility, he says—you could do it. Please, Gilbert?" He was watching her closely when the intensity expanded into a huge smile. "Hey," she said.

"Hey," said Gilbert softly, smiling back. He had missed seeing the tall rosy boy who had appeared from the adjoining room and now came to sit at their feet.

"Hey, Owen," said Margery. "Stand up. This is Mr. Fairchild from the White House. Did you know Mother had a beau once? Where's Petey?"

"Dunno," the boy said to Margery. "Hi," he said to

Gilbert. "Hey, Mom? I'm going up to the Hill and lobby. Want to come?"

"How many are there?" asked Gilbert, conscious of sounding like somebody's old beau. "How many lobbyists?"

"They're twins, Owen and Petros. They'll be fourteen next month. Can you imagine? Hey, Owen? I want you back here at three, okay? I promised Daddy we wouldn't be late tonight. Did you check out of your room? I'd love to go with you, but I can't."

Gilbert immediately rose. "No, no," she said. "Don't you go away. Run along, Owen. Did you check out of your room? I bet Petey's up there."

The boy kissed her, waved at him, and left, without answering any of her questions. Margery shrugged at Gilbert. The boy, he had noticed, was beautiful. Gilbert was secretly afraid that if he had children, they would be awful, awkward, shy, homely versions of his very young self, exposing him to the world, and yet here was dumpy Margery with a beautiful child and apparently another to match. The boy had kissed her, too, voluntarily.

"Did you know he was in there?" Gilbert asked, realizing that with her son in the adjoining room, Margery had probably not intended to seduce him. Even Margery.

"I hope he isn't rude if he goes around knocking on doors at the Capitol—did he say why he was doing that? I wonder. I don't know why he has to nap in Petey's room. He made such a point of getting a separate hotel room, and Petey was perfectly happy to take the second bedroom here, and now I don't even know where he is."

She took up her glasses and her notes, and Gilbert took them away from her. Well, she said, in answer to his questions, she had married Buddy, as he knew, and then— then she stopped. "Then I guess I married Gower."

"What do you mean, you guess?"

"You don't know anything about it?"

"How could I?"

"I guess Buddy didn't tell you. He's still sensitive. I thought maybe you had seen something in the papers. It was kind of a mess, although, of course, it was a long time ago."

It seemed that when Margery and Buddy were interns, Gower was being a radio personality in Boston, married to a fashion model. They met through Buddy's sister, and fell in love immediately. Gilbert had a hard time picturing it, but that's what Margery said. "And so we got married. I was pregnant with the boys, of course."

"Why didn't you have an abortion?"

"Oh, no, you don't understand. We did it on purpose. It was the only way to get Buddy to agree to a divorce. Look, Gilbert, this was a long time ago. We celebrated our fourteenth anniversary this winter. See?" She put out her capable hand, with its close-clipped nails, and showed him a digital watch surrounded by diamonds.

"Are you happy?"

"Not entirely," she said. "I'm happy when I'm seeing patients, making the rounds, talking to students—you know. It's a luxurious life. But it drives me crazy every time I go into some obstacle course, like the damn school the boys go to, and they purposely fill them with carpeted hallways and then say they can't educate children who can't walk. I feel so frustrated all the time, Gilbert. And I'm not really a crusader type."

"Margery, can I ask you something? Your other boy. He isn't sick, is he, in some way?"

"Oh, no. He'll turn up, probably five minutes before the plane leaves."

"You know what I mean. You obviously know these things first-hand. It must be somebody close to you."

"You're just like Buddy," she said, taking back her glasses and getting up.

Gilbert was stung. "How can you say such a thing to me?"

"Motives. Everything has to have a childhood something or other. I'm a surgeon, Gilbert. I see lots of sick people. Sure, I get fond of some of them. Others not. Why does there have to be something personal in it for me? I didn't expect this of you, Gilbert. You're supposed to be in the public service, you know."

"I was just asking."

"No, Gilbert, I run into this all the time, and it really makes me mad. That's what finally made it so I couldn't stand Buddy any more, always looking at himself. It was just another version of Gretchen, Gower's first wife. This is nothing against her, and I must say she was marvelous about everything, much more mature than Buddy. But she thought her life depended on her looks, so she was always examining her face for wrinkles, and she wasn't twenty-five yet when they got divorced. I'm not criticizing her—but she was looking in the magnifying mirror all the time, and God, we were so sick of the two of them. I'm sorry if I sound heartless. Really, we didn't mean them any harm. We just fell in love—people do. But we tell our boys, 'Don't come around and tell us how bored you are, or how depressed. There's a whole world out there.' They're nice-looking kids, and there are always people at the network who want to put them on the air or something. I said absolutely not. There are too many people in the world employed at doing nothing. Just being on television talking, or something.

"I know you're going to say I married one. But believe

me, Gower hasn't had an easy life since we met. His parents were rich, and he got into broadcasting at the right time, but he had to take care of the babies while I was a resident, he runs the household, he gets jobs for my people, he does lots of things. And the main thing is, he cares about the world. He cares what happens. That's what makes him so good reporting it. You know, grown people have got to be interested in something besides themselves. Kids, too, for that matter. Owen's gotten interested in my Disabled Marchers lately. He's probably getting thrown out of people's offices right now, bullying them about it. Petey doesn't care about that, he wants to be an actor, only he's really serious about the theater. He reads, he goes, he hangs around backstage and learns lighting and sound and everything."

"Margery, please don't tell me I'm Buddy again, but Buddy's sister—she was your sister-in-law. She was handicapped. Wasn't that even a little influence on you?"

"That's right, I forgot. She's partially blind. So?"

"Nothing."

"She's as bad as he. The only worthwhile thing she ever did was to introduce me to Gower."

"What made you think of me again, Margery?" He was looking at her plump arms, her energetic hands, then up to her bright eyes. Her glasses were the kind that had been considered smartly severe decades ago, when she had gotten them: black frames, but slightly turned up at the outer corners. What were then dowdy, no-nonsense spectacles with round gold frames, were now what Wanda wore, on a velvet ribbon around her neck.

Margery rested her head back on the sofa, and Gilbert moved closer to her. "Well, of course, the first thing that made me think of you was that Buddy wrote me he'd seen you and you were interested in his project, and then

Gower said maybe if you were that hard up for something to do, you could help me with mine. Does that sound selfish? That was the great lesson I learned from you, Gilbert, to be selfish. Remember that fall I discovered I could have two lovers?" She laughed. "A nice girl in the Fifties with two lovers? My boys would die if they knew, even now."

"If you liked it so much," said Gilbert coldly, "why did you marry Buddy?"

"Well, Gilbert. You know. It was still the Fifties. He was ready to marry me, and you weren't. I would have felt kind of left out, not being married, especially in medical school when you don't have time to fool around. I liked having Buddy to come home to. I guess it was because medical school was so rough. I ended up having to work my way through, you know, because my father died two months after I entered. I'm glad he never knew his savings didn't amount to anything. I needed Buddy for a while. But meaning well isn't enough. I moved on, and I just wasn't a little girl any more who needed anyone."

"And Gower?"

"Well, yes. Believe me, he's wonderful. I hope you'll get to know him. But even he accuses me of forgetting he exists. I had to get my practice going, and I was having the babies, and for a time there, I wanted to make money. I did, too. Stinking lots of money. And then it was my group. I'm ashamed because I forget to watch the news some nights, and he comes home and says, 'How was it?' and I say, 'How was what?' Isn't that awful? I was brought up to believe that it was the job of a wife to be understanding, and if she wasn't, she got left. It's a good thing we can joke about it. Ah, well. Yes, I do need him. He's kind of cute, isn't he? Lots of people think because he's so handsome he couldn't be all that smart, but it isn't true."

"Margery, you've got a sex object."

She giggled. "Tell me about you. Your wife is kind of odd-looking, isn't she? I mean, old-fashioned. I think it's neat. What does she do?"

"She's going into the fashion business."

"Oh-oh. Gower's first wife went into the fashion business once. I guess I told you. Listen, Gilbert, can I ask you something? Please? Can I get you some stuff to read? Can I send you some people to talk to? We've got people who can tell this much better than I, and we believe in having disabled people handle everything. I'm just talking to you because I know you."

"Thanks a lot. But sure."

While she was emptying a big briefcase of reading material for him, the telephone rang. "Honey," she said into it, "I told you I want you back here. Now. Daddy said he'd pick us up if we can get the four o'clock shuttle, but he can't do it later. That's great, but you tell me about it on the plane. Owen went off some place, but he's going to meet us here, and he promised me he was all packed and checked out. See if you can find out what happened to Derry, will you? Daddy left her here because he doesn't think I'm capable of getting you all to the airport, and I think he's right, and now I can't find her. No, my friend is still here. Why don't you call Daddy as soon as Owen turns up, and tell him we're on our way? No, dear, I really want to get home and see Daddy before he goes to the studio. Come on, I want to talk to my friend now. Good-bye. Tell Daddy the lunch was delicious. I don't know, shrimp, or something. Okay, honey, good-bye."

"Good-bye, Margery," said Gilbert. "I like the way you turned out."

"Oh, I have a few more minutes. I was just trying to hustle the kids along."

"I work, too."

"That's right, you do. Will you really talk to people if I send them?"

He kissed the shiny tip of her nose and left the suite and the hotel, just another middle-aged man going back to his bureaucratic job after eating too much lunch and failing in his fantasies.

When he got back to the White House, he found a request to prepare a summary of television themes they had used in the campaign, and the ratings of different shows on which each had been emphasized. There was a message from Liane, asking if he wanted to talk about the entertainment for the British dinner coming up, and one from Wanda, asking what he thought of the name Eighty Days. Toby took long messages.

"For what?" he asked when he called Wanda at home.

"For the store, of course. In a boutique, the name is everything."

Chapter XI

"LET'S GO through this once again," said Gilbert. "Me boss. You secretary. You do what I say. Not do what you think."

"I can't stand that man," said Toby. "I'm very sensitive to vibes, and you should take advantage of it. I'm telling you, I get bad vibes from him. B-aaa-d."

"All right, let me explain this once again. I know it's hard, but pay attention. I do not care what you think. I don't care. You can stop vibrating. I'll see whomever I please, and I am not asking your advice. It's a free White House; understand that. I am asking you to make his visit here comfortable—in fact, I am ordering you to do so—and

I resent having to say it. This is the same courtesy we extend to anyone who comes here."

"It's not the same. Last time, that man cranked at me from the moment he got here. He didn't like being carried down the stairs, and never mind that I had to beg people to do it. The carpet was too thick for his wheelchair. He didn't like the threshold on your office. I'll spare you the trip to the bathroom—that was beyond belief. I am not a nurse. And do you think he was the least bit grateful? He is, without a doubt, the rudest creature I ever met in my life."

"Tell me, Toby, are my other visitors grateful to use the bathroom? What are you doing, collecting tips? I don't know if that's dignified. Why don't we put in a pay toilet, instead? That way, they wouldn't have to be grateful, and we'd make more. Don't you think we could probably charge a dollar? After all, it's the White House.

"Listen to me, Toby, I want a ramp on those steps, and I want you to find one, and I want it there at three-thirty —no, at three, so I can inspect it. White House secretaries do not tell their bosses that something can't be done—they find out, and they do it. I'm going to send you back to Katie Gibbs for a refresher, you punk. Of course, there are ramps. I've seen them myself, in the East Wing. You ever heard of President Roosevelt? Probably not. But you better believe he went to the bathroom whenever he felt like it, and he didn't have to thank the clerical staff for letting him do it. Now you either get a ramp there, or you will lie stiff on the steps and let Mr. Wollonby run his chair over you. Is that clear? And while you're at it, why don't you take out your manicure scissors and give the rug a haircut? On your hands and knees. Where's my tea?"

Toby, tight-lipped, turned on his heel. When he reappeared, he shoved a used Lily cup with a tea bag tag hanging out of it at Gilbert, instead of the china cupful of English Breakfast he usually served in the morning on a wicker tray with the mail. But the ramp was in place when Gilbert sneaked out for a look after lunch. "You're the best secretary a boy ever had," Gilbert said to Toby's haughtily averted head when he returned to the office. "I could just give you a big old kissie."

"I'm on my lunch hour," said Toby. "I don't have to talk to you now. Sir."

NEVERTHELESS, John Wollonby arrived angry. The ramp had been narrow and set at a perilous angle. The two colleagues he had brought with him had been insulted. The double amputee veteran had been called Son by a tall Secret Serviceman, and the guard at the gate had not talked directly to the one with cerebral palsy, but had put his questions about her to Wollonby, as if she were his child.

The gold carpeting had been bad enough on the wheelchairs, but television cables laid across the entranceway made it impossible for the three chairs to cross until the cameramen, who had been found in the lounge playing a two-administrations-old game of gin rummy, had grudgingly removed them.

"I'm very sorry," Gilbert kept saying. "You see how much we have to learn."

"When are you planning on getting started?" Wollonby replied. "This year? This Administration? This century?"

Gilbert, who had begun to accustom himself to the woman's slurred speech, was grateful to make out her suggestion that they not pick on Gilbert, but get to the business at hand. "This *is* the business at hand," snapped Wollonby. "I pay my taxes, Mr. Fairchild. I think I should be allowed access to the White House when I try to come here on important national business at the express invitation of someone who purports to be interested in it. I did not request this meeting."

"I can only say how sorry I am," said Gilbert, who was getting edgy at having to keep being sorry when he had meant to appear magnanimous. He had always enjoyed having visitors because he was good at putting them at a disadvantage, with little waits and carefully positioned chairs and strategic interruptions, all the time being faultlessly polite. But this time, he had felt his heart sink when he heard the commotion in the hallway. He looked at them now, their scruffy wheelchairs in a semi-circle in front of his desk, contrasting with the band-box cream sofa on which he usually put guests who were too brisk, so that they realized they had to be on their best social behavior. The veteran was good-looking and robust—what there was of him—and meticulously polite. Gilbert hoped it was military deference to a superior, but suspected it was contempt. Gilbert felt the woman would be the easiest one to charm, if he could establish a line of contact to her obliquely hanging face, but he couldn't get through his own curiosity and embarrassment.

He had said he needed facts, and they brought him reams of material—messy photocopies of statistical reports, pasted-up newspaper clippings, letters, diagrams, bent photographs—all documenting lost battles. Architectural barriers, educational barriers, health care inadequacies, fights with transportation systems, bureaucratic battles, individual cases written up in optimistic feature articles in publications no one had ever heard of, letters politely expressing disinterest and refusing appointments.

All this unusable junk was crisply presented. Just what was the White House interested in? How did this relate, if at all, to the President's Committee on the Physically Handicapped? Was that to be expanded? Was there going to be a real commitment at last?

"Well," said Gilbert weakly, "we're just beginning. Leave what you can with me, and I'll get back to you." His voice sounded to him like the tone of those awful letters he had been glancing through while they talked. "You have my personal commitment," he added recklessly, but still, he imagined that the three were exchanging cynical smiles.

"Dr. Dale spoke highly of you," said the veteran. "That's why we're here."

"Really?" asked Gilbert. "Did she?" He was also thinking that they came because it was a thrill to do so, but stopped because it occurred to him that they might really think it no bigger thrill than using the White House bathroom.

He supervised their painful exit from the West Wing, wishing he had stuck with the arts.

''You see?'' said Toby. "I told you. No matter what you do, it doesn't satisfy them. If you ask me, that man likes nothing better than to make people like us feel guilty. He had himself a field day, making everyone run around just for his convenience. Even you. I hope you're happy."

"Toby, I want you to remember what went wrong, so it doesn't happen when they come again."

"Yes, sir, Mr. Fairchild. They're coming again. Our *casa* is their *casa*."

"Toby, don't give me a hard time. It's no extra work for you, and you know it. What's bothering you?"

"I'll tell you what's bothering me, Mr. Fairchild, sir, if you really want to know. It makes me sick to see you playing the phony like that. After all we've been through together, it's the first time I've seen you make a complete ass of yourself. I suppose you want to impress that fat old flame of yours. Gilbert, we have work to do. I'm not kidding. You're living on past glories around here, and if you don't shape up in a hurry, you're going to find yourself writing Presidential greetings to the B'nai B'rith convention, and I'm not going to type them for you, either."

A tall blond woman in an expensive tweed suit appeared in the doorway and said, "This must be your boss, Toby?"

"Later," Toby snapped. "The President wants this right away." She waved, and Toby said from between clenched teeth, "Brewster's secretary. They're moving in today. Going to be Counsel. Why didn't you at least go to law school?"

"What do you mean, phony? I didn't expect it from you."

"Phony! Phony! You know what I mean! All this bleeding-heart stuff because some jerk lost his legs, probably in a car accident on a date. These people have a free ride, my dear—it's your taxes and mine that support them all their lives, so they can run around making trouble and telling us all to feel terrible because we're normal. Look at you. I know what you're doing. You can't stand it because your girl friend married a bigger celebrity than you. I can understand that. God, that I should live to see the day when I'm scolding you for not keeping your sex life out of the office. But that is what I'm saying, Gilbert.

You have got to get to work. Look, I'll help you. We'll find something. We'll be back up there, I promise you. All you have to do is pull yourself together."

"I just noticed something," said Gilbert, who had slumped down in Toby's visitor's chair, his head on its back and his chin on his chest. "You like me. You're fond of me."

"Oh, shit," said Toby. "You're just a meal ticket to me. If you go, I go. And I like it here."

"No, it's more than that. Okay, let's talk. But you have to believe I'm leveling with you." Gilbert got up and walked to the doorway to his own office, and stood with hands in his back pockets, rumpling his jacket.

"Go ahead, " said Toby. "I don't promise anything, but I'll try."

"Good. You say I'm a phony. True. But that's my specialty. I'm a very good phony. And you're my apprentice. If I weren't such a good phony, you wouldn't be here. That's politics, kid. You know a good thing when you see one."

"Granted," said Toby. "You sound more like your old self already."

"So why should you get upset if I use a bunch of—of cripples for my own devious purposes? Isn't that a smart thing to do? That's our issue. Right?"

"No," said Toby. "That's not our issue. Wrong."

"Why not? Bleeding-heart stuff, you said it yourself. Terrific!"

"No," said Toby, who had also stuffed his hands in his back pockets, having, in the course of his job, appropriated all of Gilbert's mannerisms, so that anybody watching the two of them off-guard had the impression that they were part of a long chorus line of people all doing the same things at the same time.

"It doesn't work because you really think you really care. You're scared of the new people, so you're trying to tell yourself that you're better than they are, because you're sensitive. You can't be a phony in the honest sense if you believe it yourself, Gilbert. The best thing about you is that you're always truthful—no hidden corners, no surprises, no being blackmailed by your own soul, because there's nothing to expose that you don't already know. That makes it easy to fool others. I learned that from you, sport, and it's the most valuable thing you ever taught me. And let me tell you, it's disgusting now, to watch you, of all people, lying to yourself."

"But I feel something, Toby. I can't tell you what, but it's not just the scare, and it's really not jealousy of Margery Dale's husband. That you've got to believe. But Margery is on to something. She's happy, and what's more, she's successful."

"Margery's a doctor. It's her job to feel sorry for misfits. You want to screw her, that's your business. But don't go telling me she's found God."

"You don't think I could get genuinely worked up over something like that?"

"Frankly, no."

"Okay, but, Toby, I'm on the verge of being on to something. Not just the handicapped issue—something larger."

"The day you get born again, I quit."

"No, no. I wasn't even born the first time. My mother is too absent-minded. Besides, that's been done. But so have dirty tricks. Done to death. Any idiot can play those games now, so it's time for me to quit. Don't forget that I invented all that manipulation."

"Maybe you'll get the Presidential Distinguished Service Medal, or whatever it is."

"No, but I mean I can find the next thing."

"Like what?"

"I don't know yet, Toby. I'll tell you what. Give me, say, two days to think it through, and Friday we'll have lunch, anyplace you want, and we'll work out the strategy. Okay? I'm going to clean up my desk now and knock off and go home and think."

"Mrs. Fairchild is expecting you to pick her up at five-thirty. You're going to the opening at the Hirshhorn."

"Yes, that's right. What's opening, by the way?"

"How would I know? Art. It's an art opening. Six to eight. What's the difference what's opening?"

"Toby." He put his hand on Toby's shoulder. "Buck up, Toby. We'll get back on top. Only better."

"I certainly hope so," said Toby. "When you get philosophical, it gives me the creeps. She said you don't have to change. Clothes. For the opening. I'm going to knock off now, too, if you don't mind, and I promise you I'm not going to think."

Gilbert removed his hand. "No. I expect you to be here to answer the telephone."

"Sick leave. I'll take sick leave. Your friend gave me a headache. Oh, never mind. I'll stay." Toby flinched, however, when Gilbert brought the hand back to clap him proudly on the shoulder.

WANDA HAD their car out front, and was in the driver's seat. Toby had called to inform her when Gilbert left the office—just one of his little services. She motioned him to the passenger seat, on which there was a Florentine gilded wood tray with a plate of open-faced sandwiches, a half wine bottle, and a stemmed glass.

"Wanda, I've got to admit you're cute," he said. "Let me just get rid of my briefcase. Be right down."

The pigskin case she had given him was stuffed with papers from his afternoon visitors. They were so messy, with their coffee rings and torn corners, and they contained such messy sagas that he was anxious to get them out of his clean office and not happy about having them in his cozy house. He had no intention of reading them, and was discharging his duty by carrying them around. He owed them that much.

Back outside, he picked up his tray and maneuvered it into his lap. "Listen, it's cold. You ought to put on the dog." *Putting on the dog* was their phrase from Wanda's wearing the fur coat the senior Fairchilds had given her. It was a young matron's fur, with its mink collar and sealskin body, and she had hated it until Gilbert had succeeded in making her feel it was funny.

She shook her head. "No, it's a funny thing about art openings. I've been thinking about this, because it's the kind of thing I want to be able to know for the boutique. You have to have more drama in a costume than you would have for, say, an embassy reception. But it's so easy to slip over into being original, and that's a total disaster. Then you look like an artist's wife. Do you know what I mean? There's always some artist's wife who is wearing something cleverly improvised. Probably when she was young and she posed for him, it was some carelessly flung bit of red shawl that made the picture, and made him fall in love with her. But now she's older, and she's running around promoting him and they're living better but still above their means, and so she tosses on some gaily colored rags, instead of a real dress, and looks like something the cat dragged in. But the expensive types in the gold balloon pants and hand-painted blouses look just like her. Funny.

Still, you can't look as if you're there as an art dealer or collector or something dreadful like that, either. So that's why I didn't put on the dog."

She was chattering on as they entered the great concrete bunker and glided up the escalator, nudging him occasionally to point out examples, nodding at people they knew on the down escalator. Gilbert had once explained to Wanda the necessity of a married couple's looking as if they had arrived at a party without having been able to finish all the good conversation they enjoyed at home, so that they wouldn't have that lost look of being stuck together with their matrimony until they could ensnare an outsider. Now he couldn't tell whether Wanda's talk was one of those stretch-outs, or whether she was really anxious to talk to him.

"Hey," he said, catching a phrase. "*I* told you that. I made you this whole speech, six, eight months ago, at the East Wing. It was the—Lost La Tours show, remember? There were a lot of artists down from New York? You're a plagiarist."

"No, I'm not. I'm a student. Now that you mention it, you're right. So you see, I pay attention and it all sinks in, eventually. You should be pleased. Besides, it's community property—your ideas are mine, and mine are yours. If I have any. Honestly, I thought I'd made this all up. Okay. Tell me something new, now that you know I listen."

They had been wandering in circles, of course, as it was a circular building, looking idly at the paintings, and appraising the crowd and then deciding that no one there was worth their splitting up over. It was the worst place in town for such interplay, because the circles made people keep running into the same faces they had just nodded good-bye to, coming around the track once more. It gave everyone the sense of having exhausted the party in record time.

So they decided to go to the next floor. Wanda had her arm in Gilbert's, and he was patting her hand in fond recognition of her candidness, so he stumbled as he got on the escalator. "Stupid thing!" he cried.

"What is it, dear? Did you hurt yourself?"

"No. I just hate escalators. They oughtn't to allow them. They're vicious."

"Did it bite you? Where? You know, one day we're going to have to look into putting something in our house. I can't tell you how often I find myself out of breath from running up and down three sets of stairs, just because I've left something on one floor or another. I must be getting old."

"Yes, that's another thing. Why do we have to live in a house built like a grain shaft? It's nothing but a staircase with a few platforms attached. My father's going to drop dead there one of these days."

"Gilbert, shhh. You're shouting. What is the matter with you? I thought you were having a good time. I have an aspirin in my purse, if you want it. Or we could just go home. I've seen enough. There's nobody here."

She searched for the aspirin, but Gilbert put his hand out and stopped her. "I'm just edgy," he said, and told her about his day. "Do you think I'm faking it?" he asked at the end of what he considered to be a fair recital. "Toby thinks I am."

"Of course not. All well-bred people are compassionate. I think all Toby is trying to say is that it might not be the right cause at this time. Which doesn't mean it might not be later. Or that Toby's right. I have perfect faith in your judgment, and I don't think you should let Toby, who is, after all, just a boy, have so much say. To a certain extent it's cute that he's sassy, but I'm amazed that it could trouble you so, whatever he says."

He tried again later, while they sat at their pantry table, almost in the dark, surrounded by colorless cupboards of lined-up wine glasses. They were eating yogurt out of antique china cereal bowls.

"Two questions," he said, thinking it was nice to be married and have someone loyal with whom to share the plots he used to hatch alone, but also that it didn't seem to be as efficient this way. "One is: Why do I care? and two is: Is this really useful to me?"

"I'm glad I didn't marry someone of my own generation. This is fun; I learn a lot from you."

"Gee, thanks. Do you want to hear this or not?"

"Just teasing, Gilbert." Her eyes were smiling, and only a tiny bit condescending. "Go on."

"There has to be a point of identity for a person to get emotionally hooked, and I don't see it. I don't care about starving children halfway around the world, for instance, or here either, for that matter. I've never starved, and I wouldn't know what it was. Would you?"

"I guess I've been hungry. I can imagine it, yes."

"Wanda, you're not seriously suggesting that the hunger of someone on a diet who's thinking about the ice cream in the freezer, the way you are now, is like hunger with no food."

"There's no need to get personal," she said. "Want some?"

"Sure. So hungry babies, or war devastation, or trapping animals, or any of those things people get emotional about, or claim they do, don't reach me. That's honest. But the handicapped thing does. I'm beginning to think it's left over from adolescence, before my college experiment, say, when I was eleven or twelve, and I knew

I had this great handsome dashing soul, but the body didn't match. The struggle was to take this sweaty, bony body and use it as material to act out being the world's greatest lover, or whatever I wanted to be at the time."

"But you were a handsome boy. My God, you told me so yourself. Poetic, Byronic. So what are you talking about?"

Gilbert stopped, ice cream spoon in mid-air. It was so plain from her amused recital of this fact that she knew about his good looks only second-hand. Had he really changed that much? Was it the receding hairline, or the emotional letting down of hair? His youthful beauty had been something he felt he had willed into being, growing the body to fit the part, forgetting that the body might revert when he stopped playing that part. He had little heart to go on talking, but he saw it through. "Anyway, I think there might be empathy for a soul that has to act out its life story in a poor embodiment. Maybe. Two is: What is it in this issue that makes me feel I'm onto something new? I know that the time for clever stunts has passed—I just know it. It was smart when everyone else was plodding naïvely along, but everyone's a trickster now, and people are onto it. In fact, they're so cynical that you are automatically suspected anyway. Look at the way I seem to Toby. And yet I swear to you it's true that I feel something about these people, and that's in spite of the fact that I don't like them."

He went silent, and after a while Wanda pulled his sleeve and said timidly, "May I ask something? It's sort of related."

He had forgotten Wanda, as he talked in the shadows, and now he looked at her to see whom he had chosen as a confidante.

"Erna thinks we should ask Liane, or maybe you, if you

can get the First Lady to our opening. It would completely eliminate our media problem, and establish once and for all the specialness of it's being a Washington place, for a Washington woman. We might even give her a dress she could wear to the opening—say, making it a luncheon, instead of an evening party. My question is: Do you think she would do it, would it be better if you asked her, or should we go through Liane, or should you, and when is the right time to move?"

Wanda, who had been leaning on the table listlessly mushing her ice cream, was sitting up brightly now. "Not yet," he said. Wanda knew she could trust his judgment.

GILBERT WAS CONSCIOUS of flushing when Toby walked in on his telephone conversation with Margery, and just stood there, not pretending not to listen. "Well, that's what I wanted to talk to you about," he went on nevertheless. "It's just easier in person. I'll come up—Thursday? How would that be? Maybe we can have dinner Thursday and I'll stay over so we can talk again Friday if necessary. Is there a good hotel near you? I hate hotels. Well, that's very kind of you. If you're sure it's no trouble. Okay, then, great. See you then."

Toby shook his head.

"Oh, get lost," said Gilbert.

"Whatzisname does his big show Thursday at eight-thirty, so he won't be able to make your dinner. 'The Political Notebook,' on from eight-thirty to ten. Too bad. Why don't you make it a more convenient night?"

"Don't give me a hard time. I'm working on it. This is all connected." He had kept postponing the luncheon discussion he had promised Toby, making up for it by each day raising the quality of this non-existent excursion. "I can't make it today—suppose we go to Jean-Pierre's tomorrow?" "Wanda has some stuff she wants me to do—let's make it Tuesday, and I'll tell you what. We'll go to Jean-Louis's."

Toby arranged for Gilbert to go to New York at midday, so that he could put in an appearance at the office in the morning, seem to step out for an early lunch, and still have much of the day with Margery. Toby was a good secretary. He always assumed enemies were watching.

So it was at about two-thirty that a woman in an ill-fitting white uniform looked him up and down and conceded, "If you're Mr. Fairchild, you're to put your bags here and there's coffee on in the kitchen, that way, and the doctor will be back soon. She's seeing a patient."

"Soon" turned out to be after four. Gilbert had spent the time wandering around the apartment, which must have been put together from two good-sized apartments, because there was no end of rooms, but they were occasionally interrupted by odd hallways with red exit signs.

The theme was brown, lacquer red, and white, with throw rugs over the main rugs, and no curtains or other coverings on the windows, with their Scotch-advertisement views of Manhattan. No Margery he had ever laid eyes on, in any decade, could have had anything to do with creating such décor. There were red walls behind brown and white patterned sofas piled with red pillows, and white upholstered easy chairs (from which it would be easy to fall if you took it easy, because they were bereft of arms) with brown and red patterned pillows.

On the many tables, slabs of glass over rocks or tree trunks, were stacks of huge books with red jackets on the top book in each pile, brown earthenware ashtrays and vases with dead red lilies, and, on the biggest table in front of the ten-person sofa, a collection of different-sized boxes in dark lacquers. They were arranged so densely that there was no room on the table to park a drink.

Farther afield, the unmade nuptial bed, with brown and white herringbone patterned sheets and brown pillows piped in red, was on a platform, and had empty posters at the corners, like natural wood flagpoles. The door on one side led to a man's mirrored dressing room, with shoes and suits lined up according to a color spectrum of grays, blacks, browns, and dark blues, and there was a brown bathroom; the opposite trail led to a red bathroom, and, finally, a real Margery room, lined and paved in loose papers and textbooks. The front rooms of the apartment were neat but dusty, while the private rooms were clean but messy. So were the housekeeper and the cup of instant coffee with dishwasher-bent spoon she had handed him when his explorations led away from the kitchen. She had an air of knowing that he had no right to be in the back room, but of being uncertain whether she had the authority to expel him.

Margery came in wearing a fur coat like Wanda's dog, only in two colors of mink, instead of mink on seal. It also had a fur bathrobe tie. The effect was of an animal coming down to breakfast after hibernation.

She looked pleased to see him and unsurprised to find him in her husband's dressing room. Perhaps the master's wardrobe was considered one of the sights. "Did Mary get you a cup of coffee?" she asked, without seeming to expect an answer. The gesture was supposed to represent the full range of hospitality, for she had no other suggestions to make for his comfort. She pointed to a brown leather chair in the bedroom, the best-smelling piece of furniture he had ever encountered, and outlined her program.

Gilbert had trouble paying attention while Margery tugged at her galoshes and sighed gratefully as he took each foot and pulled. She loosened the belt of her dress, a complicated knit job with braiding that outlined her tummy, and pushed a solitary gray forelock out of her face and into the rest of her dark hair. He sat at her feet after his gallantry with the boots, and stared smilingly until she said mildly, "Gilbert, are you really not listening?" Remembering how uncute he thought it in Wanda to substitute caresses for attention to his words, he retreated to the chair. The room was growing dimmer, and nothing was occurring, except that a White House policy on the disabled was being outlined for him, when Gower Dale walked in and turned on the lights.

"Hello, Fairchild. Making time with my wife, I see."

"I wish," said Gilbert.

"Why don't you guys take a break tonight and go out? I have a show or I'd go with you. Want me to arrange something?"

"I'd just as soon keep working right here," said Gilbert. "This is fascinating." He put all he could into this lie, and it seemed to succeed. Margery looked pleased.

"I'll tell you what," she said. "Gower's got to get ready, and if you'll just excuse us for about an hour—let me give you some stuff to read—then we'll have a nice dinner sent in, and we can eat here quietly, just the two of us. Did Mary show you the guest room? Want a bath? Gower's car comes at seven forty-five."

Gilbert was miffed. Who the hell was Gower Dale to have a car "coming" for him? But he acceded in order to set up his revenge, and went obediently to the guest room with its private bathroom, in which there were no towels. It was only ten after six. He searched for Mary, but by now the vast series of rooms showed no signs of a maid, or even a loafing cleaning woman, being there, or, for that matter, ever having been there. Running out of ideas and patience, he marched toward the master suite, intending to demand a towel from Gower—who was more likely than Margery to know where they were kept —or, failing that, to steal one from him. He had noticed that the red bathroom had red towels monogrammed in brown, and the brown one had brown towels monogrammed in red.

The bedroom door was shut, and Gilbert was startled when he heard noises, and prepared to leap to someone's aid. Then the blood rushed to his face. Only a fool could have misunderstood that human cry. He stood at the door and listened. Gower must be producing the moans, but Margery was the back fence harmony. He tiptoed backwards until he was in her study, making sure he could still hear. It was certainly unattractive, he tried to tell himself. Margery, who never had had an ounce of graceful restraint, had grown into a barnyard. Then he heard whimpering. Was it possible, he thought with desperate hope, that she was only crying? Perhaps she and Gower were having a fight? He listened again, over his own heartbeat. No it wasn't possible. He sat down angrily at Margery's desk, straining, but the sounds had ceased. He was still there, a good time later, when Margery and Gower emerged, as if nothing had happened. He was freshly shaven, and both of them were decently dressed.

"I couldn't find a towel," said Gilbert accusingly. He was angry now. "There are no towels in my bathroom."

"That Mary," said Margery. "Gower'll get you one."

"No, thank you," said Gilbert. He remained sullen all evening, as Margery was oblivious to his expectation of being mollified. Same old slutty Margery, he kept thinking. Only now that everyone's screwing around, she has to be shocking by being virtuous.

H E L E F T before they were up on Friday, scorning to touch the red lacquer tray with its carton of cornflakes that the maid plopped on his bed before he was quite awake. He called in sick from the Washington airport, realizing that Toby assumed he was calling from Margery's apartment. He was anxious to see his wife. If marital love were the fashion of the day, she seemed the logical choice. Fleshy Margery was obscene, anyway, compared to delicate Wanda.

She was in the drawing room with Erna, who always treated Gilbert warily now, as if he might give away something that would endanger her friendship with Wanda.

"Come join us," said Wanda, accepting a cheek kiss "You didn't say hello to Erna. Guess what we're talking about?"

He could guess. So he sat down on a needlepointed footstool and entertained them with stories about the First Lady, and the information that she adored, above anything, receiving things for free. Perhaps Liane could proffer the bribe for them. As he talked, he felt the flattering attention of the two women, looking more rapt than he had seen either of them in bed. No, he admonished himself. Erna was a simpering mess, but not his Wanda, who looked so guileless in bed, in her crushed silk nightgowns, tortoise hairpins scattered on the bedroom floor.

It took a lot of First Lady stories to get her there. She and Erna had listened enraptured, carefully wrapping up each anecdote, tagging it with outrageous price, and imagining the customer for whom it would be fitting. Finally, he steered Erna out the door and asked a pliant Wanda to put him to bed, since he didn't feel good, skip the tea tray, let's just go upstairs, you and me.

They did. He luxuriated in their puffy bed, contrasting Wanda's embroidered white-on-white trousseau linens with the flashy colors of the Dale establishment on which he had had uneasy rest the night before. There was no nightgown at noontime, and Wanda, too, was white, her little china breasts delicately poised on her narrow rib cage.

He watched her face, through everything. It, too, was lean and white, with all the emotion put into the triangular tilt of her eyebrows, which were auburn and only two or three hairs in width. It was the essence of sexuality— the look of a tortured saint. She uttered no sound but one melodious trill. It startled him into self-consciousness, and he realized that his face, too, was arranged in that peaked-eyebrow triangular look, and that he, too, was stifled silent. His expression must be a mirror image of hers. Hers of his. Perhaps she had copied it. They were beautiful lovers, who ought to have gossamer veils blowing across them from an open garden window. Margery was a sloppy animal.

"What's the matter?" she whispered.

"Nothing. I told you I don't feel good."

"Of course. I'll get you some tea." There might have been impatience in her voice, in the way she got out of bed and put on her dressing gown, but it was muted, and, anyway, Gilbert didn't care. He wanted to be left alone. He had done enough for her, with his political stories.

At dusk, after a fitful nap, he got up and went to the White House.

TOBY HAD GONE for the day. After sitting alone at his desk for some time, without turning on the lights, Gilbert stood at the window and stared at his reflection against the dark outdoors.

He had gotten fat. Not fat, exactly, but out of shape. He felt like going outside and letting the wind slap him, but the choice between walking outside the grounds and being mugged, or walking inside the grounds and being stopped every few minutes for his pass, made him cut across the back arcade, without a coat, to head for the East Wing of the White House. Liane was still there, putting away papers in her office that looked like a ship's lounge, and looked pleased to see him.

"Liane," he said, "I've come to a decision. Things have got to change. Life is going to be different from now on."

"Oh?" she asked, and he liked the look with which she watched him, as if she always expected pleasure from him. This was his tried-and-true best friend. But she seemed to think he was going to follow up the statement.

"Oh," he repeated. "Well. It's like this." He was stalling. He hadn't gotten that far. "Liane!"

"Yes, Gilbert? What is it, dear?"

"Liane, I've always been in love with you. I was crazy not to see it. I did, but you were busy, remember? You've always been off with someone else. I've been off with someone else when you needed me—it's like some myth where we're always condemned to miss each other. No more. You and I are going to start life afresh together. Now. We have no choice."

She laughed, and Gilbert, already disappointed at what he had said, at the fact that it turned out to be the same old idea of another romance, when he had expected something really new of himself, got furious. "I mean it," he said, grabbing her arm and pushing her back into her desk chair. She stared at him, and he looked defiantly back. Then her eyes filled. That morning, George had made one of his pretty speeches about how he was trapped into having dinner with some pathetic creature out of simple charity, and Eric reported unflattering things he had said about her to his therapist. "Don't tease me," she said slowly. "I'm a little shaky."

"I was never more serious in my life."

"Gilbert. You know how much I—I care for you. I always have. But, Gilbert, I'm too battle-worn to go through anything. I'm not young, but it isn't even that. Please try to understand."

"Let's go away. You can tell me then."

"How can I? Where?"

But Gilbert had exhausted himself, and he sank back into her sofa, closing his eyes.

"I'll tell you what," she said timidly. "On the eighth I'm supposed to go up to Stony Lake and get it ready." She was referring to the President's private house, his former summer house, and to the upcoming visit of the former and maybe future Chancellor of West Germany. "I'll go up a few days early, and you join me there. You'll have to make some excuse for going, because there'll be no hiding the fact that you'll be there, but once we're inside the compound, we can have it pretty much to ourselves. If you want. Gilbert? Gilbert, please tell me you were joking."

"Are you? Are we really going to use the President's house as a motel?"

"Why not? He's the President of all the people, isn't he?"

"Why not, indeed? Liane, that's why I love you. You could be my twin sister. Sure, why not?"

Chapter XII

THE HOUSE had been a cheap summer place, soon
abandoned by a family who had never developed the
affection to compensate for its deformities. It was a retreat
owned by people who were busy trying to advance. First
the father of the family had deserted it, arguing the ir-
responsibility of subjugating solemn national duties to the
capacities of a whimsical, flimsy, local airline. Then the
children, who were supposed to be deriving some un-
named benefit from the ramshackle neighborhood and cold
lake, got old and bold enough to have other summer plans.
Only the mother had kept up the pretense, using it for
what she called rest, but what was actually the last re-

maining loyalty to the idea that the family wanted to get away together, if only outside obligations would allow them. "Mother needs it because she feels the heat," they all said in justification of the failed hope the house represented.

That was before the Campaign. When Gilbert and a few others needed somewhere secret to hatch their plan of snatching at history, they were delighted to discover the boss's summer house. Conspiratorially they tracked in sand with their bare feet, placed their carry-out cartons over forgotten paperback novels, and enjoyed the contrast between the humbleness of their surroundings and the audacity of their plans.

After the Nomination, others came, and the airline was forced to behave more professionally. Great loads of television equipment arrived and were somehow plugged into the otherwise unyielding ground. Famous people—media, movie stars, and other political celebrities—patronized the local pharmacist, who patronized them back. The lady who ran the newsstand discovered, for the first time in her seventy-nine years, that she was a character. She developed a satisfactory sideline in out-of-town newspapers and local pithy remarks.

Election night, it never got dark near the house, where candles had always been kept in drawers and on kitchen shelves because the electricity, too, had local character. An imported electric sun was focused on the front door all night, and when the younger son opened it, he miraculously set everything into motion. Extra lights, cameras, and microphones came forth to record this event, until the boy, who had forgotten why he had opened the door, retreated behind it.

The next morning, while hot lights and frantic attention were still focused on the front door, crews of a more

silent nature arrived to turn the cottage, originally purchased for its distance from Washington, into a center
of the universe. Plans were laid for equipment that would
make the dusty living room, in which the fidgety family
had never discovered anything more interesting to do than
play Scrabble into a place where nuclear war could be
efficiently declared to the world, if necessary.

It was only after the inauguration that the badly made
house finally became what its owners had conceived it to
be so many years before. While the First Family was still
wallowing in the good White House life, they had begun to talk romantically, first to newspapers and then
among themselves, of what they called home. It had to be
the summer shack; they had no other. Their true dream
house, in a nearly racially segregated pocket of Maryland,
had been sacrificed to the ideas of Gilbert and Liane, who
had chosen them a more appropriate residence on a spring
lunch-hour lark. It was a huge, triangular, renovated
Victorian house on Logan Circle, near transportation, the
White House, and most press offices. It had a porch suitable for impromptu outdoor press conferences. The
neighborhood was still in the stage where it boasted of its
mix of the down-and-out with the up-and-coming. The
children, removed from their offensive public school,
were placed in a private school whose parent community
represented a good range of races and of the political
affiliations of lawyers, psychiatrists, and journalists.

It would have been unthinkable not to sell that house
after the election. The children were grown, the new
job came with a house, and, besides, the place had suddenly jumped $175,000 above its real estate value for
being a historic artifact. So when the family now sighed
for home, as they had previously yearned for the White
House, it was for the poor old summer house.

Liane had been there several times after the inauguration, once with the First Lady and then with teams of decorators and their assistants, all valiantly trying to retain the look of being honored, so as not to look horrified and amused at what they found. In record time, the floors were stripped, and a country theme was developed—a floral pattern in white and shades of green that was manufactured into a limited edition of unpretentious chintz curtains, slipcovers, and careless mounds of pillows. The local utilities were forced to go on a standard White House work schedule. A wing was added for the grown children, who had a new longing for family life. The President and First Lady had grown in stature too great to occupy their old corner bedroom, and required a bedroom and study each. A White House miracle worker made the fireplaces perform and cured the drafts and smoke clouds that the local fireplace genius had declared hopeless.

The house next door was bought by the United States government and turned into a guest house with its own red and white floral country theme; and the house next door to that was made into a Secret Service station, brightened by color television sets. The lady across the road had also received a handsome offer for her cottage, but refused to sell, having become immensely fond of the mediafolk to whom she had been dispensing free coffee, telephone service, and sandwiches since the nomination.

But the fickle newspeople were beginning to drift back to the village for their wants, the inn there having been purchased by a hotel chain that understood about running massive switchboards twenty-four hours a day and taking accurate messages from editors. Two other chain hotels were being slapped into place nearby. A souvenir stand and a citizens' protest movement had been newly founded in town. Most of the residents had been quoted in news stories as bystanders, and some of them had been the subjects of feature stories. From the mayor to the village idiot, they all were at work on their images.

When Gilbert disembarked at the airport, threading his way through the construction work, the rent-a-car clerk gave him only a minute's glance before returning to her book, the just-out analysis of the mechanics of winning: *The President We Deserve*. She knew who Gilbert was, but was used to seeing people whose names her parents, at home, also recognized. She had noted the arrival of Liane Beaufort, too, but had been cool to her. She blamed Liane for the fact that the King and Queen of Belgium were not stopping there on their American visit. Liane was beginning to be the focus for town complaints—that the place was being turned into a circus and that it was not receiving proper recognition.

Gilbert had not been there since the election, and remembered the house as a political headquarters, where layers of papers and paper cups decorated the floors and windowsills. Now, having trudged through the snow, and past the checkpoints of ear-muffed guards who gave it a Russian outpost look, he discovered a country mansion with fires blazing, kitchen stocked, and pure Early American furniture. It was suddenly a house worn smooth by many generations and a century or two of weather for the ease of a homespun American statesman. The odors of untold numbers of carry-out fried chickens that had given their patriotic all had been absorbed into the flavor of a house where special things were always being baked and roasted, and honest homemaking had been preserved.

The honest homemaker in residence was a member of the White House household staff who, like a colonel at the Pentagon, had found that her rank meant little in

Washington and that she had to go afield if she wished to exercise her proper authority. At the moment it was being abused by Liane, who, rejecting all camaraderie, told her to serve trays in the upstairs sitting room and that would be all for the night. The housekeeper retaliated by pointedly calling Gilbert Mr. Beaufort.

He had been given a staff room in the guest house, while Liane, who had come up the day before, had a side room in what was now called the main house. As soon as the house was quiet, they got into the First Lady's four-poster bed, recklessly sprawling on top of the antique American quilt.

"We'll ruin it!" Liane giggled as they rolled about, laughing as much as they were kissing in the thrill of breaking a twenty-some-year taboo. "It won a national prize!"

But they didn't manage to ruin it. "I'm a little tired," said Gilbert. He disengaged himself and settled back against the headboard, putting out his arm for Liane to come and lie beside him.

"Are you nervous?"

"Just tired."

But he didn't know what he was, so they lay together, half-clothed, as if they were spent. After a while, Liane suggested supper, and they found the trays by a carefully constructed unlit fire. Gilbert lit it, poured wine, lifted the covers from the plates, and sank back into the loveseat next to Liane. "This is more like it," he said.

"More like what?"

"I don't know what I'm saying. I mean it's good to be near you."

"It's good to be near you, too," she said, cuddling up and spilling her wine on his pants. She mopped it with her napkin and said, "Hi."

Gilbert did not acknowledge this introduction to a new Liane, but looked for the one he knew, in the way he knew. "Liane, I've been thinking. You want to hear about it?"

"Sure, let's talk."

There was something about the tone he didn't like, because it seemed to replace their former bold frankness with a vulgar new intimacy, but he went on. "Okay, listen. I'm going to go in for virtue." She took back her napkin and ostentatiously spread it on her own lap. "Well?"

"Well, thanks."

"Oh, my God. No. I'm not talking about that. Liane, no, listen, I'm talking about something more important. Oh, God, I didn't mean that, either. Can I go home and go to bed? No, wait—all I mean by that is I need to start this day over again. I'm making a colossal mess. Liane, you just have to remember that there's nothing personal in what I say. That doesn't help, does it?"

"Never mind, Gilbert. I'll try."

"Thank you. I really do love you. Now, what I'm saying is that everybody in the world is trying to do now what I used to do alone, and a crummy place it's gotten to be. Besides, I don't like going with the crowd. So I'm going to abandon it and try the opposite—virtue."

"And you think I'm being wicked."

"No! Come on, Liane, you're not trying. Sexual virtue can be one of the meanest tricks I know. If I got you up here to say I wouldn't sleep with you because it's wrong—why, that would be about as evil as a person can get. That was my genius as a manipulator—I could tell the difference between bad right and good wrong. But why is it when anyone tries to talk about philosophical and moral questions, it always gets sidetracked on sex? You know, that is really a very trivial aspect of behavior."

"Forgive me. I cannot think what brought it to mind. I shall never mention it again."

"You're cute," he said, and kissed her. "Look, I tried evil. At least a moderate amount in a gentlemanly way. I never liked it for its own sake. And where did it get me? All right, the White House, but where else? The summer White House. But seriously, it no longer works because everyone does it, which means that everyone knows the way I think, which means that I can't operate successfully. My whole previous success was based on my knowing how others thought, but their not knowing how I worked. So that's out. Anyway, it's a bore. I never did want to go along with the crowd. If I start doing good things, for good causes, I'll drive them crazy. Get it?"

"Virtue, the ultimate decadence."

"You got it, sister. Let's go back to bed."

This time, they drew out the caresses and the peeling off of clothes, not as anxious as they had been to gallop to a conclusion of which they were wary. Liane seemed to be going through an encyclopedic routine when Gilbert shifted back into his position against the headboard and held out an arm again for her to come up beside him.

She looked up from deep in the covers at the bottom of the bed. "Don't you like me to do this?" She looked both anxious and blazingly cheerful, like an aspiring actress standing beneath a light bulb on an empty stage, refusing to admit that the audition was over. Gilbert felt like the director who has long since made up his mind, and now has the disagreeable task of getting the smile off her face and her body off his stage.

"Liane, please stop. It isn't going to work."

"I'm having a lovely time," she said brightly. Gilbert saw how badly she wanted the part, but he badly needed her to move along. The price would be having to talk about it. He would have to reassure her that it wasn't any lack of talent on her part, but simply that he couldn't use her. If she insisted, he would have to supply reasons why. Why not, actually. He didn't know why not, and personally, he didn't care.

No amount of popular psychology was going to make him interested in this miscalculation disguised as a problem. He was not going to worry over it and fuss over it and classify it as a personal disaster, the way girls he had known in college made pageants out of the Loss of Virginity. He couldn't even work up an interest in what effect his impotence had on Liane's feeling about him, any more than he had been able to interest himself in the ex-virgins' inquiries of "Do you still respect me?"

Yet there was Liane, his own dear friend Liane, looking at him with false eagerness, as if a discussion of the act would do just as well as the act.

He tried to tell her he was older now, skimming over her rejoinder that she was older than he by mumbling that it was different for women. He said that he supposed that it was Wanda, but she made a bigger declaration of her love for George. They were too much alike, he said, which was why he would always love her best, but it made lovemaking incestuous, if not narcissistic.

That helped some. Indeed, to the extent that Gilbert took time away from his discovery of virtue to consider this lesser matter, it seemed the most likely explanation to him, too. But as he walked back to the airport the next morning, he was sorry about it all because he was afraid he had lost his only friend.

Liane had been wildly solicitous. She insisted he take a cashmere scarf—the President's?—when she found he hadn't brought one of his own. She ordered the housekeeper to pack him a lunch, as if he weren't going to switch planes in New York City forty-five minutes later, and be home an hour after that. She kissed him good-bye with abandon, as if she couldn't get enough of him. Gilbert patted her kindly on the backside and left, feeling bereft as he looked at the foreign expression of romance she exhibited for him.

A WEEK LATER, Liane burst into Gilbert's office, shut the door behind her, and announced joyfully, "I did something terrible. You're going to hate me."

"Please do me a favor," said Gilbert. "Don't tell me. All right? As long as you're happy, I don't think it's terrible, I think it's wonderful, and I love you madly and support you in whatever you do. Okay?"

"I told George."

"You told George?"

"I told him everything. Please don't be mad at me. He won't dare say anything to Wanda. This is the best thing that ever happened to him."

"Wait a minute. You told George I couldn't get it up, and now he's so excited he's like a young man again. Terrific. Congratulations. And thanks a lot."

"No, no, no, no, no. Oh, Gilbert. I wouldn't do anything like that."

"Whew. So what did you tell him?"

"The truth. I mean, I didn't really tell him the truth, of course. I told him we spent the night together, and I promised not to do it again. That's all."

"Okay," said Gilbert. "Always glad to be of service. Let me know if there's anything else I can do for you."

"Gilbert! Aren't we brother and sister?"

He took her in his arms, happy to have her back. "Forever. Yes, I love you more than I can say. But I've got a lunch date, so go away."

"Will you come to dinner a week from Saturday?"

"Oh, Liane." He dropped his arms. "Liane, sister dear, what do you want of me? I'm too old for these games. You young people go frolic by yourselves."

"I'm only asking you to dinner. Please, I need you."

"To do what, for God's sake?"

"To eat dinner, of course. You and Wanda. You had us last time. Just a regular dinner party. I promise there'll be other people there and George will be charming. I'm going to tell Wanda you said yes," she added, blowing him a kiss and closing the door behind her.

TOBY CAME IN immediately. "No cheating in the office," he called out. "Shutting the door in my face! Shameless! What'll you give me not to tell?"

"Tell what?"

"Oh, I know. You don't even cheat on your expense account, do you? It's not natural. People notice; don't you think they don't. You're trying to spoil things for them."

"I don't cheat on my expense account because I would like, if you please, to get caught for something more worthwhile."

"What?" asked Toby. "And when?"

WANDA and Erna had been busy with rental agents when Gilbert returned from Stony Lake, and it wasn't until ten days after the trip that he noticed with surprise how Wanda looked at him when she accused him of not really telling her about it. It was only an overnight excursion, and he had been away from home for weeks at a time all the previous year, from the time of their marriage until after the election

"What should I tell you?" he asked ingenuously.

Wanda was sitting by their fireside, making sketches for the interior of the boutique. Unlike Liane, whose talent was for hiring fashionable talent and giving them free rein, Wanda fussed with things herself, putting on her own stamp. He appreciated the quality of her stamp. It was visible in the scene she set for an evening at home. With her hair done up in rolled braids over her ears, the firelight flickering on her face, the soft folds of her brown panne velvet dressing gown contrasting with the primness of its starched white collar, and the work in her hands passing, in the dimness, for some sort of gentlewoman's craft, she looked like the kindly rector's daughter in an early-nineteenth-century novel. Gilbert imagined her cameo head full of wry observations on people and society, although he knew that she was busy planning a store front that would photograph well.

He was supposedly reading, but he preferred to defer his work to enjoy the fragrance of his tea, which she had solemnly poured from a genteely chipped pot. He pictured Erna slapping down a cold Martini for Walter, and even Liane and George with their chrome French coffee-maker, and he gazed fondly at his wife. The gamine who had rushed in breathlessly earlier, with the painted red mouth and jaunty beret, had been another good picture. When Wanda changed her costume, an appropriate backdrop always fell mysteriously behind her.

For this scene, she wore a flirtatious half-smile. "Oh, you know. You and Liane up in the woods together alone. You can't expect a jealous old wife not to pry."

"Alone if you don't count staff and guards and a chorus of local yokels," he said mechanically, noticing the feeling beneath her banter. It was touching to see her worried. His interest in Margery became broad comedy, and his fiasco with Liane, pitiful. To his mental pictures of other married couples at home, he added Margery and Gower, mixing instant milkshakes from packaged powders in a futuristic kitchen they didn't know how to operate. He was happy where he was.

"Liane was funny," Wanda began. "She invited us to dinner, but she sounded urgent about it, and said you had okayed it. You never mentioned it; had you?"

"Yes, she came by a day or so ago. I forgot. We can cancel, if you want."

"Oh, no. The whole thing just sounded odd."

Gilbert tried to think what she was saying. Wanda's ears functioned well, and if Liane had floated her story anywhere into the air, if she had only whispered it to George at home at night with all the doors and windows locked, it was possible that the echo had wafted across the river to Wanda. That was the only explanation for her clumsiness, which he found sweet.

There was no hostility in her question, just a slick of anxiety on top of her graceful wifely demeanor. Gilbert asked himself whether he trusted Wanda's sophistication enough to tell her what had happened. She would have to be clever to understand that the truth was an affirmation of his commitment to her, but he wondered whether anyone except himself was complicated enough to skip

over the tedious question of infidelity, the letter of the
law, and see the meaning.

He did not ask himself, as he sat admiring her troubled
face, whether her reaction would be like George's. He
and Liane might be twins, but they had not married another set. He was used to thinking of George as a buffoon
whom Liane, by some potion, had been beguiled into
thinking a prince in spite of his ass's head.

Wanda was a lady, but it was a gamble. If he told her
and she wept or threatened, it would damage something
between them. But if he won, it would remove her sensing
an absence of truth, and after all, the truth was that he
loved her dearly. Bringing the candle to the center of the
room would illuminate that. It was the crookedness of
Liane's and George's twisted ties that made the glare of
truth between them ugly.

Besides, he had sworn himself to virtue.

"Liane is my oldest friend, as you know," he began.
"Over the years, I've heard all her troubles, and she has
mine."

"I know what's coming," Wanda said, smiling shyly.

"Maybe," he conceded. "It was idiotically stupid, and
I almost lost a good friend. You know, Wanda, sometimes
you have to grab something to know if it's real. We're all
such terrific frauds in our charming way, you and I
and Liane, and you wonder if we can really mean something to one another, or if you'll just close your hand on
air. Look at us. What do we do? I'm tired of all that
sleight of hand. The truth is, I never enjoyed it. Never.
It was just a way of getting to the goals when the honest
methods didn't work. I never did anything mean for its
own sake. The goals were all right, too: getting an education, being respected, engaging in politics—whatever.
But they all were supposed to be preparation for some-

thing, and we never got to the something. All we're supposed to do at the office is explain away whatever goes wrong and organize the re-election. Well, I find I'd finally like to do some good in the world, and I'm going to do it openly and honestly."

"You're losing me," said Wanda, climbing onto his lap, as she hadn't done for some time. She bent her head against his chest. "What does this have to do with Liane and you doing it—in their bed? Was it in their bed?"

"Yes," said Gilbert, and they both laughed uproariously.

"Well? Go on. You can't stop there. Your wife doesn't understand you, and you're trying to break it to me gently. You're going to say that I'm too good for you, and it's your mission in life to make Liane happy."

She spoke with good-natured confidence, and Gilbert, triumphant in his choice, bent and kissed her head. "Not exactly. I mean, yes, she's happy now, thank God, but not with me, thank God. Liane has got to live by subterfuge. She's stuck in it—and I admit I encourage it, because she needs the self-protection—because that George is a natural-born sneak. It's the only thing that gets through to him. But not me." He noticed that Wanda was giving him an exasperated look. "Oh, yes. Where was I?"

"In the President's bed?"

"Wanda, it was funny. It was the funniest thing you ever saw."

"I'll bet." But she was, indeed, laughing, and at the same time slipping her hand under his robe, which had the effect of proving again, if Gilbert had needed proof, that any time spent worrying about his capabilities would have been wasted. He felt happier than he had ever been.

"Shall I go on?"

"By all means. Kiss me first, please. Deceived wives need a lot of reassurance. Was she awful?"

"No, I was. My friendship with her is real, but anything beyond it isn't. It's like my needing to know, in this business with the handicapped, how much I feel is real, or whether I was just trying to blow up and decorate a feeling that was too small to matter, or wasn't even there at all. This is sort of rambling, isn't it?"

"It sure is. When do we get to the sexy part?"

"Ah, yes, the sexy part. But is there a sexy part? Or did I just learn, early in life, that the only way to get anyone's attention is to take my clothes off? And in another sense, do I really want to call attention to myself, or is it a need to focus my own attention elsewhere?"

"Gilbert, dear! This is the most awful gibberish. Either tell me or don't tell me. What happened?"

"Nothing."

"You mean, nothing—nothing?" He nodded. "Why not?"

"Didn't work. Proof that my deepest desires are to be honest, aboveboard, your own faithful—through no fault of my own—happy, loving husband. Intact."

"I don't understand."

"I didn't do it."

"Why not?" She had risen in his lap and was looking at him as if he had just confessed to not having mailed the letters she had given him that morning.

"I didn't feel like it, Wanda. What don't you understand?"

"I understand that you and your friend Liane have been off making a fool of me. And George, too, although as you say, that job was done long ago. I understand that's what you were doing."

"Oh, Wanda." The unfairness of her being retroactively conventional outraged him. "A minute ago, you said it was all right."

"I didn't know then what you'd been doing." She got up and walked swiftly to the other side of the room, where encountering a sideboard decorated with carved wooden antlers that pointed at her, she spun around and walked swiftly back.

"It's what I wasn't doing!" he shouted.

The noise alone shocked him in a household where voices were never raised. Wanda sat forward on the sofa cushion, her hands clasping each other in her lap. "A momentary . . . impulse for an old friend, I can understand," she said in a defiant but quavering voice. "But a deliberate desire to do something you don't even want to do, showing an intimacy, a weakness, which is not the business of outsiders, is something different. I really don't care, Gilbert. If you want to have your little confession, guilt, remorse scene, please go right ahead. It's really charming the way you have to make it into a philosophy, or whatever you call that crazy blabbering. Just be kind enough to leave me out of it. I don't care for what you call honesty."

Gilbert was nearly felled. He started to protest, but didn't. Instead, he moved and sat beside her, attempting to unclutch her hands so that he could assume custody of at least one of them. "You're hurt," he said. "Let's forget it. The whole stupid incident isn't worth talking about. I thought it was funny. Let's drop it. Just tell me whether you want to go to the Beauforts' dinner or not—I couldn't care less. Liane and I are back to where we were before, George deserves whatever he gets, and if you can't understand it, try to accept my apology and my assurance that it was an isolated incident and no such thing is likely to occur again. I'll tell Liane we're not coming. Under the best of circumstances, their dinners are a bore."

"We have to go. Does George know?"

"Yes, he knows. I don't think there's much danger of his shooting me, though."

"Does he know what really happened?"

"Yes. No. Wait a minute. I don't think he does. No. I forget now. It's all so ridiculous."

"It doesn't matter in the least. Not to me. Only I'd think you wouldn't want to look like a fool in front of someone like that."

Gilbert was beginning to understand that no conversation on the subject was going to lead anywhere, and he poked the fire and settled back with his book. Wanda continued to look offended. Even when he had peeked at her after she had fallen asleep that night, her lips were tightly set. She had looked at the proof that he wasn't impotent with her as an added insult of some sort, so he had let that go, too.

He let go of the idea of trying to explain himself to anyone at all. They all were going to take honest human complexity for hypocrisy and deceit. Wanda could not be trusted with the literal truth—she took it too literally.

At breakfast, grasping at the remnants of his half-asleep nighttime wisdom, he said quietly, "Sexual prowess, if I may call it that, has nothing whatever to do with political power. That is a myth, invented by homely old politicians for dumb young girls. The two are quite separate."

"Then why'd you do it in the President's bed?" she asked bitterly.

"You mean, why didn't I do it, don't you, dear?" Gil-

bert asked charmingly. He kissed his hand to her and
went to his waiting White House car.

Telling the car to go on, he walked the route
it would have taken him. He had once admired an old
lady in New York, window-shopping on Fifth Avenue
while a car and chauffeur, both as old as herself, crept
slowly along at her pace, as a back-up system to her careful steps, ignoring the screaming yellow taxicabs behind.
But the White House driver merely nodded and sped
away.

It was a freak warm day, and Gilbert thought of it as
the beginning of spring. He wanted some sort of omen
to assure himself that this was a new page and a fresh
chapter. He welcomed the weak sunshine, expecting it to
be chemotherapy on his messily spreading thoughts.

He didn't believe in Wanda's anger, classifying it as
an absurdity. Her pique had to do with vanity, but it had
developed only after his confession of technical inno-
cence. He hoped that some bubble of an excuse for
Wanda would surface within him, showing that her reaction was essentially different from George's. The memory
of Wanda's kittenishness when the tale was only half-told
continued to nag at him.

Was he expecting too much of her? She was just learning to play by the old rules, and he wanted to change
them—to change posing and fooling into goodness and
sincerity—in order to make the game harder. Was it for
sport? Or was he simply indulging in the officious queru-
lousness of the ex-smoker?

A few petals were showing on the dogwood trees.

Soon they would be in glorious bloom, to be pointed out by spring tourists as the famous Washington cherry blossoms. He saw himself years ago, walking through Cambridge with the same lonely feeling, except that he had to walk differently now, because his clothes were different. He couldn't stick his hands in his back pockets, the way he used to, because of his coat or cradle his head against his shoulder, where his hand used to hold an extra sweater. The pockets in his Chesterfield were discreetly flapped slits. It was a narrow, expensive coat, worn over a slim, costly suit, worn over a tapered shirt with a silk solid-color tie. He began to sympathize with Wanda's contempt for him. All he would need would be a thin, carefully tended mustache, in order to make himself sick.

He was walking down Sixteenth Street, the re-cycled mansions forming a solid background to his important-person stride. He could turn off to his clothier's and get himself re-done, but into what? Gilbert had studiously avoided pseudojeans and open shirts; his weekend concession to informality was a collarless dress shirt, with linen or velveteen slacks. One had to avoid Buddy Loomis's hoary boyishness, and any change in the other direction would leave him resembling his secretary, Toby.

Toby greeted him coldly. "They've been asking for you," he said without sympathy.

"Let me tell you something, kid," said Gilbert as nastily as he could. "I happen to have responsibilities that They, and even You, don't know about. We are not in a simple Senate office anymore, and the quicker people understand that, the longer they'll last. I thought you understood my position. An employee at your level ought to be able to make it clear that I am not to be watched or summoned. In the future, if people ask for me, please tell them I am not available."

Toby blinked at him. Gilbert threw him his coat, and Toby caught it without taking his eyes off his employer.

"All right," snapped Gilbert. "Tell Them they can come now."

But he ended up going to Them. His game was rusty. Toby was enough for one morning, without Them during the day and Wanda at night. Toby's hash did look settled, though; perhaps if he did one such performance every day, the time would come when he would have them all settled, and he could settle back in his chair and rest.

Today was not the day to settle Them. Lipscomb, the one with the meanest face and the two haughtiest secretaries, put it to him. He was presiding, with Brewster sitting to one side, smiling silently. Lipscomb had Gilbert's neatly bound report in his hand and threw it on the table, with a practiced flicking of the wrist, while Gilbert had to watch.

"Boy, I love you young idealists," said Lipscomb, shaking his head negatively. He was two years Gilbert's junior.

"It's going to be the new issue," said Gilbert. "Civil rights in the Sixties, women's rights in the Seventies, rights of the disabled of the Eighties. This time we're going to bring it up before they make us."

"Make us?" Lipscomb laughed, and Brewster broadened his smile. Two of the older staff members at the table looked away. "No, my friend, we are not."

"This is going to be bigger than any of them," Gilbert persisted. "This is not a minority—this is everybody. Every single voter. There's nobody in the world who hasn't been sick, or who isn't hoping to grow old."

Brewster put up a hand to silence an incipient outburst from Lipscomb. "And they don't want to be reminded of it," he said reasonably. "But you're right, you're right. You ought to be working on something you believe in." Gilbert understood that this was practically the definition of something of no importance. "Think about it. I'm sure we can find a comfortable place for you over at Health and Human Resources. People like you are needed over there."

Gilbert felt himself flooding with inarticulate misery. "Just give me the word, Fairchild, and I'll make a call and settle it now."

"May I remind you," said Gilbert, hating the thin sound of his voice, "that I developed the issues for this campaign?" It sounded weak, even to him. The campaign just won, the one that he had personally launched from its audacious beginning, that he had invented and then skillfully wrapped around an unlikely bit of raw material who happened to be a senator, was boring history. No one remembered it.

"That so?" Brewster confined himself to that, and waved his hand toward Lipscomb, who continued.

"We shouldn't have to tell you this, then, Fairchild. People don't like to see cripples. It's as simple as that. That wheelchair crew you have in to tea—we've all seen them. We've all heard them. I don't want them around the President." Lipscomb had looked for confirmation to Brewster after daring to use the word *I*, and he received a nod. "The Easter Seal child is one thing; this is another. It's a lousy photo opportunity—anyone who can't see that doesn't belong in the business. We're not arguing against whatever it is you want to do for these people. That's fine. It's just not a personal issue for the President's attention. I don't know how to make it any plainer. We all know the President has a special tolerance for you, but just don't push him too far."

Gilbert locked eyes with Brewster, ignoring Lipscomb, and picked up his report, and left. In the world of White House pronouns, the *him* in *push him too far* stood for Brewster.

But Lipscomb had used the word *special*, in describing Gilbert's relationship with the President. The word was in his official title, too: Special Assistant to the President. Not wanting to go back to his own office and noticing that the Oval Office door was open, he watched the President's secretary slipping noiselessly into the Presence, and he followed her.

Gilbert did not have dropping-in privileges, although it now occurred to him that if he had taken them from the beginning, probably no one would have stopped him. His old self—a brash young political star, still another old self he fished out of his memory for support—would have done so. This was another instance of his having lost his grip.

They all looked at him in mute shock: Himself, His secretary, and another one of Them who was present. Gilbert gave his speech. The two minor people in the room dissolved, and Gilbert didn't know whether they had actually disappeared or had adapted to the wall coloration. The President was trapped at his own desk between two flags.

Once or twice, Gilbert emerged from his speech enough to look at the man, and finally, he was able to catch His eye. They both breathed deeply, remembering that they were not antagonists, but old comrades. It wasn't as if the President were sitting on his desk top, as he had in the old days, swinging his legs while Gilbert paced the room outlining a new battle plan, but the scene was familiar enough to them both.

Gilbert began again, more in the old way. The senator

had been used to accepting instructions from Gilbert, and there seemed to be a touch of that person left in the President who now watched him. Gilbert caught in a flash the idea that He, too, might be nostalgic for days when His campaigns were hand-made by craftsmen and not produced by huge machinery. He trimmed from his speech any disinterestedness, and painted the disabled lobby as a natural resource waiting to be tapped by the clever opportunist. Woven in was Lipscomb's objection of its being unpleasant for people to look on mis-shapen bodies. With his old talent, Gilbert spun a story that was one part Buddy, and one part advertising-level wisdom about the sexual advance-retreat fascination that the malformed body held for the subliminal mind.

The President looked spellbound. But the sun was streaming through the long windows, and they were shaken back to the present time when a butler entered with a silver coffee tray.

"Great talking to you," the President said.

"Well?" said Gilbert. "I need a go-ahead."

The President looked at him icily; Gilbert watched the spell freeze over. He tried to will the President into offering him a cup of coffee. There was a second cup on the tray.

The President sipped alone, but the trick of not moving or speaking worked, and finally even a President had to fill the silence. "I have to staff it out and see what everybody thinks," he said humbly. There was a wistful quality to his voice, and Gilbert registered the fact that he had won him personally, but that it wouldn't matter any more. The man was not free. Perhaps he never had been, but Gilbert hadn't minded so much when He had belonged to him.

They parted, and Gilbert returned to his office. He

wanted to weep walking, back into the city streets and his past. He was practically in tears as he shuffled past Toby, but he did notice the new note in Toby's voice as he said, "Mr. Purcell was looking for you, Mr. Fairchild, and I told him you might not be able to get back to him today." It was said with firmness and faith.

"I was in the Oval Office," said Gilbert. "You know. Where your friend Prez hangs out." He watched Toby as the plaster cast of a respectful face was cast into permanent form.

Gilbert shut his inner door, planning to despair, but his lips curved when he thought about Toby. It's a sad day, he thought, when you have to congratulate yourself on winning civility from your own secretary. He thought what a poor figure Toby cut next to the figure of Gilbert Fairchild at his age.

The rest of the day he spent sitting in his authoritative desk chair, at his historic desk, moving only occasionally, rotating just enough to look out the window. Virtue wasn't working out. Every now and then, he heard groups of voices in the hallway, meaning that people were going to meetings, meetings of which he hadn't been notified. Toby still put his schedule in the silver frame every day, but the entries were written larger and were more grandly spaced.

Now was the time to quit it all, go abroad to some place cheap and charming and live the good life. Yes? With what wife? Or we could have a baby and I could take paternity leave, he thought. Anyway, they don't fire people at the White House for lack of productivity, like some crass industry. Only for being an embarrassment, or a potential embarrassment, to the President. If he didn't do anything at all, he wouldn't be responsible for anything going wrong. Yes, but someone else would, and would desperately need a scapegoat, and a person who wasn't doing anything, wasn't even paying attention, was too choice for that. Lipscomb would screw up, or Brewster, and would pin it on him, or some unknown person quartered in the Executive Office Building, who envied him his little West Wing office, would do it.

Dusk came, and he hadn't put on the lights. His listless eye fixed on the beams of a car pulling into the parking area between the White House and the EOB. Another car pulled up next to it. Out stepped two women in typically durable Washington dinner dresses and day-length coats, each carrying a black garment bag. For the first time in hours, Gilbert got up and pressed against the window, squinting over his glasses.

The two women were conferring pleasantries on the guard at the inner gatehouse who was charged with the superfluous task of checking the credentials of people who were already within White House boundaries. The tall, flashy young blonde was Mrs. Lipscomb, Gilbert knew; he and Wanda had picked her out as the quintessential Second Wife. So Lipscomb was invited to the state dinner tonight. Well, there would be a lot of them—Liane had mentioned the press of heads of state anxious to check in with the new President—but Gilbert had been to the first.

The other lady was older, her odd, bony face still just like her father's, familiar for decades to Gilbert as the Majority Whip and then, when he had supposedly been turned out to rich pastures, as an ambassador who was kidnapped, found, and hero-ized. It was Mrs. Brewster.

Mrs. Brewster! *What?*

The Brewsters had been at the first state dinner, and now they were going to the second one, too?

Ten minutes later, Gilbert smacked his door open.

"Okay, Toby," he barked, "here we go. If you have a date tonight, animal, vegetable, or mineral, break it. Call Mrs. Fairchild and tell her I'm having dinner with Mrs. Beaufort. You and I are going to get the prize for working late. Order sandwiches and yogurt, and get back here with your notepad. Do I have to give you a loyalty oath?"

"You know me, sir," said Toby.

"That's what I'm afraid of. Nobody in the world is ever going to know of this. I mean it. The campaign was just fooling around—time to get to work."

"Yes, yes, I'm ready. What can I do?"

"Make the calls, will you? I'm waiting."

"Sir? Do I understand that I tell Mrs. Fairchild you're going out with Mrs. Beaufort, but we're really going to be here working? I'm just asking to get it straight."

"That's correct. Some people can't face the truth. This is kinder."

Toby went out, shaking his head. When he returned, he found Gilbert leaning on the desk, hands over his eyes. "Gilbert! Are you all right?"

When Gilbert looked up and said, "Sir—you mean sir," his eyes were glittering, and focused beyond Toby, who had to scribble wildly to keep up with the dictation.

"Number one. This is a memorandum from Mrs. Beaufort to the First Lady. You'll have to get the style from Liane—not from her secretary; you understand?—but hold off till I break it to her. Here goes:

"Let's include the ambassador of (Toby, find me a smallish country, diplomats not well known; family not in Washington) on the next major guest list, and I suggest you make a point of talking to them. We have a delicate situation here, but I think it can be smoothed over if you show them some special attention.

"I was at their dinner last week (Toby, it has to be

a country with a dinner last week) and was present at an informal conversation about the White House policy on the physically handicapped, which they seemed to believe is now being discussed as an issue in the West Wing. Mr. Lipscomb (check his schedule, but I know he goes to everything), who is a fixture on the party scene, thoughtlessly remarked, 'We don't need the freak vote.' (No, make that—'seems to have made an indiscreet offhand remark.' Let's make her ask what it was. I'll brief Liane.)

"It was nothing—we all know his outrageous sense of humor—and would have passed unnoticed if not for the fact, which he couldn't know, that the ambassador's son has polio. In fact, nobody said anything at the time, and I may be worried for no reason, but I feel it wouldn't hurt to be extra-gracious to them right now. They have an acute sense of etiquette, and I think it would be a mistake to mention the incident or the child's illness. Let's just include them when we can."

When Gilbert paused, Toby looked at him transfixed.

"Let's do the other, and then, when you've got the information, no later than tomorrow noon, give me this typed, one copy only, and destroy the ribbon, and we'll go over it. Ready for the next one?"

Toby nodded.

"I think I can do this one right off. It's a letter to Dr. Dale in New York, but you'll have to wait until we get the memo done, because the copy of it will be enclosed. Amend that copy to include the freak quote. When we finish, the only copies of this existing will be the one Liane sends and the one to Margery. All drafts and notes to be destroyed."

Toby's head bobbed slowly.

Dear Margery,

Believe me when I say that I left you full of admiration for what you are doing, and for what you have become.

I hate like anything to disappoint you, and I haven't given up yet. I just want to show you what I'm up against. Show this to Wollonby, too, because I told him I had hoped to have something positive for him to announce at the Disabled Workers' Convention, and I can't. Tell him I tried. God knows I did. I'm still trying.

I'll have to ask you to destroy the memo and this letter after you two only have read it. Don't let Wollonby copy or keep it. It would cost me my job, and I may yet be more useful to you both than I would be on the street.

My best to your husband,

Love.

Toby remained transfixed. "Okay, move!" said Gilbert. "That's all until I call you. What kind of sandwich did you get me?" The carton of yogurt said "JAN 22." "My yogurt's expired," he called, but Toby had shut the door.

HE BUZZED TOBY every half hour with another list of information he needed, some of it existing only in other people's White House files. "Feather fingers?" asked Toby.

"I thought you had friends," said Gilbert. "You always told me you were well connected."

"Yes, sir, I am. Ready for another sandwich?"

Gilbert looked up from the mess of papers and torn sheets of yellow legal pads that were covering the usually pristine surface of his desk. Across the way, he could see lighted offices in the majestically whimsical structure that was the Executive Office Building, so much more impressive than the plain White House. "No, I may get something from the Mess myself. I'm going to walk around a bit and stretch."

"Let me get it," said Toby. "You stay out of the halls. There's a dinner tonight, and the place is full of cameramen and people reporters running back and forth to phone in."

"I see," said Gilbert. "Say, Toby? Do I have any evening clothes here?"

"I do," said Toby. "If you tell me what you want them for, you can have them. Provided you don't ask what I've got them here for."

"Are you kidding? You're a little squirt."

"Same size as you, Mr. Fairchild."

"I'm talking stature," said Gilbert. "I don't want them, but leave them anyhow. It's just in case I get restless and want to socialize, or maybe I'll feel like dressing up tonight."

AT TEN THE NEXT MORNING, having spent the night on the sofa, Toby gave Gilbert, who had been home and changed, the finished memorandum and a stack of other papers he had prepared. His eyes were sparkling. "When do we get Brewster?" he asked.

"Never," said Gilbert. "I like Brewster. He'll understand this, and we'll be able to work together." He was leafing through the stack of papers, lifting the nosepiece of his glasses to wipe away the perspiration. "I didn't ask for anything on Brewster. I want this destroyed. He's not a bad person like Lipscomb, just too caught up in the mechanics of life to deal with morality." He laughed.

"I'll tell you what I do want. There are going to be a lot of people traipsing through here. I'm looking for issues; the disabled thing is good, but it's not enough. So I'm going to be interviewing the downtrodden. The word will get around, and anyone who seems to have a halfway legitimate cause gets a full, intelligent memo, stating it as that person does, with no judgment exercised by you, and I will review them. We are looking for instances of unfairness or whatever that affect large numbers of people; huge numbers. Eventually, I'm going to be working with the President's Counsel to get the legal angle on these things, or at least on the ones I choose, so bear that in mind when you keep records. And remember, I don't want your rotten opinion on who's pretty."

"Yes, sir, yes, sir!" called Toby, blowing him a kiss.

"Come back here. One more thing. Stop enjoying this. I'm not kidding, Toby. We're going to phase this sort of thing out. Bear that in mind if you want to keep working for me." Gilbert's glasses were sliding again, and he peered at Toby like a nineteenth-century schoolmaster. "You still think I'm kidding, but you're going to find out otherwise if you try to get smart. We're going to do good around here, and we're going to earn ourselves the luxury of doing it in a scrupulous way. I don't like what happened last night. I didn't like cheating in college, and I don't like it now. But I'm not willing to give up and let the bad guys have everything. I'm not saying we can't have our little ploys, Toby. They're neither good nor bad in themselves, and we need to be effective. I don't see what's wrong with being clever. Oh, hell. I'm just sorry this particular thing had to be so stinking. Now go."

"Gilbert? Can I say something?"

"No."

"Gilbert, you've always been basically honest that I know of. I mean, basically. And compared to others—you don't even know what some people do."

"I don't want to know," said Gilbert. "Get out of here. And don't let me catch you smiling."

TWO WEEKS LATER, Gilbert passed the palest Lipscomb he had ever seen—even his bushy beard had turned to ash—on his way to answer an 8 A.M. summons to the Oval Office that Wanda had relayed to him when he was in his bath. The color Lipscomb had lost was in the President's face. He was wildly waving a newspaper.

"That God-damn Wollonby is a friend of yours, Fairchild," he screamed. "You did this!"

Gilbert flushed. Half the inner circle staff was standing around, looking at him. Gilbert had had indulgent parents and had gone to progressive schools. It was the first time he had been dressed down by a superior since a big kid did it in grade school.

"This could kill us! It could kill us, do you hear me?" The President hit the newspaper with his left fist. It folded over his hand, and he flung it all over the room. Nobody else moved or spoke. "That idiot Lipscomb!" shouted the President. Lipscomb was standing in the doorway. "Who brought him in here? You, Fairchild? Is he another one of your precious friends?"

"I didn't hire him, sir, but sure, we're all working together here. Except that he killed my program. Which is fine, except that he shouldn't have told people and created expectations."

The President gave him a narrow look, and it took all Gilbert had to keep himself from flinching. "Your God-damn program," said the President. "All right. You have yourself a God-damn cripples' program. Get busy. Take whoever you need. I want to know tonight what I'm doing for the God-damned handicapped. And, Gilbert!" he shouted, as Gilbert had been turning to leave. "If that freaks' convention of yours is still going on, you give me a speech to deliver there this afternoon, and I want it now! Three minutes of goodwill, and no jokes. Got it?"

Gilbert waved his hand as he scooted out. He could hear the President yelling again, but only at the world, not at him. There were footsteps behind him, and Brewster, catching up, put an arm around Gilbert's shoulder, shaking his head sadly.

"It's not right," said Gilbert.

"No," said Brewster, "it isn't. But these things happen all the time. I'm glad your program was at least saved."

"Yes, well, thanks," said Gilbert, leaving Brewster to go up to his office, while Gilbert headed down to his. He hoped that Toby wouldn't immediately realize that an office on the main floor had now become vacant. He was happy with the one he had, where Wanda had spent the previous weekend putting in flowering plants and cushions. Besides, it had that much more quiet in which to plan the improvement of the world.

For a complete list of books available from Penguin in the United States, write to Dept. DG, Penguin Books, 299 Murray Hill Parkway, East Rutherford, New Jersey 07073.

For a complete list of books available from Penguin in Canada, write to Penguin Books Canada Limited, 2801 John Street, Markham, Ontario L3R 1B4.